D1456648

three
witches

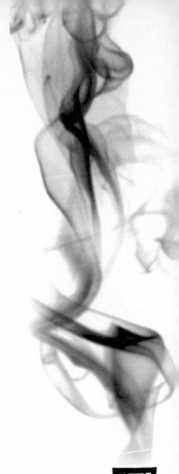

ROARING
BROOK
PRESS
NEW YORK

Three Witches

PAULA JOLIN

THANKS TO:

Chris McCarthy Roberts, my first reader and best friend.
Andrea Somberg, who said "I LOVE this idea."
Ben Tomek, for spotting potential in three crumpled chapters.
Kat Kopit, with the vision to see this book as spookier and more powerful imagined.
Mark Osborne, my chunkalunks, who taught me Trini phrases and All Fc me the best damn curried goat in the world.
Sandy Smith, for the careful attention she gave to every page.
Robin Hoffmann, for her inexhaustible patience and the lovely design v
Greg Stadnyk, who came up with a cover beyond my wildest dreams.
Virginia Jolin, who never fails to tell me I'm brilliant.
Paul Jolin, who never fails to make me *feel* brilliant.
Sumie Yano and her innovative idea to make the third witch Japanese.
Lynette Osborne, always ready with the perfect soca or calypso.
Tessa Ropp, who never fails to answer the phone.
Helen Matamoro, the first Trini to share authentic obeah stories with me.
Hazel Matamoro, always up for a good lime, a game of Spades, and some rum punch.
Wendy Williams, for advice on tea ceremonies, tatami mats, and kanji characters.
Nabila Najjar, who introduced me to jinn one eerie midnight in Damascus.
Neji, Sylvia, Christen, and the taxi driver who drove us all to the top of the mountain outside Meknès.
Jamie Lankford, for all that she does for aspiring writers and especially me.
Tracy Abell, Shirley Harazin, Karen Kincy, Donna Koppelman, Christy Lenzi, Doug Osborne, Robin Prehn, Bunny Ray, Vanitha Sankaran,

And finally:
Julien and **Maia,** just 'cause I love dem.

PART I

ONE

ALIYA KNELT on the hardwood floor. With trembling hands, she checked her scarf, careful to tuck every strand of hair beneath the fabric, almost as though she was getting ready to pray.

Prayer was the last thing she should be thinking about tonight.

A crisp breeze swept in through the open window and blew over her knees, across the back of her neck. The wide sleeves of her *abaya* billowed out, and she caught a glimpse of her watch—11:58 and counting.

She unclasped the band and tossed her last link to modern technology under the bed. No clock ticking, no computer humming, no electric blanket toasting cold feet. Just the frigid air outside, roughing up the leaves, and the faint sound of an animal howling far away.

Her fingers stumbled as she struck the first match against the back of its wooden box. Strike one fizzled, but strike two

1

caught and held. Aliya moved the flame from one candle to another until five lights glowed, safe and stable, at their points of the pentagram. The wooden floor gleamed in the dark.

She took a deep breath, flipped the Qur'an open to her favorite verse, the one about the elephant. *Recite it backward*, Great-aunt Reem had told her all those years ago. *Letter by letter.* Wasn't this the kind of thing she'd go to hell for? Such an innocuous act, it couldn't be.

She read the words under her breath. Wind whipped through the window again, fluttered the flames.

Start at midnight, Old Aunt had said. *Carry on until you're done.*

Next up: blood. Aliya picked up the ice-cold silver pin, jabbed at her left index finger, and failed to make a dent. Freshman Biology all over again. Was she going to faint now, too?

Not the time for that, and especially not the place. If the thud of her head hitting the floor woke her parents, if they came in and found her out cold, surrounded by candles and a needle, dressed all in black, they'd think . . . Correct that. They'd know exactly what she'd been doing. Something good, pious Muslims never took into their own hands.

Though she hadn't been much good as a Muslim lately, had she?

She jammed the pin into her left thumb with such force that the blood gushed out. A crook of her arm, and she found the scrap of cloth, pulled it forward. In pin and blood, she drew a series of careful strokes on the fabric. God help her, she was going to run out before she reached the end. Squeezing the thumb—*oh, that hurt*—she got the last few drops she needed.

Done. The letters of his name, etched in blood, made the fabric so beautiful it almost pained her to burn it. She fed it to the nearest flame anyway, a silver tray poised beneath the candle to catch the ashes. Almost there. She lifted the tray up to her face, puffed on the ashes once, twice, three times, watched them rearrange themselves. Then she mixed them with freshly ground tea.

All very simple, nothing gross or improper. Aliya scooped the mixture into a covered mesh teaspoon and dropped it into the teacup. She leaned between candles, stretched her hands to the wall, plugged in the kettle. *No modern conveniences*, Old Aunt had told her. But the kitchen door squeaked, and her mother slept in fits and starts.

Empty your mind. Let the jinn hear your call.

The kettle boiled. She flicked off the switch and poured the steaming water into her cup. Swirled the mesh spoon around till the water turned brown and browner still.

Blow across the top of the cup three times.

Puff.

Puff.

Puff.

Recite the Beloved's name three times.

"Trevor Sanders."

"Trevor Sanders."

"Trevor Sanders."

Tell them what you desire.

"I need to speak to Trevor one last time. Five minutes, that's all." Five centuries was more like it, but she doubted the jinn could bend the rules that far. "Five minutes."

She drank it all in a single gulp, not caring that the hot liquid stung her tongue. Stretching out across the floor again, she blew out the candles one by one.

Then she sat back to wait.

TWO

ALIYA GOT HER ANSWER the very next day.

The family room, center of the Najjar household—squabbling kids, gossiping aunties, the incessant TV talking to itself—was a strange place for the dead to choose to communicate. A strange place for Aliya to do her homework, too, but Mama insisted the computer stay in sight. "I know all those crazy things online kids do," she said. "Meeting up with criminals and sending secret sex messages. You don't like it, work in your room." Try telling Mama that the teachers at Fillmore stopped accepting handwritten assignments back in 1992.

So Aliya struggled on in the family room. She reread the last line of her overdue History essay, a line she'd typed more than a week ago—*Another terrible oppression of World War II took place in our own backyard, the Japanese concentration camps*—then clicked back to her e-mail. Nothing.

"Hey, Aliya," called out Cousin Mariam. She sat on the couch, flipping through a newspaper. "Did you know this boy who died?"

Thank God, this once, for the noise. No one heard Aliya's sharp intake of breath. No one could see her face, either, since she was practically pressed up against the computer screen. *Calm yourself*. She'd prepared for this. "How would I know him? He was a party boy, the kind of guy who'd throw bottles out of the back of a truck—not someone you'd find in AP classes."

4

How would she know him? Little drawings she doodled on the side of her desk in Calculus—snails, seagulls, cranes. Two periods later, he'd add the captions: *Supersnail's cape catches on a clam shell, saves him from certain death*; *Wanted: Seagull. Stole a million sand dollars.* And one day: *Meet me out by the bus lanes, after all the idiots have gone home. I'll be the one in the green hat.*

"But you must have known who he was," said Mariam. She took a sip of tea, making a face because Mama was so stingy with the sugar. "It says here he was very popular, lots of friends, leaving some huge bash in Wilcrest when he drove through the railing and right over the cliff."

Almost a stunt car, he'd introduced her to Mitsu. *Almost human.* She could imagine it, couldn't stop imagining it, Mitsu with her blue doors open like wings, soaring off the edge of the cliff, a daredevil at her wheel.

"Aliya?" Mama came into the room, set a glass of warm milk by her elbow. Felt her forehead for a fever. "Drink this, I know you're not feeling well."

"Flu?" That was Mariam, from the couch. "Have you taken any Tylenol? Or you know what's even better, Nabile told me about this, heat a towel over the radiator and then wrap it tight around your head."

"Have you tried it?" asked Mama, clearing a space on the couch and sitting beside her.

"Haven't been sick," said Mariam.

Aliya clicked on her IM account. "U there?" she asked Sherine for the third time in twenty minutes. No answer. She tapped the edge of the table. Tabbed through a whole series of pages: MySpace, Facebook, Muslim Girl World, letting images flash across the screen, reading nothing. Out of the corner of her eye, she made sure that Mama was busy with her tea. Then she typed: **Teenwidows.org**. Not that she was a widow, not exactly, but it felt like it.

"I'm not surprised," said Mama to Mariam. "You've had a very lucky year."

Mariam preened on the sofa. She'd been married just three weeks. "I think the best thing was taking the semester off. The dean wasn't happy about it, not happy at all, because I got into the honors program and everything, did you hear about that?"

He's dead and I can't tell anyone, she read in a forum entitled: Just Bereaved. *I mean, everyone knows he died in a car crash, but they don't know that he was with me.*

"Oh, you did hear?" Mariam preened a little more, even though she'd told Mama the honors thing herself. "I figured I needed a semester to get used to being married. It's a lot of *work* being somebody's wife." Mama, married twenty years, kindly held her tongue. "Especially somebody like Nabile. He's so surprised every time I mention takeout. He wants a hot meal every night and, by God, it better have meat."

"Boys raised in Syria are different from Syrian boys raised here," said Mama. "Of course, Nabile is a very good husband, and a doctor, and as soon as he gets his American qualifications, you'll both be well off. And it's nice that you didn't make a fuss about him being an immigrant, like so many girls do."

Aliya paged down. No replies.

Mariam giggled. Last spring, frantic with exams, she'd holed up in Aliya's bedroom with a stack of textbooks and growled when anyone came near. Nowadays, she talked a lot less about radiation and a lot more about relationships. "Arab-American boys don't understand about the *mahr*. The

dowry." Aliya felt Mariam look up at her back. No need. She
knew what *mahr* meant. Bride-price. The amount a man paid
for the right to touch you. "So helpful to make it college
tuition, if you know what I mean. It's lucky I have my schol-
arship, but med school will be so expensive. Girls back home,
they go to college for free, but here, even the state schools . . ."

Mama's mouth pulled in, not quite frowning. She blew
across her teacup. "Your uncle wasn't thinking just about your
education when he suggested Nabile. He thought you'd fit
together nicely and, from what I heard from Nabile's sister, I
thought this too."

Mariam's bridal gold jangled on her wrist. "Oh, Auntie, I
didn't mean that. I love Nabile."

Loved him? Loved him enough to walk three miles to the
only store that sold Worstley's wool socks because he com-
plained his feet were cold at night? Enough to set a paper bag
of rose petals in his locker so they'd flutter down when he
pulled open the door?

Enough to spend half her soul in salty tears when he
died?

Aliya jammed her fingers on the keys as she typed, blocking out Mariam's singsong voice as she said words Aliya
couldn't bear to listen to: *so sweet, tender, devoted.* Aliyaalnaj-
jar92@yahoo.com—still nothing. Her fingers danced over the
keyboard, and she wound up at her school e-mail. Somewhere she hadn't been since . . .

You have 1 new message.

Click. Open. Big, black, bold letters jumped out: **Trevor
Sanders**. Of course, it could have been, must have been, sent
before . . . what was the date?

9/9/2099.

He'd set his computer to the future on purpose. *I don't want my mom tracking me down—'You sent this on day X, when you were supposed to be in detention.' You know what I mean. Plus, now my e-mail will always go straight to the top of your inbox.* He'd kissed her on her forehead. That had been near the beginning of everything. She'd swooned.

She was swooning, now. Good thing for Mariam's babble, or someone might have noticed her hands frozen above the keyboard. Could she read this? Not like she had a choice. After all, she'd set it all in motion: blood, candles, pentagram.

Hey Aliya, it began.

You're probably pissed that I didn't show up last night—but please don't be. There's all kinds of crazy going on here, shit you wouldn't believe. Shock you out of your pious Muslim girl mind. Look, can you do something for me? That envelope in your locker, can you give it to Gillian Smith? She's in your Am Civ class, tall black girl with a funny accent, the one who never takes her coat off. And don't get your knickers all crumpled thinking something crazy—you know I don't kiss girls with attitude. This is business baby. Tell your parents you're meeting Sherine to study and take it over this afternoon—don't worry about wasting the Sherine excuse, because I can't come tonight either. But soon. I promise.

Love Trevor

She read it again. A third time. No protests of undying love, no sonnets about how much he missed her? Not even a rhyming poem—*Roses are red, violets are blue, heaven is stinky, because I'm without you*? Sent before, it must have been.

Back in the day, when she and Trevor were young and in love.

"Aliya? Is everything okay?"

That was Mariam, emerging from her rhapsody on her oh-so-breathing husband. Lines of concern etched the edges of her mouth. Aliya clicked the corner of the screen and killed the evidence. "Just an e-mail from school," she said. She stared hard at the desktop, then managed: "About that boy, there's going to be a memorial service. It *is* sad. Even though I didn't know him, I can't imagine what his mom must be going through."

Except that she had an excellent imagination. Every other moment she imagined that the phone was going to beep, that the text would be from him.

She found herself at Peoplefinder.com, typing in a name: *Smith, Gillian.*

"The boy who died?" asked Mama. "What was his name?"

"Trevor Sanders." The screen in front of her blurred at the words. "A kind of stoner who blew off class and grabbed girls in the parking lot." Not girls, a girl. A girl named Aliya. Not in the parking lot, either, but over at Stoney Community Par-k, in the shelter of the gazebo. With sun shining through, like the last page of a romance novel.

Why couldn't she think about something, anything else?

The page came up. *Smith, Gillian: 42 Roosevelt St.*

"I'm going to Sherine's to study."

"Now?" said Mama. She looked around the room, still searching for the clock they'd moved last August. "We're having rice with *bazalia* tonight." A handful of green peas. Not long ago, that's all it took to keep Aliya home.

"I'll eat there," she said. She took her green jacket off the back of the couch and slid her arms into the sleeves. Mama didn't protest; Sherine was the only approved friend left on the list. At the door, Aliya remembered her cousin. "See you later, Mariam."

"Don't you need your books?" Mariam called, her voice as suspicious as her eyes. Or maybe it was all concern. Either way, the front door had closed behind her. Aliya wasn't going back.

Sherine would be hunched over her computer right now, researching colleges west of the Mississippi. "No way in hell I'm going anywhere within a day's drive of home," she said every day at lunch. "I am so sick of playing the dutiful Arab daughter and sleeping three to a room. I'm going to get to the dorm and think it's huge." Sherine covered her hair and never missed morning prayers, but she was adamant: "Only God has the right to tyrannize me."

Aliya trudged down the driveway, out into the street, dodged a couple of puddles on her way to the corner. Not Sherine, not today. Take a stretch around the block to work her legs, that's what she'd do. Tell Mama that Sherine's family was having beans with *lebin*—why was it everyone gobbled up that fool yogurt dish except her?—and come home in time for the peas she loved. She would. She wouldn't go anywhere near Gillian Smith's house. What would she say to her? *I got this ghostly e-mail . . .*

Gillian Smith—what had Trevor been thinking, hooking up with her? Not *hooking up*, hooking up, but "business baby," he'd written.

Aliya looked up in time to just miss the wet branch hanging over the sidewalk. Tiny icicles danced across the back of
her neck.

What if—she let herself think it for one second and then,
she promised, never again—it really was a message from
beyond the grave? *Shock you out of your pious Muslim girl
mind*—that suggested something, didn't it? Their first conversation in the bus lanes, she'd given him the rock-bottom
truth: "I don't, you know, I don't go with boys."

"But you wear jeans and T-shirts, not like that . . ." He
didn't say "ninja-freak Sherine," but the words hung in the air
between them. She turned to go. He put one hand on her
arm, touched her through the fabric of her jacket, and it was
like a vise grip, pulling her into another world.

"I'm religious," she said. "It's not my parents. Well, it is,
but it's me, too. God says no boys."

"God doesn't say anything against talking, though, does
He?"

He did, actually. But Aliya let it go, and she let the hand
stay, and that was the beginning of her new, secret life. They
never talked about religion again, not when she asked him to
stop smoking up and he did, not when she went on at him
for hanging around Glimmer Collins and he said, what was
he supposed to do, when Aliya was too ashamed to be seen
with him? Not even when he kissed her for the first time. Or
the second time. Or the third . . .

A car swerved, splashed through a puddle, honked. The
driver rolled down the window and leaned out. "What
are you, high or something?" The words, the accent, were

American, but Aliya ducked her head anyway, hoping it wasn't someone she knew. The Arab community was full of people who spoke perfect English and would still ask Mama what she meant by letting Aliya meander the streets alone, and almost at night.

Meander, that's exactly what she was doing. Just because this was Armitage, three streets before Roosevelt, didn't mean anything. She wasn't going there. Well, if she did, she was just going to walk past Gillian's house. After all, what was that about an envelope? He never slipped an envelope through the slits in her locker. At school, the day after it happened, she went straight there. She couldn't stand even one more second of knowing that his notes were piled up inside, with the drawings and the jokes and the pineapple-scented stickers to remind her of the afternoon he'd introduced her to virgin piña coladas. Her locker, more full of him than anyplace else in school.

She took everything out that day, and she hadn't been back there since.

She cut through the library parking lot, jumped the railroad tracks behind, moved into the chic part of town: rows of old tenement houses and duplexes remodeled into single family homes. The illusion of city, with all the comforts of suburbia. Aliya looked up and down Coville Street, sure that she scented dog, which made her think about Rambling. Dirty, wild things, dogs, always slobbering on you and leaving stains on your pants, and her parents said it was irreligious to keep them in the house—*Godless Americans*. But she liked Trevor's dog. He was the not-too-friendly type, keeping his

distance until he got to know you, and even then, he didn't
slobber.

She turned the corner. Up ahead, three duplexes away, she could make out the Roosevelt sign. *Shock you out of your pious Muslim girl mind.* Maybe he was in heaven, and the Christians were right all along. No virgins (not that she wanted any, thank you very much), no rivers of honey, no olive-tree gardens. Just men in white robes, wandering through clouds and strumming harps.

Of course, Trevor might've found himself in hell.

Roosevelt Street, thank God. She put her hands in her pockets, pushed them down hard. This was 41, which meant 42 was right over there. Gray house, not big, not small, empty driveway, black front door. Wildflowers blowing in a foot-long strip of garden. An open window right above it.

Was it Aliya's fault the voice with the Caribbean accent floated out loud enough to reach the islands? Or that it was saying something that sounded like, "Trevor wouldn't want—"? No. Of course, crouching down, skirting her way past the rosebush and into the nook below the window . . . hard to blame someone else for that.

No time for quibbling. She sent a little prayer of thanks to her God—He was still there, even after all she'd done— and settled herself down to hear something.

THREE

"LOOK, EMMIE—NO, I get that." Gillian flicked her cigarette ash into the silver pen case her father had won at Games Day twenty-three years ago. An empty peanut butter jar sat next to it, but why bother? "I get it, but really, suicide? Don't be ridiculous. Who told you such rubbish?"

Emmie squawked on. Not answering Gillian's question, of course, but going on and on about how she was through. ". . . It's over, Gillian, I'm done with it, and nothing you can say will change my mind." Stupid drama queen. The sort of bitch Trevor *would* sign up.

"I'll look into it, Emmie, I will, but we've got you lined up for three—" Interrupted again. Gillian looked down at the list of ten names in her hand. Seven were crossed through with large *Xs*. *Emmie Randolph* had been written across the top, in capital letters. See what came of going partners with a white boy? You never knew what they'd do, those damn white people. Drive their cars off a cliff as likely as show up at your door with flowers and a scheme.

Tears? Not Gillian Smith. She barely knew the boy.

She shivered. Stupid wind. Stupid too-thin sweater. Stupid cold weather, enough to drive a person mad. No wonder people went off cliffs up here. She shot a glance at the half-open window across the room. Easy enough to close it, but then her clothes would smell like smoke. In Trinidad—oh,

those magic words—people didn't have this problem. They
kept their windows open all night and fell asleep to the scent
of the ocean breeze.

She shifted the phone from one ear to the other. "What?
Secret girlfriend? What's a 'secret girlfriend'—she worked for
the CIA? Girl, you're talking shit. Who's telling you all this?"

Squawk, squawk, squawk. It was Trevor's fault that Emmie
was freaking out, all of it Trevor's fault, really. Why did she listen to him in the first place? So many empty promises. Too
bad the dead don't make deliveries.

"Emmie, Emmie, calm down. Do you really think I'd be
involved with a druggie? . . . What? I'm from *Trinidad*, girl,
not Jamaica, and no, people don't make a living 'smoking
rope' back home." *Damn Americans. Get a map, learn some geography.* "No, look, let me keep your name on the books—
you're down for Arthur at Chelsea Prep, Matthias at the
Jewish Day School, and Nick . . . Emmie? Emmie?" What the
fuck? She shook the phone. Damn girl had *not* hung up on
her. "I'll keep you on the list then," she told the phone. Then
she snapped it closed.

Another girl, one whose bank account was not sinking
into double digits, would have thrown the phone across
the room and damn all if it broke, but no way was Gillian
picking up the pieces and asking that man for another
cell phone.

No need to be cold one more second though. Who was
here to smell her anyway? A last drag on the cigarette and she
crossed the room, chucked the butt through the open window, and lifted her hands up to slam it down. Caught sight of
the girl hiding below.

Was she for real? Gillian blinked hard—girl still there. A tramp, a beggar, a nowherian? Did they have anything to feed her? There was leftover curry in the pot and maybe some rice in the fridge . . .

Except, wait, not a beggar. This was a girl from school, from the other side of her own Am Civ class even—what was her name, Aisha, Amira, Alina?—one of the ragheads, anyway. Of course, Americans wouldn't say "raghead"; they talked all pretty with their "Arab Americans" and "African Americans," but it was other words they were thinking, and they'd spit in your face as soon as offer you a ride home. In Trinidad, they said the words, and then linked arms and headed off to the beach. Gillian stuck her head through the window. "What are you doing, spying on me?"

The girl jumped so hard she bumped her head against the window ledge. "I'm just cold," she said. "There was warm air coming through the window, so I figured I'd—"

"You think I'm stupid?" Gillian pulled her head back, yanked the window all the way up, and gestured at the girl on the ground. "In."

She didn't move.

"Get your butt inside."

One more minute and the girl bent her head, braced her arms, and wriggled her skinny Arab ass through the window. "What?" she asked, getting to her feet. She pushed masses of dark, curly hair off her face.

Wait her out. Except that waiting, well, not exactly Gillian's hand full of high cards. "You're out there spying on me, and you ask *me* what?"

"I wasn't—"

Gillian picked up the phone. Everything happens for a reason—if she'd thrown it against the wall, where would she be now? "I'm going to call the police. Or better yet, immigration."

Spygirl raised her eyebrows and power shifted. "I was born here," she said. Too polite to add *idiot*. "Could you please close the window?"

Gillian wavered. She was freezing, too. *Slam*. "So? What the hell is Nick's problem? He doesn't have the balls to stalk me himself?"

"Huh?"

Gillian waved her cell phone in the girl's face. "You think I won't press charges?"

"Are you nuts? All I was doing was sitting under your window. What do you think the police would do? Tell me to run along home and stop bothering you. Then they'd tell *you* to stop bothering *them*."

Gillian turned away. The list was still in her hand. Scratch Emmie's name off? Really, what was the point? She crumpled it into a ball and sent it arcing toward the wastebasket, except that it missed, hit the carpet, rolled under the bed. "Whatever," she said. "Get the hell out of here. Tell Nick I don't give a flying—"

"I didn't come here because of any Nick," said the girl. "I was sent here by someone else." She was staring at the wall over Gillian's head, her eyes unfocused, almost as though she was in a trance. Was she on drugs? Gillian'd heard a million stories about the shit they did in Saudi Arabia—or maybe that was Pakistan. Opium laced with cyanide, make you the highest kite in the atmosphere.

There she went, sounding like Emmie, mixing up parts of the world she'd never been to and labeling them "druggie." When did she turn into an American?

"Trevor."

"What?" Gillian stared. "Who?"

The girl lowered her eyes, turned her head aside. "Trevor Sanders, you know, he was, uh, he passed over last week."

Passed over? She sounded like some kind of fake medium. Still, how did she guess Gillian and Trevor were anything to each other, anything at all? "What's that? Trevor Sanders told you to come here?" No way Gillian was discussing business with this girl come out of nowhere. "Are you sure you're not looking for that cheerleader Shimmer, or Shimmy, or whatever, the one he was all over at the last football game?"

Spygirl wasn't looking dreamy now. "Glimmer, her name is Glimmer, and he didn't have his hands all over her—she chased him, but he, he had other, other things on his mind."

Gillian dropped down onto her bed. She didn't invite the girl to take a seat. "It's Aisha, right?"

"Who? Me?" By now she was picking at a broken nail. "No, I'm Aliya. Aliya al-Najjar."

"What has Trevor got to do with me—or you, for that matter?"

The nail came off, and Gillian watched Aliya start right in on the next one. Could have used a manicure, that girl, dark red polish would look great on her. But Arab girls were all hide-your-light-under-a-veil, even the ones who didn't scarf. "I got an e-mail from Trevor today," said Aliya. "He wanted

me to give you some envelope he left in my locker. Said it
was really important."

Gillian stared. Stared again. Stared some more. "Uh, dahlin," she said at last, in her most gentle voice, "you know Trevor's dead, right?"

"I know."

Right. Gillian wanted to think about that envelope—was it full of money, *her* money, or maybe a passkey to a safe-deposit box somewhere? But she put on the breaks, because the girl looked about to pass out, and Gillian didn't trust her anyway. Not a centimeter. "So Trevor's dead, and he's sending you e-mails from heaven? Who knew God had wireless?"

Aliya looked down at the carpet, up at the ceiling, at the first window, the second window, and finally settled on the carpet again. She blinked those big dark eyes a couple of times, even wrinkled that sharp Roman nose, but she didn't say anything.

"Tell me this, then," said Gillian, when she couldn't stand to look at the hesitant girl another second. "Probably a hundred thousand people died in the last twenty-four hours, all with devoted loved ones wailing and ripping their clothes. How come Trevor's the only one who learned how to send an afterlife e-mail?"

Still nothing from the girl but blinking eyes, wrinkling nose.

"And why, of all the people Trevor knew, why pick you?"

Spygirl broke. "We were friends," she said. "Closer than anyone knew."

"And the e-mail from heaven?"

"You wouldn't believe me."

"So?"

Aliya bit her thumbnail so hard, Gillian thought the whole nail would come right off. "In Syria," she said, "we have this stuff we do, kind of like magic, but it's all caught up with Islam—I mean, strict religious people like my parents wouldn't go near it, they think it's *haram*, that's forbidden, but my great-aunt, well, some other people, they see it more like a shortcut. To getting the things you really want. I mean, you should only do it if you're desperate."

Gillian knew all about desperate.

"So, well, last night, I was a little—I was out of my mind. I really needed to talk to Trevor, and since my great-aunt taught me how to do it, well sort of, I, well, I tried it. Some of the magic."

"Nowadays magic's on e-mail, too?"

Aliya rubbed her lips together. Bit the bottom one. "I told you you wouldn't believe me," she said. "All I know is, last night I tried to contact Trevor, and this afternoon I got an e-mail. And the e-mail said to give you the envelope, so here I am."

"And you never thought, could be a glitch in the program and Trevor sent it, oh I don't know, last week, when he was still breathing?"

Silence. Gillian would bet her life savings—all the money Trevor had been keeping for her until the end of the year, all the money that was, maybe, in that envelope—that Aliya had thought of the glitch thing herself, knew that was the truth. She just didn't want it to be.

"The important question," Gillian said, "is why Trevor was writing to you at all."

"No," said Aliya. "The real question is why he was writing to me about you."

"Trevor and I were running a business together." Gillian talked tough, but she almost always folded first, damn it.

"What kind of business?" Did Aliya look relieved? That girl had it bad for a dead boy. "A start-up?"

"A none-of-your-business business," said Gillian. Then, because she couldn't wait any longer: "So, Secret Girlfriend, where's my envelope?"

Aliya's eyes fluttered up. "Well, that's the thing, he never left me any envelope. He said he did, in the e-mail, but I've been all through my locker, and—"

The cell phone was out of Gillian's hand, skimming across the floor, crashing into the corner, before she could stop it. "Jeezan ages—do I look stupid to you?" The whole thing was lunatic. Gillian's suspicions of Nick Loring came roaring back, and she spoke too loud. "Get out. And tell whoever sent you, I'm not as stupid as they obviously think I am."

Aliya headed to the window.

"Not the window. I do have a door, you know. No *broughtupsy*, that's what's wrong with you."

Aliya stopped in the doorway, looked over her shoulder at Gillian. "He really did send that e-mail today. I came here because—well, never mind." Then she said it anyway. "Because any connection with him is better than none."

Aliya's footsteps clipped down the hall. Gillian pictured the unwashed dishes lining the kitchen counter and wished she'd shown the girl a careful route to the front door. What did Aliya know about living with a man who thought that bowls and spoons and cartons of milk made beautiful decorations? She probably had a stay-at-home mom who spent all day filing things in cupboards.

The footsteps faded. Gillian fished the crumpled paper out from under the bed and smoothed it out. Then she sat down at her desk, flipped up her laptop, and turned it on. Two minutes—stupid slow computer—and she was opening Firefox. Her fingers tapped out an address and she ended up at the Fillmore High Web site. The prompt asked for her name. *Aliya Najjar.* Password: *Trevor.*

Bingo, first try. Trinidad primary schools taught logic so much better than the Americans. She opened Aliya's inbox, found Trevor's e-mail at the very top, dated more than ninety years from now. Some ghostly trick, or just Aliya's prank? She leaned across the desk and switched on the printer.

Way out past Hilton Street, somewhere on Kelly Boulevard, there was an *obeah* man. She'd never been—she didn't believe that nonsense, she was an educated Trini—but desperate times and all. And she'd pit Caribbean black magic against Middle Eastern mumbo jumbo any season of the year. Even winter.

FOUR

DING-DONG. The door swung open, and the heavy scent of garlic and lard came out to meet her. Gillian caught her breath. Garlic and lard, a lethal combination in obeah. Behind the door, a hallway stretched long and dark before her, candles flickering behind wall sconces. She got a whiff of murder-mystery novel before the tall, thin man came into view. He wore a white robe that came to his knees and a white turban wrapped around his dark head. The skin on his face was like paper; crepe-thin but not wrinkled. "Come in, Gillian."

Now that was creepy.

She covered fast. "Hi, I'm Gillian Smith, you know my father, Derek Smith? He's an architect over at Mowbray Associates. Anyway, I have a problem, my cousin Kevin, Kevin Durrani, maybe he's the one you know? He thought you might be able to give me some advice." Some cover. Hopeless, that's what she was.

"Come in, Gillian," the obeah man said again. He moved to the side, and Gillian entered the dark hallway. The door slammed shut behind her, candles flickered, and Gillian shivered. What the hell had Trevor gotten her into now? If he'd kept his damn eyes on the road . . .

She followed the old man down the hall. He shuffled along in leather sandals that had to be imported from

Trinidad—and who was he kidding, sandals in a New England winter? Although the house was toasty warm. Trust a Trini to know something about heat. Probably scamming the electric company, getting twice the heat for half the price. Then again, maybe he was heating it by obeah.

Was that even possible? If only she'd paid attention that night, a few weeks after her father left, when her mother snuck out of the house at midnight, hair covered, face bare of makeup, a box of blue—yes, blue, the stuff you use to whiten clothes—in her hand. Her mother had woken her up with kisses, an *I'm doing this for you, chunkalunks*, but Gillian had just buried her face in the pillow and gone back to sleep.

The end of the hallway, finally. The obeah man opened the very last door and they entered a room with a high ceiling, its only luxury. The wooden floor was bare, and there was no furniture. A makeshift clothesline hung in one corner, pieces of bright cloth dangling from it. No sconces here: Dim light filtered through the black velvet curtains that covered the windows. Stone face masks with slanted eyes and big noses stared down at her from the walls. And on the floor over there—was that a chicken? *Scratch, scratch.* It was. Two chickens off in a corner. Good thing she liked animals. Another thought: maybe the garlic and lard had nothing to do with obeah but were all about overwhelming the smell of chicken shit.

But then, why keep chickens in the house at all?

The obeah man eased himself down onto the floor, sitting cross-legged. Gillian followed suit. Stupid floor, all hard planks and poking nail heads—what, did he tear up the carpet himself?

"So, Daughter," said the obeah man. "What's this malevolent force that brought you to see me?"

The faint sound of drums filled the silence that followed—or was that her heart? No, drums, upstairs somewhere. She took a deep breath. "Malevolent force?" Hopefully he'd pass right on by the shakiness in her voice.

"I can feel him hovering over you. Some kind of boy, lined with silver, smelling of soy sauce—" She flashbacked to Trevor, chowing down on sweet-and-sour chicken as he swerved his Mitsubishi around the sharpest corner. "Something black, crowing in his ear," added the obeah man. Black crow, powerful symbol of death. The obeah man frowned. "So sorry," he said. "There was more, but it's faded, I've lost it."

Not-quite-silence settled over them. *Malevolent*, the obeah man had said. What did Trevor have to be mad about? Unless he was angry that she was alive and kicking it up, while he clanked around in chains somewhere. "It's this friend of mine, this boy who crashed up his car. He and I were working a business together, and when he died, he took all my money with him." Maybe he had, for all she knew. Maybe it was in the glove compartment of that thirdhand Mitsubishi he was so damned proud of. How could she have been that stupid, letting him keep the money?

"Has all this fury brought him back?" asked the obeah man.

"Huh?" Gillian scratched her arm. Across the room, the chickens scratched the floor. "I'm not angry. I want my money—I'm going back to Trinidad, you can understand that, right? I left my mums there. Opportunities, that's what everyone said about up here, that's what my big-man father always claimed." She snorted. "What opportunities? The math I'm doing in AP, my cousin did two years ago in form three. Up here, white people want to put everyone in a category—they line me up with four black girls and sing, 'One of these things is not like the other.' And the weather—"

But the obeah man wouldn't let her go on about the cold. "Your father, what category is he in?"

"Jumping hoops for the man, that's the game he's playing. Suit and tie to work every day."

"You think he should go to work dressed up like he playing *mas* for Carnival?"

Enough. She hadn't come here to talk about her father. She wouldn't stay in her own room to talk about her father, not even when Mums called. *Is he there? Is he seeing anyone? Not that it means anything to me, but if he's going to be taking care of my baby, he better be taking care of her, not out every night with some* bumsey lambe. *Gillian's response: I'm outta here, Mums. Library, you know, project on South America.*

"This isn't about my father. It's to do with my, uh, my friend. She got an e-mail, and she thinks Trevor sent it to her after he died. It's completely mad, she's not even a Trini, just messing around." She leaned to one side and pulled a folded piece of paper out of her pocket. She hadn't wanted to leave it in her backpack. Mad herself, but still, what if the backpack got stolen? No one was going to steal something out of the pocket of her jeans. "Here it is. It could have been sent before he died. It was, I'm sure, but if not . . . well, then, he's trying to get in touch with me. And I'm figuring it must be about the money, because we weren't like that, together you know. So he must be feeling guilty—I know you said malevolent, but it could just be guilt—that he hid my money and died and now he's trying to tell me where it is. Don't you think?"

She held out the sheet of paper, but the obeah man didn't take it, didn't even look at it. "You sure you want to do this, Daughter? Obeah's not for taking lightly."

She wasn't sure at all.

"I thought this force was hovering over you—but now I see the truth. It's you, isn't it, trying to reach out and overturn things."

Gillian felt her heart go a little cold.

"You can still walk away, you know . . ." He frowned. At her? At the sounds of the chicken across the room, pecking at the bottom of the wooden clothesline? "This boy, what was he to you? Nothing, you say, this is all about the money—but money can be replaced. Go to McDonald's, put on a paper hat, and you go get money. This money you're talking about was not honestly come by, I think. Then let it go, honestly." He half closed his eyes. "There's no place for obeah in this. Obeah is to ease hurt, emptiness, longing—for someone whose emotions have taken control. Not for money. You're talking greed, girl, and obeah, obeah's not about greed."

No superpowers here. He was so wrong about her. This was all about hurting, about the emptiness she felt every morning when she woke up and heard the cold rain battering the roof above her head, the longing for her island, for the bacchanal and pounding soca of Carnival. Money wasn't for color to outline her eyes, it wasn't for a nice car or good-time pills; it was to go home. But the obeah man was still talking: "Obeah is not some kind of game, Daughter. You play the fool with obeah, you change the world. You start small, and you end up with snowstorms in the tropics, or sweltering heat in the middle of January."

She wished. "Anyone who changed the weather up here would be doing the Americans a favor." Ah, the balmy weather of Trinidad. Fresh skies, cool breezes, sea like bathwater. Storm-free, safely located outside the hurricane belt. God is a Trini, after all.

Gillian looked up to find a storm brewing across the obeah man's face. "You playing me *mamaguy*, girl," he said. "Go your way."

A chicken pressed her beak hard against the wall, as though looking for a way out. Gillian didn't move.

"You didn't hear me? You need a Q-tip or something?" The obeah man's shoulders went back. "I won't be caught up in the schemes of an ignorant girl."

But Gillian wasn't scheming. All she wanted was the way things used to be. The reason she listened to Trevor was because he'd promised her that. If only things had stayed on course. She grit her teeth, made her own promise to the obeah man. "No schemes," she said. "But they told me, my cousin said, well, I thought you could tell me whether my letter is from the dead boy or just an e-mail glitch or even that raghead—I mean, Arab girl—playing me."

"*Chupidees*, the two of you." But the obeah man leaned forward, fast, and snatched the paper from Gillian's hand. He shuffled out of the room and was back before she'd had time to think *going where?* Back with a small incense burner in one hand and in the other, the paper. The burner was lit, glowing in the room, though you could hardly smell the scent of lavender through the garlic, the chickens.

The obeah man was so tall Gillian had to scramble to her feet to see what he was doing. He held the paper over the burner and waited. One long moment, two, three—scratch scratch chicken, breathe breathe Gillian. "No secret writing," he said and handed it back to her. "No MapQuest directions to your money. I can't help you. Go please."

He was already holding the door for her. She didn't have to walk through. She could jump him, pound his head on the floor, hold him up with the gun she didn't have, and make him work his magic. Or she could accept that the whole thing was *dotish*. What had he done, after all, except keep some chickens in the house and predict wild swings in climate? Hell, Al Gore could've told you heat wave in Alaska was coming.

Obeah man was just trying to drive her *basodee*. She walked down the hall and showed herself out. The fact that he knew her name? More *dotish*. Man probably kept an eye on all the Trinis in town. Those revelations about Trevor? All in her head. If he said he'd smelled barbecue she would have remembered the time Trevor came by with sticky fingers, waving a sheet of paper with his new business plan in her face.

SHE CLOSED THE DOOR behind her. Even the cold walk to her car wouldn't wring the garlic out of her clothes. If she were back with Mums, they'd make curry, drown the smell of garlic in all the spice. They'd do fresh roti too, fold their hands into the dough, kneading it together. Finish off the best pieces before the men even got to the table.

Down the walkway, back to the sidewalk, *move your feet, Gillian*. An ominous feeling hung over the sunny suburb. Not the scene she expected when she'd wrung the obeah man's address out of Kevin. Trinidad-style row houses, that would've been more like it, crammed close together, lining a street impossibly narrow and impossibly steep; soca music blasting, lil boys playing cricket in the road. She turned her head, took one last glance over her shoulder. Had the obeah man's villa looked this creepy when she drove up? Did the curtainless windows really grow darker while she was inside, did the chimney tilt more precariously?

What was so disconcerting? The fact that the obeah man had never denied the letter was ghostly? Or was it—

"*Eons.*" The thin trickle of a word warbled in the air behind her. What the hell? No, wait, not *eons*—"*Gillian.*" Someone was calling her name. Had the obeah man raised a *jumbie* from the grave and sent it to follow her?

Don't be ridiculous. But it was a heartbeat, then two, another "*Gillian!*" before she finally forced herself to turn around and face whomever—*whatever*—was behind her.

FIVE

NO OBEAH-RAISED JUMBIE shimmered in the afternoon light—a skinny girl stood there, alone, black hair whipping around her face like a mask, lips full and pouty. Spygirl. "What, you were just going to ignore me?" she asked.

Gillian stared at her. "What is this?" What was the girl thinking, following her all the way out here? Gillian couldn't believe it. Horror thought: What if the Trevor-wrote-me-from-the-dead dilemma was all a cover and Spygirl was really mad for Gillian? Maybe she should have asked the obeah man for a Make-Me-Ugly spell. "You can't just say 'hello'? 'Excuse me'? Why the hell you stalking me?"

"Me? Stalking *you*?" Aliya brushed her hair back; two angry black eyes stared out of her face. "I'm not the one breaking into people's e-mail accounts and reading their private letters."

"What are you ranting on about?"

Aliya came so close up in her face that Gillian had to step back. "Yesterday, I came back upstairs to ask you if you knew, beforehand, that Trevor was going to be at that party. You were so absorbed in printing out my e-mail, you didn't even hear me at the door."

Had to say something. "Why didn't you come crashing through the door, challenge me then?"

"I'm not you," said Aliya. Gillian expected her to look away, but her gaze never shifted. "Besides, I wanted to know what you were going to do with it—didn't figure you'd tell me if I asked."

Gillian shoved cold hands into her pocket. Girl wasn't the piece of fluff she looked like at first glance. Still, time to put her in her place. "It's not that I believe in your afterlife e-mail, don't swell your face up so. But the house I just went to, there's an obeah man living there—you know what obeah is?"

"Like voodoo, isn't it?"

"Something like. I wanted his take on your wild imagination. That's all." Gillian turned her back on Aliya and headed down the street. What had possessed her to park so far away? What was she thinking, the old man was going to do obeah on her license plate?

Aliya scrambled to catch up. "Well? What'd he say?"

Gillian could let it go. *Chupidees, the two of you.* Run with that, why not? Then again, the last time she'd checked, a one-way ticket from Boston to Port of Spain cost $699.

Aliya's sad eyes, her hangdog face, those had nothing to do with it.

"He said Trevor's a 'malevolent force' hanging over me." Gillian stepped down off the curb, swerved past the puddle spreading in the street. Aliya swerved alongside her, and they jostled elbows in the middle of Kelly Boulevard. "But if I just leave the whole thing alone, he says, it'll probably sort itself out. Still, I think he saw something, he just doesn't trust me—" Aliya's lower lip had jutted out, her face screwed up. "What? You're the one who followed me here, now you don't want to hear what I have to say?"

"'Malevolent' is not a word I'd use to describe Trevor."

Ow. Gillian's feet crashed into the opposite curb. "By the time I left, obeah man seemed pretty sure the malevolent one is me," she said. Four steps down the sidewalk and her car finally came into view. *Malevolent.* Aliya was right, the word didn't suit—wouldn't have suited—Trevor. "Willful," "whiny," "white"—all were a better fit. Obeah man didn't get Trevor, just the way he didn't get her; all she wanted to do was set things right. And all Trevor wanted was to lime, party, have a good time. Nothing malevolent about that.

Almost there. Gillian clicked the unlock symbol on her key ring.

"Well? What are you going to do?"

Gillian took in the car parked right behind hers, up against the bumper. Aliya's car, had to be. *Stupid Gillian. Couldn't you have looked in the rearview mirror just once?*

"Do? What do you mean, what am I going to do? Go home and take a hot shower." The getaway car at last. The door opened, but it wasn't Gillian who'd opened it. Aliya. Climbing into the passenger seat.

"What are you doing?"

She didn't answer. Gillian found herself inside, repeating the question.

"You haven't told me anything, not even what your 'none of your business' with Trevor was." Aliya ran her finger across the top of the door, found the lock and pressed it down. *Click.* "You think I'm going to just give up and fade away?"

Not anymore. Anyway, what difference did it make? "A prom business," said Gillian. "Boys like Mac Stevens or Al Winthrop, guys who could never get a date, pay us to fix them up with someone really hot from another school. And now, hot girls from Fillmore, we're fixing them up with boys from other schools. It's been very . . ." She paused for the right word. "Lucrative." She wanted to finish up by ordering Aliya out—but it hadn't worked before, so why would it now? Sure enough, the *chupidee* was asking for details. Gillian slid the key into the ignition and pressed Play on the CD player. "Jumbie," Road March winner at Carnival 2007, pounded against the doors and roof of the car. *Jumbie.* Too much coincidence for Gillian's taste. She started the car. Music blaring, car ready to move—surely the fool girl would jump out? But of course she didn't. Gillian drove smoothly down the tree-lined street, hit the corner, and only went faster. By the time she took a hard right onto Route 1, she knew exactly where she was going.

Aliya asked something else, but Gillian couldn't make out more than a moving mouth with the music so loud. And then they were there, pulling up alongside a green house with an open front door and so many leaves in the driveway you could barely see the pavement.

Aliya's mouth was still moving; she covered her eyes with her hands. Gillian turned the music down. "I can't" exploded into the car. "His mother doesn't even know me, and if she did, I mean, I just can't."

"I'm not saying we should go in," Gillian began. Then someone came out the front door, someone taller than Trevor, with glasses, but the same pointed chin and the same swinging, almost-an-athlete walk. "There's Luke," she said. "Have you talked to him?"

"I haven't talked to anyone," said Aliya. But she dropped her hands and leaned forward, watching him. Something moved across her face: quiet tears.

Luke wore a black cap pulled down on his forehead and a black backpack slung over his shoulder. Slung low, like it was heavy. Could he be carrying her money?

Gillian flushed in some kind of shame. Trevor was dead—couldn't she spend half a minute in front of his own house, mourning him?

Then Aliya was grabbing her arm—"Duck!" A car rumbled to life up the driveway as both girls pushed their heads down. *Thwack*. Gillian's hit the steering wheel. Stupid wheel, stupid head, stupid, stupid, stupid Spygirl. The car roared past.

"Jeezan ages—"

"Well, what if he saw us?" said Aliya, sitting back up.

Gillian sat up too, checked her forehead in the mirror. Big red spot growing there already, damn it all. School counselors would be slipping her thin pamphlets with "Abuse: you can make it stop" on the cover for the next six weeks.

"Don't just sit there," said Aliya. "Follow him."

"Follow him?"

Aliya leaned over and turned the key. Down the road, Luke's car stopped at the stop sign. "Hurry up."

"Are you crazy, or stupid?" But Gillian pressed her foot on the gas. "What, you think he's headed out to a council with the jumbies?" She paused. "Ghosts, you know." She was kidding—*kidding*—but she noticed Aliya didn't tell her no. After a minute, the girl said, "Who knows, maybe Trevor contacted him, too."

They reached the end of the street. Gillian looked as far as she could in one direction; Aliya peered around the corner in the other. "Right," Aliya said. Gillian's car jumped to the right and sped up. "What are you doing? Do you want him to see us? Don't you know how to follow anyone?"

If only Gillian had gotten in off the wait list at Spygirl Institute.

Luckily, she only had to duck and swerve for three more streets. Then Luke took a right on Daimler and headed toward Route 1. Where the hell was he going? A quick look at Aliya's white face told her what the girl was thinking: out to the state forest, to Trevor's last resting place.

Except that here he was, turning left on Old Post Road. Not two minutes from the center of town, but it felt like country. On one side, mansions with rolling front lawns; across the street, thick woods. "There's no one else on the road. He's a complete *cunumunu* if he doesn't know we're following him."

As though he'd heard her, Luke pulled over, stopped short. Gillian shot past him, staring straight ahead, but Aliya turned right around in her seat and gave a play-by-play. "Don't worry, he's not even looking up. He's getting out, slamming the door . . . now he's walking in front of a small brown sign—hey, I know where he's going. Stop the car."

For some strange reason, Gillian bumped over onto the grassy shoulder.

"There's a path over there," said Aliya. "It leads to Fuller's Lake. Come *on*." They were out of the car, Aliya running, Gillian scrambling to catch up. After all, there was something in that bag, maybe, something he might be about to consign to the depths of the lake.

They entered the woods and tumbled down the path. "Do you have to break every freaking twig in the forest?"

Aliya jabbed her with an elbow. "Shhh." Girl had some nerve, when she the one making all the noise.

They came out onto a grassy hill, and below it, a sandy beach. It took a couple of seconds to find him, but she saw that Luke was walking toward a thin figure sitting at the end of the pier. Even from behind, Gillian recognized the pink hair. She couldn't help looking at Aliya; sure enough, Aliya was looking right back.

Miya Chonan. Once blue-ribbon speller, ace math tester, hand waver beyond compare. Today: slut of the year, complete with little red horns and black sash.

What was Luke doing, looking up Miya? Did they really want to know? One more look at the girl beside her, and Gillian guessed they did. Aliya tilted her head toward a nearby clump of trees, her meaning clear.

SIX

"CAREFUL YOU DON'T fall in," said a voice behind her.

Miya sat at the very end of the pier, swinging her legs over the two million gallons of Fuller Lake. Home to trout, bass, catfish, crappie, and—wait, what was it?—oh yes, tadpoles. That was local geography for eight hundred points, thank you very much.

"This is a funny place for a meeting," said Luke, taking a seat on the plank beside her. Almost beside her. A small pile of rocks sat between them. Miya sorted through the pile, picked out a small round one, and tossed it. One second, two seconds—best of rocks, heading for the sunset horizon—and *splash.*

"Don't you remember?" she said. Almost four years ago now, that fateful company picnic where they'd talked Arthurian legends and her mother had met his father for the first time.

Luke didn't answer. Perhaps he, too, was trying to swipe an eraser over the blackboard of the past. He divided the pile into round stones and smooth stones—very methodical, Luke. She'd forgotten that.

"I feel like some kind of spy," said Luke. "All this, 'meet me at the pier, four o'clock, come alone.'" He pushed brown bangs off his forehead. "What's up, Miya?"

"Just wanted to tell you how sad I am about Trevor," she said. Held her breath, wondered if by some supernatural chance he knew. She snuck a glance at him out of the corner of her eye: no sign of *gnosis*, as he passed a flat rock from one hand to the other. "And I figured your mom wouldn't be too thrilled if I showed up at your house."

"Huh?" Luke skimmed the rock across the water. Four, five, six hops—he'd always been the best at skimming. It had been Trevor on distance, of course. "Oh, that. My mom's a bit of a basket case these days. She doesn't recognize me even, most of the time. The doctor's got her high as a kite on 'ludes. She's even fawning all over that damn dog, the one she used to threaten to euthanize day after day."

"Oh," said Miya. "Sorry." She was, too. She pictured Trevor's mother, prostrate, sobbing on her bed—not difficult, since she'd seen her that way before. It had been Miya who'd sent her rushing there, then . . . "Were you at Mal's that night?" she asked Luke. "Was that the last time you saw him?"

"Why are you asking me? Weren't you there?"

Miya sat so still on the pier that she might have been frozen to it.

"Talking to Trevor—that's right, all intense, in the corner of the TV room. I saw you. It just never occurred to me . . ." He leaned over, tugged on the ends of her hair. His cologne, something musky and male, spilled off his shoulders. "Give up the nonsense about condolences, Sim. You called me down here for a reason, didn't you?" His eyes flashed, his voice had a bite to it.

"To tell you how sorry I am, about Trevor." Had he really seen her talking to Trevor? They'd been hidden behind the high-backed sofa, hemmed in by that glass curio cabinet. She closed her eyes, sank back into Mal's living room—hip-hop pounding in her ears, couch reeking with beer, Trevor shouting. Shouting loud enough for someone else to hear? But no one had been nearby. No one she'd noticed, anyway.

It had been a long time since she'd noticed Luke.

"You're the secret girlfriend, aren't you?" Luke stared at her. He'd grown taller, broader, more commanding since middle school. "I thought it was just Glimmer playing the drama queen, but it was all true, wasn't it? That's why you called me down here today."

Glimmer Collins had done some sobbing at the memorial service, wailed that Trevor'd never kissed her, never even touched her; he was in love with somebody he couldn't have. Typical Glimmer scene. Not that Miya'd dared to go to the service. Savannah Lucas, Glimmer's best friend, had run a useful play by play on her MySpace page.

Miya twisted her head with the wind. Let him think her heart was broken, why not? Better that than the truth. But instead she said, "Don't be ridiculous."

"It would kill my mom if Trevor was with you. I thought Glimmer was just talking out her ass, but this, this makes sense."

"Me and Trevor?" Miya's hand slipped, sent half the stone pile into the water. *Splash, gurgle, klunk*. Eighty-seven hundred liters of water swallowed them up. "You have it all wrong, we didn't, we weren't . . ."

Why should he believe her? Her big mistake, stripping for the Cavalho twins. No better way to confirm the school rumors that Miya would do anything.

At least she'd said no to the videotape.

"Someone saw him up on Standish Road, you know, that little clearing just before you reach the access road to the forest? After he left the party, an hour or two later—"

"The Crescent?" Miya's teeth slid into her lip. At school, in the library, she chewed on pencils, but here she was stuck with nothing but body parts. "Bastard, he said he'd given up."

"Given up?"

Miya looked across the lake, where the sun was spray-painting everything pink and purple. Her butt, ice-cold against the top of the pier, had begun to hurt. She should get up, go home, make some dinner. Get out her Calc book and do those last eight problems. Check her e-mail, tell Rod Crew to stop sending her those stupid blow-job jokes.

"You know the Crescent. Trevor and Mal used to hang out there and smoke pot, and maybe, well, you know Mal, she'll try anything. Some people like their reputations wild. But Trevor was supposed to be through with all that."

"He was with a girl, wasn't Mal. They were standing in front of a car, a white Buick, the girl's car, I guess, and arguing. She was shouting at him."

"Could have been Mal."

He reached out, tugged her hair again. An electric shock—or something—must have passed between them, because her hair stood on end and she shivered. He told her, "The person who saw her, who told the police about it after Trevor—well, after all the stuff in the paper about Trevor—he only caught a glimpse of her face in the headlights, but he said she had red hair." She half turned her head, found herself looking into his gray eyes. "Was it you?"

It had been a long time since a boy had stared at her like that—as though she wasn't a girl at all, just a means to some information. Miya unbuttoned the top two buttons of her jacket. Ignored the cold that brushed across her v-necked chest, slouched her shoulders till a bit of rounded breast showed through.

"It wasn't me," she said. "We did talk at the party, but it wasn't all intense." She always sounded her most truthful when she told her biggest lies. "Why are you asking? You don't think—Trevor wasn't depressed or anything, was he?" Her gaze drifted until she was staring back down into the lake, which seemed to have grown black. She was unprepared for his fingers on her chin, for him to wrench her head around. "What the hell are you insinuating?" he asked.

"I didn't say anything." She leaned forward, tucked her trembling hands behind her knees under her thighs.

"I can take melodramatic shit from Glimmer, but you're too intelligent to try to pull this crap. Trevor was driving too fast, flying up the road like a maniac, just the way he always did." The same unconvincing story she'd been telling herself all afternoon.

He stood up. "You'd better forget this stupidness."

She peeled her jeans off the wooden pier and scrambled to her feet. Moved close to him, as close as she dared. "I don't see why it matters now."

"Jesus," said Luke. His foot swung out, and he kicked the remaining rocks into the water.

"Luke, I'm sorry." She leaned over to clutch his arm, but somehow she missed. He was already shoving his hands into

his pockets, striding down the pier. She watched as he
reached the rickety steps, jumped them two at a time, headed
up the steep path that led to the street.

Then she started after him.

SEVEN

AT THE TOP of the path, Miya looked right, then left: no Luke. He must have parked on Davis Drive. Why was she chasing him, anyway? Just to hear herself say *sorry, sorry, sorry* out loud? He could never give her what she needed—the words *it wasn't your fault, Miya* could only come from Trevor.

She rounded the curve anyway and almost banged knees with a blue, mud-splattered car. She would have thought it belonged to Luke except for the two girls attached, their butts balanced against the back door. One had her arms crossed, and the other seemed to fade into the fur-lined hood of her black jacket.

Their faces came into focus. Two girls she knew, sort of. Aliya had been on College Bowl one semester, before she quit, claiming late practices hurt her grades. The island girl, Gillian, was in her Calc class. Write it on the board, and she'd complain: problem was too easy, chalk too squeaky, teacher too lazy.

What were they doing here?

"Hey," said Miya. They must have seen Luke, watched him disappear. She'd just ask where he'd gone, all casual . . .

"So what was the deal between you and Trevor?" asked Aliya.

Miya stopped. They couldn't have overheard her conversation with Luke, could they? Anyway, she hadn't said . . . what had she said? All she could remember was her pounding heart, her scattered thoughts; Luke's gray eyes not quite seeing her. God, she hated that. She'd given up playing the Invisible Asian Girl long ago.

"Well?" said Aliya.

"No deal," said Miya quickly. She'd remember it if she'd given herself away. She would. She was famous for her memory. "I've known Trevor since middle school, that's all. We met down there, at the lake." Her mother and Mr. Sanders flashed across her mind, dancing that exuberant salsa on the shore, all their colleagues studiously looking away.

"You were with him that last night," said Aliya. Her dark eyes shone with suspicion. "If you know something—"

Maybe you're right. His last words echoed in her head. Miya turned, tried to find something to look at. Nothing but dirty gray road below, dismal gray sky above. What business was it of theirs, anyway? Spying on her, eavesdropping, and now trying to badger her into leaking gossip.

God, Miya hated girls.

She pulled her jacket closed. "I don't know anything," she said at last. "There isn't anything to know. He was hanging out at Mal's party, and we said hi. Maybe I asked him how his family was or whatever, but it's not like we were friends. Not anymore." *Maybe I told him to stop thinking about himself for once. Maybe I—*but no. There was no going back.

Aliya opened her mouth to say something that sounded like "Didn't—" but Gillian kicked her. "Look, we're just trying to sort out what happened with Trevor that last night, and since."

"Since? He went over a cliff and his car exploded."

A little harsh, that. Aliya rubbed her lips together, blinked rapidly, and Miya was sure she was crying. Playing the drama queen? *A boy died in my school and I'm so sad, sob, sob, sob.* She wouldn't have credited Aliya so, back when they squabbled on College Bowl and Aliya was right that the first sociologist was Ibn Khaldun, not Emile Durkheim. Annoying, sometimes, that Aliya, but she was no Glimmer Collins.

Not that it mattered. Miya had never known what to do with girls. She took in gray road again, gray tires, gray, gray sky before she finally managed a short, "Sorry."

"Here's the thing," said Gillian. "We were wondering, you know, if you've had any out of the ordinary experiences." Aliya elbowed her, a short, sharp jab; Gillian pushed back. "Anything you can't explain, something supernatural, that sort of thing."

Miya yanked her hair hard enough that it hurt. "What are you, Ghostbusters or something?"

"It's not like that, Miya." Aliya intertwined her slender fingers; it almost looked like she was praying. "We just . . . we think—"

"We have our reasons," interrupted Gillian. She shook her head so fiercely her earrings jingled. "And they're not necessarily the same ones. Some people are looking out for themselves, others are just crazy."

"Sorry, I can't help you," said Miya. The street was wide open, but she started feeling hemmed in, all those trees. Or maybe it was Gillian's menacing look. The island girl plunged her hands into her pockets, came out with a well-worn piece of paper. She unfolded it, looked it over. Just a couple of typed lines, Miya could see through the back of the page. Gillian read it once, twice, three times.

"What's that?" asked Miya.

Gillian didn't look up. "Did you ever wonder if we know the truth about Trevor's death? The whole truth?"

Had the whole world been at that damn party, listening in? Either that, or Trevor had worn a wire—

Or written a note.

Miya's eyes returned to the paper in Gillian's hands. Its creases and smears seemed to take on a sense of weight, an aura of seriousness. She squinted, trying to make out the words through the back. Was that *I can't*? As in, *I can't go on*?

"Can I see that paper please?"

Gillian peered over the top of it. "The evidence on this paper offers a whole different way of looking at Trevor's death," she told Miya. "Why should I share it with you—you won't even tell us what Trevor said to you at Mal's party."

Evidence.

Gillian started to fold back the paper. Folding away Miya's chance to find out Trevor's last thoughts, his reasons for, well, for whatever it was he'd done.

Not if she could help it. Miya opened her eyes wide, looked over Gillian's shoulders, and said, "Oh my God" in a half whisper. The oldest trick in the world's most predictable book, but Gillian and Aliya both turned their heads. In that half second, Miya leaned forward and snatched the note out of the other girl's hand.

Then she spun around and ran.

EIGHT

MIYA CRASHED BACK through the woods, but instead of taking the path down to the pier, she veered left, toward the Daqri Apartments and Court Street; right after that she'd hit downtown. Less of a walk than school to Fuller Lake. Were they following her? If the note were as vital as Gillian claimed, surely they'd be panting at her heels. The crunch of broken twigs echoed in the woods, followed by the crash of someone parting leaves. She sprinted past the Daqri sign, leaped the fence, took off down Court Street. She turned the corner. Downtown Fillmore was hardly New York City, but there was always a crowd shuffling on the sidewalks, especially late afternoon. She ducked into the doorway of the ToeShoe Shop and stole a quick look behind. No one there. She uncrumpled the paper in her hand. An e-mail. *Hey Aliya*, it began. She read through it to the *Trevor* at the end. Then, cheeks cooling, heart back to regular beats, she read it again.

Of course, *Aliya* was the secret girlfriend and Gillian was—well, some shadowy connection. Their behavior made a bit more sense. But why the secret? Aliya was smart, confident, verging on beautiful: willowy figure, clouds of dark hair, that fragile look. Sure they ran with different crowds, but everyone threw over caste for love. No need for Trevor to make such a fuss.

But if Aliya was the girlfriend, who was the redhead at the Crescent?

Da-da-di. Miya's cell phone rang. She swung up her purse and pulled it out. **Mom**. Hardly time for a chat, was it? But Mom didn't easily accept being ignored. She'd call back. And call back. And call back—

"Hey."

"Guess where I am?"

Miya sucked in the sides of her cheeks, walked past the Papeterie and the *halal* butcher shop. Got assaulted by a wave of fried food from Fries With That, all the way across the street.

"Miya-chan? I'm at the Gallery, and they have the sweetest little black dresses. I mean, perfect. I'm going to get one for me; do you want one too? What do you think?"

Just what she needed. Her mom over at the Gallery, not three blocks away, ever-ready for that bonding moment.

"Miya?"

"Well, I'm sort of in the middle of something, Mom." She reached the plastic chairs at Starbucks, dodged the line that was already out the door. A swift glance at the sidewalk behind her showed that Aliya and Gillian had definitely been left behind. "I think I've lost them."

"Lost what?" Mom's voice came a little breathless, as though she was squirming her way into a dress even as she spoke. "Where are you?"

"No, just these two crazy girls, following me. They were telling me lies about someone who can't defend himself. Anymore." Trevor wouldn't have made a date with Aliya, wouldn't have promised her *soon*, if he was planning anything drastic. "I'm just trying to get them to leave me alone."

She waited for Mom to start babbling about Alone in the Dark, that new nightclub in Boston. But her mother surprised her. "Is it Perry's son?"

Perry. She hated that her mother called Mr. Sanders that, as though they were still friends, after everything he'd done. "Why would you think that?"

"If it is, your friends should be careful. Sometimes a restless spirit can chase after people who tormented him when he was alive."

A sharp wind whipped past Miya's ears. Ridiculous, to think that last part was directed at her. She'd never tormented anyone. But she remembered that look on Trevor's face, heard her own words—*Why blame everyone else for what happened? Your mom's fault, my mom's fault, everyone conspired to drive off your dad. Now you're saying it was* my *fault because* . . . But she'd never finished that sentence.

"Maybe you should pray for him," said Mom. Prayer? Mom? But she was going on. "I don't mean in a church, those scary cult prayers. Proper prayers, to help him rid himself of the jealousy and anger, so he'll leave your friends alone."

Not my friends, Miya wanted to say. She didn't get the chance. Mom launched into some story about her grandfather, Ojii-san, and how he had bad luck for seven years, until he went to see a *kitoshi*. The kitoshi explained that it was a cousin who died abroad, and no one had ever said the necessary prayers for him. Buddhist prayers to help the dead rest easy, she gathered.

She stopped gathering, tuned Mom out. Twisted her head to view empty sidewalks. Why were Aliya and Gillian chasing her anyway? The sorry-I-missed-you e-mail was hardly revelatory. That menacing look of Gillian's, that desperate plea of Aliya's . . . their behavior shifted, began to seem bizarre again.

Mom twittered away. "That's what your friends should do, find a kitoshi," she finished.

Yeah, right. Gillian and Aliya were modern girls, American girls. They'd be no more interested in kitoshi foolishness than she was.

Miya passed Ye Olde Furniture. "I'll be home soon," she told Mom, and she meant it. A little wave of guilt, for blowing her mother off, hit her. She'd make her vegetable curry for dinner, with those skinny Chinese eggplants that Mom loved.

A glass door swung open and almost hit Miya in the face. Funny, she'd always thought this door was a second entrance to the antique shop, but no, it seemed to lead someplace else. No sign, but a thick, musky incense wafted into the street. Inside, crystals glittered and bells tinkled; a stack of dusty old books rose up from the floor. Someone had opened the one on top and flattened it against the window. *The Tale of Genji*, how funny. And opened to the story of Aoi . . . Miya swallowed hard. Aoi, the neglected wife who killed herself, then came back and haunted Genji. Poor Genji. He grew so sick and drawn and pale, he almost died himself.

Miya found herself drawn into the shop, her boots clicking on the tiles. Japanese people believed in omens—wasn't Mom always telling her that? But Miya was only half Japanese. She'd probably remembered the story all wrong anyway; she'd just take a look at the book, refresh her memory, and be done with it.

A whoosh of air, some heavy panting—the door slammed shut behind her. Miya whirled around.

Gillian and Aliya.

NINE

THE STORE, piled with dusty junk and heavily scented, so reminded Aliya of Damascus, she looked around for a kettle, a sugar pot, half-filled cups of tea. But the counters, crammed with little glass baubles in boxes and revolving jewelry cases, had no room for kettle or canister.

Gillian sidled right up to Miya, fists clenched as though she were going to punch her in that belly-button nose. "What the hell do you think you're doing?" she asked. "Why did you take off like that?"

Miya crumpled the paper she held into a little ball and threw it at Gillian. "Here's your pointless e-mail," she said. The ball bounced off Gillian's chest and hit the floor. "The way you were acting, I thought it was a confession to murder—and it's nothing but a pack of excuses for standing someone up."

Aliya drew her breath in quick. To someone not drunk on love and death, her otherworld, last-touch-of-Trevor experience was nothing more than lame excuses. She reached her foot out and kicked the paper ball hard, rolling it to oblivion under the counter.

Miya edged away from them, making her way toward a window crowded with a precarious stack of books. Gillian followed, so close behind she scuffed the back of Miya's boot. "Could you just leave me alone?" asked Miya.

"Let's get out of here," Aliya heard herself saying. The small rush of excitement she'd felt all afternoon, confronting Gillian, following Miya, drained away, leaving a raw, howling spot in her chest. "This is crazy."

Gillian turned on her. "You're the one who thinks Trevor is some kind of ghost."

"You're the one who believes in obeah."

"Obeah is nothing to mess with, girl."

A crash from the corner, and they both swung around to see the books on the floor. "Ghost?" said a shiny-faced Miya. "Obeah?" She had a book in her hand—Aliya squinted and made out the title, *The Tale of Genji*. First novel ever written, by Murasaki Shikibu, in eleventh-century Japan. She'd never read it, but during the College Bowl Miya had drilled them on trivia, all those Wednesdays after school.

That glitter in Miya's eyes; how annoying. "I thought you weren't interested," Aliya said. "You told us—"

"You really think Trevor's a ghost?" Miya's voice dripped with scorn.

Aliya felt more like a fool every second that Miya stared at her. She tried to explain—the midnight ceremony, the e-mail, the direction to find Gillian, the obeah man. She'd reached the part about Gillian and Trevor's business plan when a young woman with a tight mouth, hair falling out of her ponytail, pushed open the door at the back of the store. "What's going on out here?" she asked.

"Sorry," said Miya. "I knocked the books over, I'll pick them up." But she made no move. Her raised eyebrows turned on Gillian instead. "You believe this magic stuff, too?" she asked.

"Obeah isn't magic, not exactly. It's—"

"Yeah, yeah, kind of like voodoo, but in the English-speaking Caribbean."

"If you've come for magic stuff, you're in the wrong place," said the woman, now behind the cash register. "We sell crystals and candles and silver jewelry, things like that." She shot them a suspicious glance.

Aliya found herself migrating to Miya's corner. It was worth one last try, wasn't it? "Tell us what happened at the party," she said to Miya in her lowest voice. "And then we'll leave you alone."

"Nothing happened!" Miya was still holding that book, one finger tracing the raised title. *Cha-ching* came from behind them, as the cashier opened the register. Miya fell to a crouch, started picking up the books, and Aliya dropped down beside her. *The Iliad. The Odyssey. The Argonauts of the Western Pacific. Witchcraft in the Azores.* Aliya snatched up the last, while Miya stacked one, two, three books. She was picking up a fourth when Gillian swooped down and pulled it from her. "Ya man," she said, sitting next to Miya. "What's this?"

Not a book at all, but a letter-sized box an inch thick, layered in dust. Gillian swept the cover with her palm, which set the dust flying. *Tarot Cards*, it read. Had Old Aunt said anything about Tarot Cards? Aliya remembered that wrinkled face pressed close to her own, breath smelling like cloves. She'd described the jinn—creatures made of smokeless fire who could fly, fit themselves into any space, bend the laws of time and physics. She'd gone on about how to contact them: fire and blood and pentagrams on the floor. But no, not a word about Tarot Cards. Aliya reached for them anyway.

"Are you girls finished over there?" called out the clerk.

"Just a minute," said Gillian. "We spilled a box of cards, we're picking them up."

The box was in Aliya's hands now. She opened it, lifted out the cards. "One for me," she said, laying the top card on the floor. It played nicely, a girl in a black fringed shawl, crying. "Grief. And one for you." She handed card number two, a dark-haired woman with a sword over her head, to Gillian. "Revenge."

"Don't make me a white girl," said Gillian.

Aliya ignored her and turned over card number three. A girl with yellow hair—pink would have been better, but who knew what Miya would do next?—and a black heart. "A girl with a secret," she said. "You won't find peace until you tell your story."

"That's not a girl with a secret," said that oh-so-irritating Gillian. "That's guilt. Look at the bad eye she giving me," she added. Aliya couldn't help it, her face froze into anger all by itself. "But it's not my fault," Gillian protested. "There it is, written on the bottom of the card."

Miya sat flat on the floor, let the book fall in her lap. "I'm not guilty of anything," she said, her lips barely moving.

"How can we know that?" asked Gillian. "If you won't tell us what happened . . ."

Miya pressed her lips together. Aliya felt a fleeting bit sorry for her. She didn't hate Miya, who'd never fit in at school. Too smart for her own good and when she toned that down, too sexy. But then Miya said, "What, do you think I'm some kind of fortune teller?" and Aliya flinched, because there was that day, the rain pounding so hard the curtains inside the basement shuddered, that Trevor ordered Chinese food. With fortune cookies that he broke open and read out loud, ridiculous things like, *You will fall in love with a man with dark hair and two silver earrings and you will encourage him to tattoo your name on his wrist—Really?* he'd interrupted himself. *You want me to get a tattoo?* And then she tickled him until he gave up the tiny slip, and she found he'd been making them up himself.

"All I want to know is what went on between you guys."

"Nothing." Miya flipped through the book in her lap. "Trevor blamed me for his parents' divorce."

"Blamed you?" Gillian tugged on the gold hoop in her ear. "I mean, I can see him calling out your mother—" She broke off, looked embarrassed. "Shut up, Gillian," she muttered to herself. "Just shut the fuck up."

Miya ran her tongue over her lips, smudged her lipstick. Finally, she said, "You know Trevor."

"You're saying he spent the party complaining about his parents? That doesn't sound like Trevor." Aliya drummed her fingers on the Tarot box in her lap.

"Look, we got into a fight, okay? Trevor said some stupid things and I said even stupider things right back." Was Miya tearing up? A trick of the light, had to be. "I'd give anything to tell Trevor I didn't mean it now."

"Maybe you can," said Gillian. Aliya and Miya turned to her in surprise, but it was a fourth voice that spoke, interrupting them. "Can I help you girls with anything?" asked the clerk, hovering behind them. They got the message.

The three girls rose to their feet and squeezed their way back to the main part of the store. Aliya wanted to ask Gillian to explain her cryptic comment, but first: "Is that it?" she asked Miya. "Just a fight?"

"Isn't that enough?"

Bells jingled. Footsteps came inside, a middle-aged voice mumbled a question, the clerk answered, "Six o'clock." Aliya didn't take her eyes off Miya's flushed face.

"I said some pretty nasty things. I just think . . . Believe me, you don't want that to be the last thing you ever say to someone. And, well, I just keep thinking, you know how it gets when you're mad about something and you can't get it out of your head?" Miya's voice faded; she almost sounded like she was talking to herself. "What if he was driving up there and he kept getting madder and madder and not paying attention. And then . . ."

Aliya pictured it: car driving up the road, radio blaring, Trevor cursing, slope getting ever steeper. Blink, blink. *Don't think about it.*

"Stop worrying your *chupidee* self over it," said Gillian. "Trevor was too much in love with himself to obsess over a stupid fight."

He was supposed to be too much in love with me.

"Never in this life," Gillian went on, forgetting, perhaps, that Trevor was no longer *in* this life. "You smoking, girl, you think this is about you."

But she did. Aliya could see it in Miya's dark oval eyes, in the flicker of—yes, they were wet—her eyelashes. Miya turned her head away, buried her face in a rack of multicolored scarves. "There, I've told you everything," said her muffled voice. "Satisfied?"

Of course she wasn't satisfied. "I don't suppose he told you anything about me?" The scarves went completely still. Aliya pounced. "There *was* something about me."

"It's nothing, nothing about you," said Miya, raising her head. "Just that Luke mentioned something, I don't know . . ." Behind her, Gillian stepped away, head tilted back as she scanned a tiny bulletin board covered with flyers.

"Tell me." Aliya would have subjected Miya to water torture if she'd had a bucket, pulled out her fingernails if she'd thought to bring the pliers.

It must have shown in her face. "Okay, okay," said Miya. She looked a little scared, but she was already hemmed in, scarves on one side, Gillian and the wall on the other. "Luke said Trevor was at the Crescent the night he died. With some girl—not Mal, not Glimmer. She had red hair and they were fighting. Oh God, I knew I shouldn't tell you. Come on, Aliya, no, don't. Don't cry."

Aliya wasn't crying. She was disintegrating. A hundred million cells in the human body, and hers were saying goodbye to each other, one by one. She'd rather he was dead than with another girl.

Except, of course, she wouldn't.

Miya, recovered, talked over her. "What was she saying about you and Trevor running some kind of business, pimping girls?" she asked Gillian. "Could the redhead have been one of those girls?"

"Not pimping, matchmaking." Gillian sucked in her cheeks and shook her head. "And no, no redheads. We had black girls, white girls, Latinas, Asians, but I don't remember any redheads. I didn't know about Aliya, she didn't know about our partnership. Maybe Trevor had a million different lives."

That Gillian, such a comfort. Except that then Gillian was putting her arm around Aliya's shoulders, giving them a little go-ahead-and-cry pressure; *comfort* had been sarcastic, in Aliya's head, but here it was, real. She shaded her face a little, but she let the tears come.

Gillian took her arm away and rooted out a handkerchief, handed it to Aliya. "Any more revelations?" she asked Miya.

Aliya blotted her eyes, avoiding Gillian's. Her gaze went up, to the right—she was the one looking at the bulletin board now. *Posessed?* read the top line of a pink flyer. *Indian swami and Japanese Kitoshi can ease your bad luck. Multiple pathways to The Power increases your optimal truth.* And underneath: *Contact Vivek Nehru at 555-7640, or Yoko Kano, upstairs, apartment 7B.* The word *contact* seemed to stand out, brighter, more vivid than the rest.

"Gillian," she said, interrupting some discussion about whether Trevor ever said sorry in his life. "What was that you were saying before, when you told Miya she could maybe talk to Trevor?"

Gillian met her eyes, then looked away.

"You were thinking obeah, right? Don't deny it—you guys want to talk to Trevor just as much as me."

Gillian shrugged. "No one has it as bad as you, girl."

Aliya rushed on. "Here's what I'm thinking." She leaned past Gillian, drew in a whiff of jasmine-scented perfume, and ripped the flyer off its tack. "Did you see this?"

Gillian's lip curled. "Indian? Japanese? What do they know about magic? No offense," she added, gesturing toward Miya.

"Actually, you're wrong," said Miya. Her voice was a little stiff, but strong, confident, the way she used to sound in class, answering some question that wasn't even in the book. "Japan does have magic. Not in the cities maybe, but in the villages, there's still a lot of old knowledge. My mom was just telling me about it, actually." She stared over their heads. "An odd coincidence, if you think about it."

"Uh-huh," said Gillian.

Aliya hardly listened. A physical force seemed to be pushing her onward. She felt it on her shoulders, pressing forward; inside her chest, clamoring to get out. "Look, something happened that night in my bedroom. I called on the jinn to contact Trevor, and the next day, I got an e-mail. Maybe I'm just not strong enough, effective enough, creative enough—*something* enough, to go it alone . . ." She waved the slip of paper in her hand, but she wasn't thinking India or Japan. She was thinking Damascus. Arabic orchestra lilting in the background, the scent of jasmine wafting in the window. What *was* it Old Aunt said? *There are Muslim jinn and Christian jinn and pagan jinn; every person in the world has their own private jinn, just waiting to tempt them into their heart's desire.* "Maybe together we'd be powerful enough to get Trevor to—to listen. To pay attention. To hear us." She held back the last words: *to speak.*

"You crazy, girl," said Gillian. But she was picking at her manicured nails, unwilling or unable to look up.

"Don't you think," said Miya, "having an unbeliever like me there would dilute the so-called magic?"

Aliya looked straight into those still-damp eyes. "I don't think you're an unbeliever," she said. One last attempt to persuade them: "Obeah. Middle Eastern. Even Japanese. It's worth a try, isn't it? What do you have to lose?"

"Everything," said Gillian. "If this goes wrong . . ." She trailed off. "What are you talking about anyway, we all traipse out to obeah man's house? What makes you think he'll even let us in?"

Miya jumped in. "If you're going to do it, you should do it right where Trevor died." She brushed her pink bangs out of her face. "I've read about the nineteenth-century spiritualists, Arthur Conan Doyle and guys like that, and that's how *they* did it, anyway."

That was, had to be, Aliya's cue. "It's right by Firebird Point. The car—well, most of it exploded, but there are still a few pieces of rusted metal poking out of the swamp below." No one asked her how she knew that. "If Trevor is, I mean if he were, looking for me, for us, anyplace, then that has to be it."

A rustle and click echoed behind them, and Aliya jumped. Only the cashier, re-aligning the rack of scarves. "We're closing in five minutes," she said. "If you want to buy anything." She shuffled past them, headed for the windows. They watched her go.

"You crazy," Gillian told Aliya, again.

"I'm not crazy," said Aliya. Felt Aliya, in her very bones. "If you knew that you could talk to Trevor one last time— that you could ask him what he did with your money . . ." She touched Miya lightly—at least she meant it lightly. "If *you* knew that you could tell him you didn't mean it, all the things you said at the party, wouldn't you do it?"

She didn't wait for them to tell her that was the whole problem, they didn't know anything. No one did, no one ever had. "My Great-aunt Reem, she lives in Damascus, she's old, I mean really old—my mother's grandmother's sister. She wears this ratty old housedress and she barely talks above a whisper and practically the only time she leaves her bed is to go to the bathroom. But you know what? She knows about the afterlife, she knows how to contact spirits." Aliya took a deep breath. A queer feeling fluttered her eyelids and her ribcage and her belly—the same queer feeling she'd gotten when Old Aunt looked over her shoulder: *There's one right there now, up above the mirror—no, don't flinch,* habibti, *it's got to be the blackest night before he'll talk to you.*

"Obeah," Gillian said. "Some people say—"

The wooden blinds at the front window slammed shut. "We really should go," said Miya. They headed for the exit: Miya, then Gillian. Aliya had no choice but to follow. The welcome bell ding-a-linged good-bye.

"So this is it?" Aliya couldn't help asking as she fumbled in her pocket for a bus schedule—she still had to trek all the way back to Kelly Boulevard for her car. They stood in a little circle on the sidewalk. "You guys are just going to go your separate ways? You're not even going to try?"

Gillian hunkered down inside her coat. Miya said, "It's been an very adventurous afternoon."

"I'll call you," said Aliya. Exactly what Trevor had said, their very first afternoon, when she'd been so overwhelmed she threw his hand aside and sprinted across the parking lot. She'd looked back though, saw his dark face, that teasing smile. If she closed her eyes, she'd see it now.

She didn't. She looked at both girls instead, still standing there. She'd win them over.

"All right," said Miya.

"Text me," said Gillian.

Behind them, the cashier was locking the door. It sounded like the end of an interview.

TEN

IndieArabGirl: Hey

Trini_in_Exile: Hey

IndieArabGirl: I was thinking body fluids

Trini_in_Exile: Yuh on crack?

IndieArabGirl: Great aunt Reem told me that things like blood and pee--oh, and feces--are conduits for contacting the jinn. I mean, you can speak to the dead through them. Does that make sense?

Trini_in_Exile: No

Trini_in_Exile: Wait...there's something about blood in obeah

Trini_in_Exile: Soaking white cloths in red blood, I think. Something like that. I'll have to ask meh cousin

IndieArabGirl: So we should get some, right? For Saturday???

Trini_in_Exile: Gyul, yuh smokin something really potent, yuh think I going into the woods with a bucket of shit

Thursday night
Aliya: So I was talking to Gillian about body fluids—Miya? You there?

64

[A crackle, some static on the line. Then:]

Miya: Yeah, I'm here. Body fluids? Something to do with Bio class?

Aliya: No, about the whole séance thing. Remember? Saturday night?

Miya: I've got plans Saturday night, Aliya.

Aliya: Wait, just listen . . . Did you ever think about the fact that all "dead" really means is that your heart's stopped pumping blood? Doesn't that suggest that blood marks the line between dead and alive? That somehow it could be used to bridge that gap?

Miya: [Silence.] It's an interesting idea. Kind of like the whole alchemy thing—living forever—but in reverse. [Another, shorter pause.] There *is* something about the idea of certain substances being able to transform the nature of life. There's a book about this, about medieval texts on the topic and why those scholars weren't so crazy after all, author has some funny name—something like Dyonsa. I saw it at the library.

Aliya: So you're in? If you've got plans this weekend, how about next Saturday, then?

[A few moments later:]

Aliya: Miya?

Friday evening

SweetnSexyAsianChik: Yeah, she called me.

Trini_in_Exile: Crazy, right?

SweetnSexyAsianChik: Crazy.

Trini_in_Exile: I was talking to meh cousin... he said, 'avoid that obeah thing like shellfish'

Trini_in_Exile: and no, I can't eat crab

SweetnSexyAsianChik: Yeah

Trini_in_Exile: What he really said was, 'stay far, far away from that––but I know you won't cuz yuh plunge head first into everything'

SweetnSexyAsianChik: Really? You seem more like the plan-it-out type to me

Trini_in_Exile: What does he know?

SweetnSexyAsianChik: Seems like this might be your kind of thing then.

Trini_in_Exile: I'm not getting involved with obeah for no reason

SweetnSexyAsianChik: What was all that about Trevor keeping some money for you, that you can't find now?

Saturday afternoon

The idea that certain substances—blood, for example; urine; feces—have an importance beyond the obvious is one that men have pondered and studied for centuries. These substances often play key roles in rituals of mysticism, shamanism, and the occult, designed to use the cast-off fluids of others to augment an individual's power. Some cults believe that these fluids make it possible to breach the gap between life and death by offering the dead person the chance to temporarily avail himself of vital life fluids. Others think that the essential roles these fluids play in human sustenance give them sacred powers.

—Martin Dyonsa, *A New Look at an Old Practice*

Aliya: You talk to your cousin yet?

Gillian: Nah, man. I'm going out there Tuesday.

Aliya: Let me know what he says.

Gillian: Did I tell you I run into this woman from Chagauramas, living up here on Prospect Road? She swears her ex-boyfriend put a thing on her, and now she has breast cancer. Nothing to mess around with, she says.

Aliya: They all say that.

Gillian: She doesn't know anything about it, she says. But if she did, she'd wear white: go on Friday night, not Saturday.

Aliya: Friday night it is.

IndieArabGirl: Did you track down the book?

SweetnSexyAsianChik: I found it in the Salem Public Library––they've got a huge collection on witchcraft. No surprise there.

IndieArabGirl: Can you get the pee?

SweetnSexyAsianChik: Me?

SweetnSexyAsianChik: What makes you think I'm even coming?

IndieArabGirl: Gillian wants Friday. I want midnight. Don't be late.

ELEVEN

IT WAS GILLIAN'S JOB to get the shit.

She snapped her seatbelt into place and started the car. Kids swarmed out of Fillmore High, zipping up jackets, snapping open cell phones, attaching headsets to ears already red from the cold. Up the hill, Miya had almost reached the bus stop, a trail of hopeful freshman boys sniffing at her heels. At the far end of the parking lot, Aliya and her scarfy friends gossiped next to someone's black Nissan.

Gillian shifted into first gear and joined the line of cars trying to get off campus. Stupid school. You'd think they could find a better way to control the traffic than sending out daily e-mails asking students to please wait patiently and not honk the horn. Only one thing to do: press Play and let the soca carry her through the crowd. The speakers pumped out "Jump and wave," but the line running through her head was: "*Feels like o-beah . . .*"

Finally, she was out on the open road, taking I-95 to Lincoln, and then pulling into the lot. She'd called last night, told him to expect her—of course, with Kevin, you never knew. But he was right there in the waiting room when she pushed through the glass front doors, steeled herself for the stink and the noise. Shrimps, man—how could he stand to work here?

"No, no," he was telling a tall white woman in a flannel jacket. "He'll be perfectly fine. You can call every day, check in, not a problem."

"And you'll put him on the phone? The last kennel he was at, they thought I was being one of those silly old women who thinks of her pet as her child. I know very well Rommel is a dog. But he'll enjoy himself so much more if he can hear my voice every day."

"Don't you worry yourself, we'll give your *boobulups* the time of his life." Gillian smiled. *Boobulups*—dog must be mad overweight. "Don't forget, I promise we give him the best Tobago love ever."

A few more comments, mostly about feeding and one hundred deft strokes with the brush, and the proud owner of the *boobulups* was out the door. Kevin turned to Gillian. "*Pachunks*, coming all this way—you don't expect me to feed you, do you? We got nothing but ground-up horse in this place." He leaned down, kissed her on each cheek. Stinking like dog, but at least he didn't slobber.

"Do you think she gets it that you just promised to beat her pup every day?"

"She smoking something, she thinks we gonna give the phone to a dog." He motioned her to the back room. "You mind coming back here, watching me work? I got Princess Chihuahua having her nails done at four."

Gillian followed him through the door, down the hall, into the wide back room, where a dozen dogs yipped at the bars of their wire cages. Kevin knelt in front of the one second from the end and rubbed his fingers up against some nose. "How's your mums?" he asked without looking up. "You hear from her this week?"

Not this week. Not last week either. Of course, Mums had just taken that second job at the roti shop in St. James to help put Dunstan through a computer course. He'd never gone to UWI, and it wasn't like jobs in Trinidad were falling out of mango trees. Plus, Mum's foot hot—she was never one to stay home, especially when there was bacchanal going on. The good life, that's what she lived in Trinidad.

"She's good, she's good," said Gillian. "It's so expensive to call from there, I keep telling her not to. I call and leave messages on her cell, but she's so busy nowadays, she probably gets them in the middle of the night."

"She still dancing with the rum bottle?" Kevin asked. He unhooked the cage, led the tiny dog out by the collar.

"She all right," said Gillian. She followed the clipped nails and Kevin's big feet to a six-foot basin at the back of the room.

"And your dad?" asked Kevin, scooping up the dog and turning on the water with one hand. "Did he make it to the game last weekend? I never see a Trini *basodee* over baseball like that."

"Why ask about him?" Princess Chihuahua jumped out of the crook of his arm and into the tub, prancing in little circles. So excited she left her etiquette back in her cell and began licking the wall.

"You a hard one, girl," said Kevin. He said "g-yul," like the Trini he was. "You the one who wanted to come up here, you forgetting that." Gillian's face went hot. She wasn't forgetting, no matter how hard she tried. Showing the girls on the playground the customized Nikes Dad had sent her from New York. *And a swimming pool in his backyard, too*, she'd told them, thinking—well, what *had* she been thinking?

Splash. Water dotted the knees of her jeans, her shins, even her lower thighs, courtesy of Princess rolling along the bottom of the tub. Gillian stepped back. Time to get this over with before she ended up in a wet winter-jacket contest.

"Kevin," she said. He sprayed the water along the dog's back, letting her primp herself. "I need a favor."

Kevin was leaning into the tub, singing, *"Bubbling, bubbling,* 71
bubbling . . . well, di doggies started jumpin'." He tipped a generous helping of liquid soap into the water. "Can't help you,
girl," he said. "I broke like a china dish on a hardwood floor."

Gillian's back stiffened. Had she asked him for money so
many times, he just assumed she was shaking him down
again? She didn't think so. But talking back wouldn't get her
the shit she needed. She swallowed her anger in a single gulp.
"No, nothing like that. Just wondering: that obeah man, the
one out on Kelly Boulevard, he for real?"

One quick snort and Kevin was singing about Melda,
who wouldn't have had to bother with the obeah means of
getting a husband if she'd just brushed her damn teeth.
Gillian let him make his joke, all three verses of it. Then
she said, "Nah, man, I mean it. You tell him anything about
me? He knew my name before I even said it."

Kevin stopped singing, stopped moving his soaped-up
hands. "You seriously went to see he? Shit, Gillian, what were
you thinking?"

"You gave me the address."

His hands dug deep into fur, stroked the dog up and
down, waited her out.

She asked, "You never went to see him yourself?"

Kevin snorted. "Of course not." He shook his head. "I
don't mess with that obeah thing. Back in Trinidad, when we
lived in Belmont, there was an old man up the road, and people would come and go, all hours of the night, but if he did
them any good, I never heard about it."

Nothing to say to that. Kevin massaged the dog up to the
ears and back before he spoke again. "Of course, there was
Auntie Asha. Remember she? Big hefty woman." Kevin
turned and spread out his arms, soap flying from his fingers.

Gillian wiped a bit off her nose. "Then she stopped eating and the next thing we knew, she thin, thin, *thin*, girl. And sleep? Gorm, man, it was like she forgot how. All night, every night, she wanted to walk. We had to take it in shifts, walking with her, night after night, street after street."

There'd been stories about Kevin's Aunt Asha. Gillian wrinkled her forehead, trying to remember. Hospitals that couldn't help, doctors who shook their heads and shrugged. Late-night candle lightings at Mount St. Benedict's.

"Auntie's sister, she was over to see one of those obeah priests, Shaker Baptist, I think he was. 'You have a sick sister,' he tells she. 'Bring she here . . .' She rushed home and dragged back Auntie Asha, out to Chaguaramas somewhere. And he save she."

Kevin waved his arms again, but he'd stopped with the dog, so no flying soap this time.

"What caused it?" Gillian asked, finally.

"Her husband's sister. She wanted Auntie Asha's money— went to an obeah man and cursed she out."

"Oh."

So it works.

Kevin recovered, lunged for the dog. Too smart for him, Princess padded across the tub. "You crazy, girl," he said. "Even if the obeah man get you a plane ticket, where you go end up? Everybody home happy happy, your mums meeting you after school with hot cocoa and marshmallow? Nah, it gonna be Mums passed out in her room, and flies all over the kitchen table."

"Kevin—"

"So your dad's not trying any too hard, so what? Wait a year, go to college—he'll pay for you to go away, why not?

What you want to go back for, except hard work and no future? You living in a fantasy world, girl."

Gillian looked down, missed the spray of water heading to her face until it was too late. "Don't you miss Trinidad?"

"I miss Carnival and Maracas Bay, and Lord what I wouldn't give for fresh doubles with peppers and hot sauce, stinging me in the mouth on a morning. And come Christmas, I miss me real pastelles, and singing parang for a drink of rum by the neighbors." Kevin tried for Princess, but she escaped this time, too. "But I don't miss living hand to mouth, hustling here and there, begging some big shot to let me work. Shit, there's no money in Trinidad, Gillian—"

"Who cares about money? You Trini to the bone, going on about food like that. If my dad hadn't lied to me—"

Kevin raised one wet hand, shook it dry. "What you need, Gillian?"

Deep breath. "It sounds crazy, I know it does but—a bucket of too too."

"Shit, Gillian."

"Call it shit then."

He laughed. "We got plenty of too too here. Grab a bucket and shovel your shit."

THE SUPERMARKET SMELLED like antiseptic even in the meager West Indian aisle, supposed to cater to the local community. Gillian scanned the bottles on the bottom shelf. Matouk's, but not the fiery habanero version. And the only thing resembling green seasoning was made in America. What did Americans know about cilantro (they don't even call it *chado beni*), green onions, big-leafed thyme? Americans, who sprinkled chicken with salt and pepper and called it gourmet.

She sighed. Next to her, two women were tossing bags of split-pea flour into a shopping cart. "He cry every time his mums come near him with a comb," said the big panty girl. "He holler like a raging lunatic. But she, she won't cut a strand of hair till he two."

"She smart," said the second woman. A final bag of flour plopped on top of the pile. What were they making— enough *accra* to feed the town of Fillmore in a siege? "Meh cousin cut her boy's hair too soon, and he didn't speak till he was five. And he lucky, you know. Sometimes they never speak again."

Superstitious Trinis. But Gillian found herself watching the women as they pushed their cart down the aisle. It wasn't all confusion, was it? Nothing wrong with protecting yourself from *maljo*, the evil eye.

She turned back to the Matouk's, picking up a bottle and passing it between her two hands. Who was she kidding? Plain Matouk's would go perfectly with saltfish buljol if Dad ever got home early enough to make dinner. She sighed. Might as well make her way to the frozen pizza aisle again. Oh, for a country where she could roll up to the corner and dash into a shop for a roti—

But it wasn't roti she was smelling now, it was the reek of cologne, a stink she'd smelled before. Gillian swung around, and there he was, lounging nonchalantly against an endcap of chickpeas. Thinking himself so sophisticated in his Sean John clothes, his so-close-it-might-be-a-Rolex, and that perfume he should have left in Paris. Skinny like hell, no ass; weak mouth, bumpy nose, zit-covered chin. Enemy of the people, Nick Loring.

Fooled from behind, for the second time in two days.

TWELVE

"YOU GODDAMNED BITCH." Nick pushed himself off the endcap and came so close, Gillian thought he'd plow right into her. She dropped the Matouk's—glass held, but the cover popped off, and a thin stream of hot sauce dribbled onto the floor. She struggled to find her courage, failed, but grabbed her voice. "What the fuck do you think you're doing?"

"I want my money."

"I'll see your ass in jail for assault and sexual harassment," said Gillian. Stretching it a little, but that was his problem. If only some stock boy had wandered by at just the right moment. "Get away from me, you mook."

Nick stopped. "Mook? What is that, some kind of racist crap?"

Gillian took advantage of his confusion to push the panty man aside. Stupid white people. They were the ones who made the racial lines, and then they accused you of crossing them. Not enough that they had all the power, now they had to be the victims, too. "'Mook,' you idiot, is you: a jackass who can't get a girl on his own. Now will you leave me alone? You want out of the program, all right with me. All the girls are quitting anyway." So much for Trevor's promise that he would keep her out of things.

She was ready to chalk her losses. Find her money—that would pay for the plane ticket, get her the hell out of here. Find Trevor's own share, it belonged to her anyway; she was the surviving partner, wasn't she? Should be enough to set her up once she got back home.

"Quitting? Which girls?"

"Lucy, she was the first one, Sierra, Emmie—"

It wasn't Gillian's face he slammed, but it was close. His fist pounded into a sack of brown rice, level with her head. The bag cracked, and a thin stream of rice spilled out. "Emmie's mine," he said.

"You talk like you're some kind of slave trader."

Slam. His knuckles must be sore. "Shit, you people are—"

Gillian drew herself up to her full height, taller than Nick, thank God. "'You people'? Who you talking to? People in black sweaters? People of the female persuasion?"

"All I want is that you hold up your end of the deal, or give me back my thousand dollars—"

"Thousand dollars? Are you on crack? It's a hundred a prom date. What are you, going to ten of them? Trevor told me you were haranguing him—"

Nick had stopped punching things. Now he was rubbing his knuckles, bent over a little, rocking and—was it?— laughing. "Don't give me that innocent routine. You know exactly what's going on."

"Of course I do." She just wished the going on was something else: her, heading off to the pizza aisle; Nick, disappearing in a haze of smoke.

"Then let's stop playing games, okay? Do I look stupid enough to cough up money for some airhead prom date? Come on." Nick pulled a black iPhone out of his pocket and took a quick look at the screen. Couldn't she make him mad enough to slam *that* against the wall?

And, um, did he really look like he could get his own prom date?

"Colin Bing paid Trevor a thousand bucks to cork Minda Allison. So I wanted in—into Emmie." He laughed at his own stupid joke. One more reason he had to look for dates in the for sale section of Craigslist. "She was supposed to come a week ago Friday, and she never showed. I wasn't harassing Trevor, I was calling him, *nicely*, to ask where my merchandise was."

Merchandise? Gillian calculated the distance from her foot to Nick's piggy.

"He promised she'd be there this Saturday. I showed up early, checked into the hotel, snuck in a bottle of champagne, lit some candles . . . and spent the night romancing the pay-per-view." The hand with the iPhone shook. *Come on, boy, throw it.* But he hadn't completely lost his mind.

"Did it ever occur to you that that was the night after Trevor's death? Maybe Emmie was upset?"

"Did it ever occur to *you* that I want my money back? All thousand dollars. He was into Colin for a thousand, too—and eight other guys. We want the money, or the girls."

"Do I look like a pimp?"

"Do you need a mirror?"

Nasty. Gillian struggled to recover. "If this money existed— and I had it—what makes you think I'd hand it over?"

"Look," said Nick. He began scrolling through the numbers on his iPhone. Probably bringing up 1-800-blo-jobs. "I have plenty of evidence. You're not interested in buying it, I have no doubt Principal George will take it off my hands for free. And you know what? He'll probably share it with his poker buddies down at the police station."

The principal wasn't really cozy with Boy Blue . . . was he? "And if the money burned up in Trevor's crash?" Gillian couldn't believe she was even saying this. "What then? Why should I be responsible?"

"Because it's the right thing to do," said Nick. Lord in heaven, he was serious. "And because I hold all the cards." He was still staring down at the iPhone, but his fingers had stopped moving. It was half a minute before he spoke. "Trevor didn't go back to school Friday night, did he?"

"Back to school Friday night? Before the crash?"

"No, after, as a ghost."

He wasn't serious? Gillian tried to read his face, found herself moving in closer, close enough to see the hairs poking out of his chin.

"What are you doing?" he asked.

Was he leaning forward to kiss her? Jeezan ages, check out a guy—a disgusting, zitty white guy with morning breath in the afternoon—to figure out whether he's talking about jumbies, and all he sees is an invite.

Nick edged in on her. The iPhone had made its way back to his pocket, and he had both hands free. "Seriously, Gillian," he said, "if you want to work things out nontraditionally—"

"Don't touch me!"

He didn't back up, but the fingers heading in her direction ended up fiddling with a packet of curry stacked on the top shelf. She wasn't exactly frightened, not in the middle of the supermarket, but even one other shopper walking by would have reassured her. What kind of supermarket was deserted at four p.m.? "I want my money, Gillian," he said. "Or I want my girl. You have till the end of the month." He reached behind the iPhone, pulled out a card. The mook had the nerve to tuck it in her pocket.

"Get the fuck away from me."

But Nick was already turning around. He gave her a casual salute with his middle finger, and the damn iPhone was

out again and up against his ear. "The end of the month,
Gillian."

She stared after him for a long time, not listening when she told herself it was time to move. Somehow pizza seemed cold and unappetizing, more suited for a doorstop than dinner. Did she sound that callous when she talked about Trevor and her money? *I hardly knew the boy.* Wasn't exactly true, was it? "I picked you out of the crowd," he'd said at Applebee's, over their first plate of nachos. "You don't put up with bullshit, I respect that. And you don't always play by the rules—that's what I'm looking for." He raised his glass to her. A Diet Coke, but still.

Her Trini pride had been stroked—Trinis were famous for twisting the rules into pretzels and braiding them in their hair. Her hand went up to her head, touched the dozen tiny cornrows there. Of course, a true Trini didn't cross the line—didn't break the law the way, according to the panty man, she and Trevor had.

Nick was lying, had to be. Trevor might be—might have been—greedy, but he wasn't a pimp. What was it he used to call the girls? Not meat, silver dragees. Those tiny little things you put on cakes but can't eat. That must mean . . . must mean what? You could take them pretty to the party, but no touching? Or you could touch their bodies but not their hearts?

Gillian bent over to pick up the Matouk's, stoppering the cap back on. She'd have to buy it now, but she wasn't thinking about that. What evidence could Nick possibly have? Photos of Trevor handing money to the girls? Footage of Emmie saying, *I am a prostitute and I work for Trevor Sanders?*

The end of the month: Nick's final words.

Seven days. The shit had better come through for her.

THIRTEEN

ALIYA'S ASSIGNMENT: blood.

She stood outside the butcher shop, chewing on the ragged end of a fingernail. Now she was the one calling this crazy. Still time to cancel. The other girls were wavering, they wouldn't care. Miya only believed in things she could hold in her two hands; Gillian feared obeah more than she wanted to master it. Of course, Gillian had agreed to the grossest, stinkiest task. And Miya just typed *On Thursday* when Aliya asked her to add a dangerous job to her to-do list. Gillian, desperate to traipse home to the land of the laughing sun. Miya, wracked with guilt over her big mouth.

Fine. Maybe they were more interested than they let on. Let one of them get the blood. Let two of them dance around the May tree like jinn. *Hey Aliya . . .* She pushed her teeth down tighter, harder. All a big lie, of course, this e-mail from beyond the grave—but what if he did appear? Told Miya heaven was so much better than life, being waited on hand and foot by houri girls. Or gave Gillian step-by-step instructions for finding his buried-in-the-woods treasure. And they were so caught up in relief, in joy, that they never thought to ask if he missed her.

"Aliya, you look like you lost your best friend." That was Mariam, coming out the door—who would have thought she'd be buying meat at this hour? She called a good-bye over her shoulder to Sami, who looked up, saw Aliya, and waved.

Should have stuck it out in Syria, that Sami; he'd be much better looking over there. Hazel eyes, light brown hair, bushy mustache—the Syrian girls would swoon. Not Aliya. She liked dark-haired men, young men with hooded eyes and shaved faces and silver earrings.

"You okay?" asked Mariam.

"Hey," said Aliya. Recovered herself at last. *"Salaam aleikum."*

Mariam laughed. Her left hand held a package of meat wrapped in white paper. Her right one swung a drawstring Gap bag back and forth. "I decided at the last minute to pick up some kabob meat—I'm going to stir fry it, see if I can get Nabile to eat it that way." She wrinkled her nose. "Lamb is more expensive every time I come in. How'd you know I was going to be here?"

"Oh," said Aliya, "I didn't; I came to ask Sami a favor." She scrambled for something better. "And I was going to see if they had anything on special. For Mama."

"A favor?" Mariam's plucked eyebrows rose. "You want to be careful about that, Aliya—the next thing you know, you'll be hearing at the *Al-Akhbar* newsstand that you're engaged to him. You know how people talk."

She did. Gossipmongers. You couldn't sneeze in Fillmore without someone reporting it in the *Arab Community News*. That was why she was getting out. She wanted to be a private person, an American. Like Trevor was. His mom took care of him—paid the rent, put food on the table (although sometimes he had to microwave it)—but she didn't announce his personal business over a loudspeaker: *Trevor clipped his toenails at 5:05, people; clipped his toenails, write it down.*

"Don't look so fierce," said Mariam. That was Mariam

these days, prodding and pushing her into line. "I'm just try-ing to keep you from making the same mistakes I did."

What mistakes? Hunkering down behind a pile of books? Sending e-mails to the AMA, the CDC, anyone she could think of, to get information for her science projects? Marry-ing a guy she barely knew?

"I know you think I'm being a pain in the ass," said Mariam. "Don't deny it, I can see it in your face. It's just that your mama has no idea—*no idea*—what kids get up to at Fill-more."

And Mariam did? "Yeah, thanks," said Aliya. "I assure you I'm not getting up to anything with Sami."

"I didn't say that." Consternation crossed Mariam's face. She swung her bag a little harder. "You don't have to be so touchy."

Aliya let it go. Get defensive, you look guilty.

"So, what's the something special for?" Mariam asked, her voice high pitched, determined to be cheerful. "It's not your mama's birthday, not her anniversary, Eid is long gone . . ."

Eid. Aliya looked away. She wouldn't bite her lip, wouldn't think about how she'd spent last Ramadan, some of it, being tickled by Trevor. *What, on top of starving yourself, you can't even kiss me?* he'd asked her in the gazebo, when she should have been doing her Calculus. Or praying. Except the scent of his cologne drove her crazy and God forbid, she gave in. Baldessarini, the scent of heaven.

Mariam was saying something about Eid. Last Eid? Next Eid? *Snap out of it, someone's going to notice you've gone off the rails.* ". . . when he comes."

Aliya blinked.

"*Ya adamiya,*" said Mariam. Oh, upright girl. How

descriptive Arabic is. And how deceitful. She snapped her fingers in front of Aliya's face. "Wake up, Aliya. I know you're an independent girl, it's not like your baba's going to force you to marry him. But I mean it when I say I think you'll like him, I really do."

Aliya paid attention in a hurry. What? Force her to marry who? People didn't do that, not anymore. Not people like her father. Sure, he had a close-cropped beard and thundered on about the forbidden, insisting "a girl belongs at home" every time she planned an innocent study date at Sherine's. But he'd also told her, "Someday you'll be Dr. Aliya," starting back when she was eight years old.

"What are you talking about?"

Mariam's eyes flickered over Aliya, from her uncovered hair to her black ballet slippers. "If I didn't know you better, I'd think you didn't want to meet him. *Rashid*, remember? Nabile's best friend? He's sorted out his visa, I was there when your mama told you that, and Nabile's already looking into buying a medical practice with him. And he, Rashid, is looking for a wife. It's an open secret that you're number one on the list."

Aliya did know he was coming—sometime far in the future, after he finished his practice rounds or whatever they were called, the equivalent of a residency. Although maybe that was last May they were talking about it, and far in the future was now? Never mind, nothing to do with her. Rashid was old, late twenties, and Mariam herself called him fashion challenged. Aliya'd spoken to him exactly once, on Nabile's cell. She'd figured Nabile handed her the phone so he could get his turn on the Wii without seeming rude.

So much for her powers of discernment.

Mariam smiled, her secret—and secretly annoying—I-am-a-married-woman smile. "It's not that bad," she said. "And after a while, it's not bad at all. Remember that game we played when we were little, when we had to pick four boys we'd want to marry? Remember I always picked movie stars?" Aliya remembered. Lying across the bed, bathing suits still damp from the sprinkler, water dripping on the page and smearing the names. It had been Aliya who'd protested then, *But he's not a Muslim*, and Mariam who'd shrugged her off, offered an easy, *Oh, he'll convert*. "After you get married, after you fall in love, it's better than being with a movie star."

Change the subject. Aliya would not, could not talk to Mariam about love. "Besides," her cousin said, opening her Gap bag and peering inside, "it's not as though you're in love with somebody else, you're not one of those girls who falls for an unsuitable boy . . ."

Aliya couldn't look at her. Couldn't close her eyes either, because she'd see herself in one of those poufy white dresses, walking down the aisle of a church. A church! Oh, the blasphemy. But Trevor was standing at the end, dressed completely in black—and she couldn't, wouldn't look up, or she'd see from his eyes that he was dead. She knew those eyes: white and without irises, soulless. She'd seen them in her dreams.

"I should get inside," said Aliya, gesturing toward Sami. He was already wiping down the back counter. "He'll be closing up soon."

"Okay," said Mariam, pulling her bag closed. She smiled, blinked her mascara-lengthened eyelashes. "I think he's mostly cleaned out, but he might have something put aside. Maybe you can coax it out of him; he's always liked you." She stepped out of the way, to let a woman in shirwal kamis step between them; the woman entered the shop and Mariam headed off down the street. "*Allah maaki*," Mariam called over her shoulder, *God go with you*, which was funny, because she was the one walking away. But maybe her sixth sense knew that Aliya was the one walking away from God.

Aliya stepped inside, smelling the pungent sliced meat, the harsh antiseptic that kept the place clean. She took a deep breath and reviewed the excuses that Gillian had IM'ed her: school project, a play about war, Gillian's cousin the vet had run out of blood.

Underneath, though, she couldn't shake the feeling that Mariam still stood in the doorway, spying on her. Once, twice, she turned around, half expecting to catch her cousin's face pressed against the glass. But Mariam was gone.

The woman in shirwal kamis took her package off the counter, thanked Sami in accented English, left. "*Salaam aleikum*, Aliya," he said, wiping his knife with a wet rag. "What brings you in here, so late?"

"I have a strange request," she said. *Breathe, Aliya, breathe.* "I'm planning a brilliant science fair project, a model of a heart that actually beats, and I need some blood." Raised eyebrows, a grin, careful attention as she filled in the details. Aliya tried to relax. She could trust Sami. The surest way to get a Syrian to spread a rumor was to ask him not to say anything—Arabic code for "tell as many people as possible." But Sami was different. He'd always looked out for her, even when he was a restless teenager, still in high school, and she hadn't hit kindergarten yet—oh God, and she used to steal his shoes at the mosque, while he was praying, and go hide them outside, under cars, behind rocks, beneath the outdoor faucet.

He'd had to take off his socks to go and look for them; then, of course, she'd stolen the socks. But he never told on her.

"I'll get the blood for you, Aliya." He held up one hand. "No, don't ask me how. Come by Friday night, around this time—I'll be working alone again. Come around back, though, don't come inside. Okay?"

"Shokran," she said. She looked over her shoulder at the plate-glass front door again. Nothing behind it. *"Shokran katir."*

"La shokran ala wajib," he told her. No thanks required. She turned, anxiety replaced by relief, relief pushed aside by anticipation. Friday. Two days away. She was floating through the door when she heard Sami call out, *"Allah maaki, ya Aliya."*

God go with you, again. But did He? As far as she could see, God didn't go anywhere. *Trevor maaki*, now that was more believable. Maybe he hovered over her, directing cars and bad guys out of the way like a traffic cop. Maybe—she gave a little gasp—it was Trevor's presence she'd sensed at the glass door every time she looked back, expecting to see Mariam. He was probably waving his see-through hand in front of her face right now, testing how far he could go before he freaked her out. Now that sounded like the Trevor she knew.

She wasn't sure whether she felt more comforted or less as she began her long walk home.

FOURTEEN

MIYA AGREED to get the pee.

The easiest of the three tasks: all she had to do was col-
lect her own. Infinite bottles of water, urgent bathroom
breaks; a stack of paper cups, later emptied into a big yellow
pail with a sealed cover. Kept in her closet and spritzed over
with Vera Wang's Princess.

But then she had to go and agree to get something else,
too.

Trini_in_Exile: meh cousin say get some strands of hair.
there's power in hair. ever hear the story of samson
& delilah? check pillowcases, the waste bin, anything

SweetnSexyAsianChik: Morbid. And disrespectful. You
think it's so important, YOU get it.

Trini_in_Exile: yuh have the least to lose.

SweetnSexyAsianChik: !!!

Trini_in_Exile: aliya's out, she gets caught it's the noose
& i can't afford trouble.

SweetnSexyAsianChik: And I can?

Trini_in_Exile: truth will out, gyul. malcolm frederick,
boys' locker room––could yuh be in any more trouble?

Trini_in_Exile: yuh there?

Trini_in_Exile: yuh mad, girl? i'm just saying, yuh the
best choice

SweetnSexyAsianChik: But break into the house? Couldn't I just get something out of the garage? Like his skis, or that nasty dog when it goes outside?

Trini_in_Exile: aliya say he never emptied his trash & kevin——meh cousin——say we need strands of hair, it's got dna, u know

SweetnSexyAsianChik: Aliya says, cousin says…what about me? Don't I have a say?

She didn't. In the end, she'd agreed to all their crazy schemes: to the pee, which would join the shit and blood as a powerful conduit for otherworldly forces, and to the life-printed strands of hair. But it wasn't because she believed Gillian's obeah nonsense. Spirits haunting the living? Nothing more than a manifestation of the living's subconscious guilt. Omens? Just coincidences, elevated by the gullible.

Odds were, Gillian didn't believe it herself, was just crossing her fingers that Miya would stumble across the money hidden in the wastebasket, and their quest would be over. That girl was all about the cash.

Trini_in_Exile: c u @ lunch tomorrow? we can brown-bag by the radiator

Okay, not *all* about the cash. She had to know what the other island kids would think if they saw her with Slutiya Chonan.

SweetnSexyAsianChik: Thanks, but I've got library.

Someone had to protect that girl.

SO IT HAD NOTHING TO DO with Gillian and her made-up obeah rules when Miya found herself on the fire escape outside the Sanders' second-floor bathroom Thursday night. It was partly the thrill of it, that slightly naughty feeling that went with cat burgling. Second, well, she didn't want to let Gillian and Aliya down. Any other girls would have said, *If Mrs. Sanders finds you in her house, she'll just assume you're twisting sheets with Luke.* But they kept their mouths stitched closed.

She'd dressed the part: skin-tight black pants, black top like a wetsuit, back-to-black hair pulled back with barrettes. So what if the wind breezed across her shoulders like it was trying to turn them into an ice sculpture? Who cared about the dog growling below, straining at his chains?

She heaved a little, sweated some under all her clothes— look at that, cat burgling took brawn as well as brains. *God, please don't let this window be locked.*

God laughed a little. *I thought you didn't believe in me, Miya?* The weight shifted, the window creaked upward, and Miya found herself crawling through. Her legs dangled a minute—it was farther to the floor than she'd expected, and she fell long enough to think about it. Then she was in the bathroom, feet tingling with the impact, eyes taking in the dark before she turned on her flashlight.

Sniff. The harsh smell of Comet, the lemon of Mr. Clean. Cream-colored towels hung on the towel rack, and the top of the sink had been cleared free for guests—the last of them went home yesterday, hugging Mrs. Sanders good-bye and driving off with a couple of bikes attached to a rack on the back. (So said Aliya, who'd been staking out the place.) No

one to hide from except Mrs. Sanders, high on the tranquil-
lizers prescribed by three doctors (info courtesy of
blog.myspace.com/SweetSavannah) and Luke, who ducked
out of the house every time the sun dropped its pants and
sank in the sea.

Miya clicked off her flashlight, opened the bathroom
door. Hesitated a moment, then left her shoes on. Made her
way into the dark, dead hallway. Took two steps and—what
was that? A creak, from downstairs. A thump. Someone was
in the house after all. She reached her hand back toward the
door, took comfort in the unbending metal handle. Deep
breath. Probably no one there but the stupid dog.

The stupid dog was outside.

Maybe it was Luke. Maybe he would come silently
upstairs on stocking feet, a cat burglar who knew what he
was doing, and he would surprise her, wrap his arms around
her waist. He'd growl *Don't scream* in her ear, and then—

What was she thinking? It wasn't like she *liked* the
bastard.

Then he'd run his finger along her neck and up to her ear
and—

Get on with it, Miya. Move your feet down the hall. Trawl
through the trash can, find some spare hair, get a move on,
get out.

What if she got the wrong hair, pulled up some pieces of
dog? Would they end up killing Rambling by mistake?

Not like she believed any of this anyway.

She headed down the hallway, stumbled over something—what poor design, putting a plant *there*—and stood
paralyzed for ten long seconds.

Nothing. Miya pattered on, arms outstretched in the dark, until she found a door. She eased it open and slipped inside, listening. No snores, no rustling as someone turned back the blankets. No one rushing out of the dark to cover her mouth with—

Enough. Maybe she'd hit Trevor's room with the first push.

Click. Flashlight on, she scanned it across the room's contents. She still wasn't sure. A boy's room, yes, dark furniture, plain blue bedspread, a pinup calendar over the bed. Miya squinted at Miss November. Long black hair, oval-shaped brown eyes—not quite Asian, but not precisely white either.

More clues: a stack of old records, a guitar—had Trevor been musical? She passed up the records for the bookshelves, always her first stop in a new room. Rows of thrillers: John Grisham, James Patterson, Walter Mosely. Some science fiction. A careful selection of fantasy, but, thank God, Robert Jordan only through volume 8. On the next shelf, some historical tomes, one on forensics of the Middle Ages. Miya was reaching for it when she saw something even more interesting. *The Encyclopedia of Witches and Witchcraft.*

Miya knelt down, pulled it off of the bottom shelf. Flipped through—she couldn't help it—looking for an entry on Japan. No time for this, of course. No entry, either. Still, the frontispiece yielded some useful information: *LUKE SANDERS*, someone had written. *OCTOBER 31st.*

Miya shoved the book back, returned to the hall. At the next door, she pressed her ear up against the wood, heard nothing for a minute, and then a series of choking breaths, or smothered sobs. Mrs. Sanders, crying into her pillow. Miya found her hand on the doorknob. But what consolation did she, of all people, have to offer? She blinked away the memory of Mrs. Sanders opening the door that day, of her shattered face as she stared at the pictures of her husband and his mistress stored on Miya's cell phone. *How could you do it?* Trevor asked her on his last night. *My dad, your mom, it was just some fling, they would have broken up, gone their own ways. What kind of bitch would go and tell my mom about it?*

Breaking and entering didn't seem like such a lark, suddenly. Downstairs, something clattered. Miya pulled back, perked her ears, listened harder. Nothing.

Must have been the wind.

Final door, at the end of the hall. She ran her fingers over its surface, came across a series of lines etched into the wood. Not lines, letters. *K* and *E* and . . . *KEEP OUT.* Left over from Trevor's pirate phase? Or had some eerie afterlife hand reached out of the ether to send her a personal message?

She was getting as bad as the rest of them.

Push open the door—*creak.* Inside, a shocker. The eerie hand—if eerie hand there was—had been doing more than scratching notes. Miya put down the flashlight, felt along the wall, flicked on the overhead. Luke's room was a boy's room, stuff everywhere. Trevor's room had been torn to shreds. Pictures, some face up on the floor: Trevor and his family in happier days, Trevor in the front seat of his car, Trevor with his arms around a floppy-eared dog—all torn, right down the middle. The pillowcases had been ripped open and the stuffing blown everywhere. Glass somethings lay broken near her feet. In the corner, a collection of model boats and pirate ships had been crunched into bits of wood and plastic. Books, clothes, bed linens lined up in piles like they were waiting for entry to the landfill. Trevor had had his own bathroom: The door was open, and dozens of bottles, pastes, and creams had been scattered across the tiles, most of them cracked, some of them oozing lotion. Shredded papers flowed out of the upended wastebasket.

Who had torn the place apart? Mrs. Sanders? Some friend or cousin, looking for drugs? Aliya, even, searching for secrets and keeping her own counsel? No matter, whoever it was had made things easier for her. The scraps of paper strewn across the floor, the wadded up tissues stuck to the bottom of the basket, they were innocent. But across the room, clinging to the fragments of pillowcase, she found what she was looking for: two strands of dark brown hair.

Miya dug into her back pocket and whipped out an envelope, slipped the hair inside, sealed it up. *Time to leave, Miya. Get going.* But she couldn't, quite. Instead, she walked across the room and knelt down. If they came in and found her, if Trevor's mom had apoplexy, if Luke had her arrested for trespassing . . . well, she'd live with it, she'd have to. She cleared a space on the floor and sat cross-legged, determined to sort out the wood and plastic parts, determined to make the pirate ships whole again.

This one here, with the black hull and the Captain Jack flag, Trevor had been sailing it that first day she met him, at the Cataplan Health family picnic. Or trying to sail it, while Luke bombed rocks at it from the shore. He passed her a handful and they pelted it till it sank, and Trevor had to splash through knee-high water to get it. *I'll get my revenge!* he'd shouted, waving his fist, but he'd been laughing.

Miya tried to swallow, but it was like one of those rocks had lodged itself inside her throat.

It took her a long time to assemble the pieces into ships, and it would have been easier with a bit of glue, a short, sharp knife, blueprints. But she finished at last. The bookshelves were clear, so she lifted up the ships one by one and put them back. Up close, parts were splintered and bent, some pieces cracked, but from a distance—in the doorway, for example, using the flashlight, not the overhead—they looked whole.

It caught in the beam when she turned to go. A corkboard on the wall, most of its stuff still intact: a football schedule from two years ago, a couple of crumpled and then flattened out phone numbers, a coupon for a car wash. And in the far corner, a girl's photo: she wore black pants, a white T-shirt that said *Boston University*, and a black cap on her red hair. *Red hair.* Couldn't be. Miya squinted and the hair curled up a little, but still shimmered auburn. She reached up and snatched the photo, but her eyes had already moved on to the next thing. In the very center of the board, a note; stark white paper covered with large, block letters: **HEY INFIDEL, IF YOU DON'T WANT YOUR HEAD CHOPPED OFF IN THE MIDDLE OF THE NIGHT, STAY AWAY FROM DECENT MUSLIM GIRLS.**

FIFTEEN

"NOT AGAIN," said Mama. "Your father won't allow it. And we're having *kibbe* tonight, and I need your help with the *tabouli*." Mama added up a long column of figures in the red account book, muttering under her breath: *But that doesn't make sense.* Then she looked up. "What?"

"I promised Sherine—"

"When? When you promised this? Tuesday night, when you were supposed to be at her house studying, but were actually seen at the butcher shop?"

Good God. Now she wasn't allowed to check out a bit of beef?

"*Ya Aliya*, I tell you and tell you, but you don't listen. People talk. You're a good girl, home studying, they have nothing to say. You hang around a butcher shop, and they call you the kind of girl who hangs around the butcher shop. And you know what that means."

She didn't.

"I should find my slippers and rap the soles of your feet till you scream."

Mama hadn't beaten her for years. "Don't be silly. So I went into the butcher shop. So what?" A stack of invoices sat on one corner of the desk, paid and unpaid bills from Baba's pizza shop. Aliya straightened them. "I wanted to see if he had any cheap lamb, surprise you with it. You know he does sometimes, at the end of the day. What's the problem?"

"Your father doesn't like it, Aliya. He hears things at work and he better not hear them about his daughter."

Aliya waited for the hot, angry, self-righteous words to come, but she wasn't innocent enough to shout them, to storm out of the room. After all, Mama was right about her. She had been playing around. She felt shame and embarrassment well up deep beneath her skin, come out red. When she'd first fallen for Trevor, she'd quaked in bed at night, prayed to God for the strength to give him up. Later, she'd buried her face in the pillows and remembered every time Trevor touched her, his fingers skimming her lips, his mouth halfway down her body . . .

Nowadays? She tried to think about nothing.

Out loud, she said, "That Mariam. Of course she went straight to you with her gossip."

Mama's eyes were back on the book. "I just don't understand how we lost a thousand dollars . . . And Mariam didn't say a word. Um Zubeir told me."

Aliya saw her opportunity. "What was Um Zubeir doing out so late, did you ask her that? Hmmm? Was she maybe going to meet up with the butcher behind his shop? Did you ask her if she was gossiping about *me* to make sure nobody believed what I said about *her*?"

"Aliya!" But Mama was giggling. Giggling so hard her hand slipped and scrawled a big red line across the paper. "Don't be ridiculous. Um Zubeir isn't the type—"

"She may have forty pounds on him, but you know how Arab guys go for the curvy ones."

"But she's twenty-five years older than he is. Don't you think Sami wants children?"

"He can take a second wife for that, a young and glamorous one."

Mama was still laughing. She caught sight of the account book, though, and sobered.

"I'm sorry, Mama," said Aliya. She was, too, about so many things. "I didn't mean to make you ruin your page."

Mama pushed her glasses up on her head. "No matter," she said. "It's not coming out right anyway."

"Should I take a look? Did you check your figures against the bills?" Aliya dragged the folding chair across the floor and propped it open. For a few minutes, neither of them spoke as she flipped through the invoices. $200 for tomato sauce, $1280 for olive oil, $1121 for gas—"There's the problem. You copied the figure wrong." Aliya felt a little rush of triumph, and something else, too. It wasn't so long ago, back before Baba was making enough money to hire more help, that they'd all worked weekend mornings in the pizza shop. Mama paying bills, Baba firing up the ovens, Aliya and Mariam giving one last polish to the tables.

Mama was muttering again. "Should have double-checked over those." But then she wasn't looking at the accounts anymore, she was looking at Aliya. "Don't trouble your father tonight, *ya binti*," she added, as though she knew the jinn were waiting for Aliya in the state forest. "Stay home with us. We'll play Parchesi, and Uno."

Parchesi and Uno. The Friday nights of her childhood. "And Forty-One?"

"And Forty-One."

"And Baba and I can drum to *'Ya Habibi'* while you and Mariam sing?"

"You can drum, we'll sing."

Aliya nodded her head, a kind of jerk—funny, because back in Syria, that gesture would pass for no. But as she kept reminding everyone, she was in America.

GILLIAN TAPPED her foot in the inner sanctuary of her father's office. Would he ever get off the phone? Thanks to Aliya's cryptic text, now *she* had to go and pick up the bucket of blood, in some dark alley in the center of town. That girl had better show tonight. Gillian didn't have patience for her "I don't know if we're doing the right thing," and this from the girl who'd started it all.

Her father had the radio on low, but since he never more than grunted into the phone, she heard every word of the evening news. Conversations with people who'd left the southern coasts of Florida due to too many hurricanes. Should have put her in a serious frame of mind, but all she could think about was how much she hated this place, where they kept the heat on low and stashed the welcome mat in the bathroom. Stupid lack of carpet. Stupid paneled walls. Stupid framed pictures of every stupid building Dad had ever designed.

And stupid, stupid phone. Every time she came in here, he had it pressed to his ear, his head bent over stacks of building plans. Why was she still so surprised? Only time he ever spoke to her was to press those *dotish* Red Sox tickets on her. Trini to the bone? More like Trini to the first layer of skin. Trinis took their cricket seriously, but they didn't watch grown men scratch and spit on a baseball diamond.

She scrunched her tangled hair between her fingers; braids were coming out. She couldn't quite picture tonight, the darkness of the state forest, lit by nothing but the moon, the cold wind whipping around her head—good Lord, maybe Aliya had the right idea: at home, in your bedroom, in clear reach of a dozen woolly blankets. Whose idea was the forest trek anyway? Oh, right, Miya's. *Do it on the spot where Trevor died.* Miya said that. They were taking advice about obeah from a Japanese girl?

Of course the obeah man had slammed the door in her face when she went back to see him. Later, he'd slammed it in Aliya's face, which freaked her out.

IndieArabGirl: how'd he know who I was???
Trini_in_Exile: nah, he think obeah doesn't work for white people
IndieArabGirl: I'm not white!!!
Trini_in_Exile: yuh lookin' white to he

How much longer was her dad going to make her wait? The hurricane people were going off air, weather experts warning that there could still be surprises, even with only two weeks left in the season. Thank God Trinidad was too far south for hurricanes. Perfect weather, cheerful people, place like paradise. "That wraps up the hour," said the announcer. *Be there by eight,* Aliya had told her, and she'd still have to find a place to park.

"Dad," she said. He didn't lift his head. "Dad!"

He raised his forefinger, waved it around a little.

"Dad? I've got to go now."

He was writing something. Good idea. Gillian took a piece of notepaper from the pad on the edge of his desk, grabbed a pen. *Going out with my friends, won't be home till late, maybe sleep at Miya's.* She tapped the edge of the pen against her palm. Would be worth it to add a curse that would make him give her five minutes of his time, if only she knew the words. Of course, the man would have to actually read her note for that to work.

He took the paper, scanned it rapidly. As she turned to leave, he gave her a halfhearted princess wave and mouthed something, maybe "Who's Miya?" maybe "Have fun."

If only Mums were here! She'd dress up in black and paint herself with bluing and be the first one dancing around the fire, asking Trevor what the hell he was doing, plunging over the side of a cliff before the world was finished with him. He'd pay tribute to her Trini spunk, her Trini spirit . . .

Was that what she was expecting? Trevor to appear in a cloud of fire and brimstone, shouting the words to "Bacchanal Lady" as they all *wined* to the soca music?

Gillian shifted her shoulder bag. Damn thing was heavy, what with the two cans of lighter fluid. She passed through the hallway, shoes clicking on tile, and tripped down the stairs—literally. Her knees buckled and the shoulder bag fell, its contents careening across the floor.

An omen?

No time to take it on. She scrambled, shoved everything in the bag, then got the hell out of there.

"I GOT TAKEOUT from the Chinese place on St. Pete's—I got you mu shu pork."

Mom swept in, dropped the greasy paper bags on the kitchen table. Miya bit her lip. Why was Mom always so sure she knew exactly what she'd like?

"Oh," said Mom, looking up, taking in Miya's leather jacket, the bag over her shoulder. "You're going out. Now I'll end up stuffing myself like a pig."

Of course, the mu shu did smell fabulous. That place on St. Pete's never stinted on the garlic. "I'm a little early," she said. "I could have some."

"Great." Mom crossed the room, rummaged in the cupboards, found some china plates with little roses circling the edges. She came back and started dishing out dinner. "So, big date with Rodney tonight?"

The games people play. Rodney had never met her mother, never been to her house, never even called her—their relationship was all about texting, as in: *U bussy? want 2 come over? something biiiig to show u.*

But Mom liked to think Miya was having that innocent teenage experience, and Miya was happy to invent the details: how Rodney held her hand when he took her to the theater, bought her popcorn and loaded it up with smuggled Parmesan cheese, sat through *Twilight* without yawning once.

"Actually, I'm going out with the girls tonight."

Mom looked up. How strange it was to see a face that was so much her own, and so much not. Same black eyes, but narrower; same flat cheekbones, but higher. Same bright red lipstick and careful eyeliner. "The girls?" Miya couldn't tell if she was pleased or not. "You and Rodney aren't having difficulties, are you?"

The problem's not Rodney, it's his girlfriend. She expects to have him Friday nights until eleven. "I'm into a new guy," Miya said. To her surprise, an image of Luke—Luke again?—rose up in her mind. How silly. Luke. Not her type at all. "But not tonight. I thought it would be fun to have a night out with the girls for once. Do a little dancing."

"Dancing? Are you trying out this new crunk dance?" Mom's eyes lit up. She was always first in line for the latest craze. She'd been a mean karaoke singer in college—she'd even met Miya's father at a karaoke bar. Salsa dancing, that had been her line for seeing so much of Mr. Sanders. *We both need a partner, and his wife, she's too embarrassed to dance in public, poor thing.* Busy being embarrassed herself, Miya never called her on it. Not until it was too late.

"I'm not sure where we're going yet," said Miya.

Why couldn't she tell Mom the truth? *I couldn't keep my mouth shut at the last party I went to—and now I'm going to the forest to try to appease a boy's spirit, or at least my own.* Or just not say anything, like so many other girls? Stomp out in silence and not answer her cell, then come home high and defiant.

She wanted Mom to love her, that was why. She'd never understood why Mom didn't post her *100%*s on the refrigerator, why she left the HONOR STUDENT bumper sticker on the counter instead of slapping it on the back of the car. Until the day Miya came home early—trust Mom not to see the half-day notice on the school calendar—and overheard her in the study. "But she's such a geek, Perry. And the thing is, she doesn't have to be. No glasses, no acne, nice slim figure. She could be beautiful. But that short hair, and she never puts gel in it. And those clothes!" A male voice mumbled, said something to make Mom laugh. "Of course not," she told him. "Boys never call, except to ask about homework. She'll be one of those girls who goes to the prom alone, wait and see. I'll be so ashamed."

Miya could hear it now, that *ashamed*, even though her mother was saying something quite different: ". . . you're going to love it, Miya-chan. The last time you went dancing, you were about five years old, and you had on a tutu. It's so much fun, the lights sparkling on your face, and the crowd. Sometimes I worry about you, you're so inhibited." *Yes, Mom, you know me so well.* "But when you get out on the floor, you'll lose all that, you'll see. But oh, you're not dressed for it! Maybe you want to change."

"It's, uh, girls' night out," said Miya, looking down at her black jeans. "We're going to help get each other ready, borrow clothes, give makeovers . . . you know, girly stuff."

She put down her fork and pushed back from the table, even though she was only half-done. "I should get going," she said. She climbed the stairs, brushed her teeth without taking off her jacket, checked her makeup in the mirror. When she came back down, her mother was already clearing the table.

"Have a good time, Miya-chan," she said. "I knew I should have bought you that little black dress the other day."

Miya filled her high heeled boots with feet, then took the time to lace them up before saying, *"Ja ne, okaa-san."* She never spoke Japanese to her mother. But it seemed right, this time, to say good-bye in a language that couldn't be misconstrued.

Then she headed into the night, on the lookout for whatever adventure awaited her in the heart-of-darkness forest.

SIXTEEN

ALIYA PUT ON her warmest flannel pajamas and crawled under the covers. She didn't take out the picture of Trevor that she'd hidden inside the pillowcase, the one she kissed before she went to sleep every night, and she didn't whisper to God to forgive him his sins. That was over. Her whole sleeping-with-the-enemy thing, well, she'd been out of her mind, but now she was back.

By God, it felt good to be home.

She'd called Sami and told him to keep an eye out for Gillian. He sputtered, as expected, but she added, "This is it, the last strange thing I'll ever ask of you, could you just do it?" and he gave a strangled okay.

Was it any surprise that Aliya won every game she played that night? "You're on fire," said Mariam, as Aliya collected the Uno cards after her third victory. "Can we play something else now? What about Mexican Train Dominoes?"

But Aliya had won that too. She settled down under the covers. That's what she'd think about while she tried to fall asleep, the surprise on Mariam's face when she had to count the pips on a dozen dominoes. Or maybe she'd remember the rousing *"Ya Habibi"* they'd ended with, she and Baba and Nabile drumming the different rhythms on the edge of the table, Mama and Mariam singing along. It was too soon to meditate on the glory of God, but she'd get there. Maybe she'd

even wear *hijab*. She'd start slowly, one day a week, Saturday,
maybe, when they went out of town. If only she didn't look
so gaunt and ugly, if only it didn't highlight the elephant-like
nose in the middle of her face . . .

Whooo. Aliwhooo.

What was that? Outside, must be, some kind of owl.
Ridiculous to think that it was calling her. Even more ridiculous to think that it wasn't an owl at all, but some kind of
spirit, raised by Gillian and Miya. Trevor's spirit.

Stop it. She'd said she was never going to think about him
again, right? Never. That's what dead meant: gone, done,
finished. Not coming back. And if Gillian and Miya thought
different, well, they had no idea what they were doing, no
idea. Old Aunt's words echoed in her head: *Midnight exactly,
burrowed deep in the darkest woods; that's the best place to talk to
the jinn.*

Aliwhoooo.

She sat up in bed. This was crazy, she was acting possessed.
What was it Gillian had said? *You don't show and I swear I'll
come break your window, Aliya, drag you to the bacchanal by your
hair . . .* That was Gillian though, bluster, bluster, no bite. No
way she was out there in the dark, calling Aliya's name.

Just like there was no way Aliya was going to the forest.
Trevor was gone. He wasn't going to remember that he loved
her, wasn't going to tell her what he'd been playing at, with
his lies and his redheads. And hadn't she had a lovely time
tonight, playing Uno and Parcheesi and Forty-One and
Dominoes? She had. Eating cake and poking fun at Mariam
for being so married and happy, she was growing fat. But
every night couldn't be Parcheesi night, could it?

Ever play Parcheesi? she'd asked Trevor, in those long ago, living days.

I've played strip Parcheesi, he told her, grabbing her on the couch, tickling her. She let herself enjoy it for one single second before she wrestled herself away, tried to escape, scrambled, was caught and loved again.

She was out of bed and turning on the lights, opening the closet door. Crazy. It made no sense that she was here, rifling through her clothes, snatching a pair of black jeans, a black sweater. It was far too late for—

But it wasn't. It was only quarter past eleven.

Now she was pulling on her socks, her black boots. Shoving her dark brown hair into a ponytail. Ridiculous. It wasn't like she could take the car. Suppose Mama got up, looked out the window, saw it was missing? Life as Aliya knew it would come to an end.

Of course, it already had, hadn't it?

Mama wouldn't wake up, anyway. Baba, that was the concern. Mama slept like a zombie ever since she got that prescription for Ambien last week. But Baba might well wake up, reach out for the glass of water on his nightstand—

Now *that* was an idea. Dissolve an Ambien in that water, problem solved.

Aliya. What are you thinking? You're going to drug your own father? You must be crazy.

Yes. She was.

Take off those boots, climb back into the bed, she ordered herself. *Pull the covers up over your head and think about something lovely: next year, your first day of college, moving into the dorm, your new best friend-slash-roommate, with the black hair and the flashing black eyes and the island accent.* Yuh finally reached! *she says.*

Aliya found herself tiptoeing down the hall, entering the bathroom, opening the medicine cabinet. The bottle of Ambien was in her hand, then the small white pill was in her palm. Surely this was illegal?

And dancing around a fire in the middle of the state park as they tried to shake a dead boy out of Paradise—they had a town permit for that one, right?

She paused outside her parents' door. *Aliwhooo* echoed inside her head. This one last night, and then she'd move on. She promised. Absolutely.

She twisted the doorknob.

TWENTY-TWO MINUTES later, Aliya slammed the car door and ran down the embankment, tripping over clumps of dirt on the way. Firelight flickered below her, to the right of the swampy side of the lake. A hunk of rusting metal rose up out of the dark water. Swallow hard, blink, blink. Don't remember Trevor, driving her home, drumming his fingers on the dashboard. *I'd die before I'd let anything happen to Mitsu.*

And so he had.

"Where the *hell* have you been?" asked Gillian as Aliya dashed onstage. Backdrop: enormous, ominous trees, stretching in all directions, swaying just enough with the breeze to block out the moon. Center stage: Gillian, bent over, fingers wrapped tight around a metal shovel, digging a pit. Stage right: Miya, emerging from the first line of trees, carrying a rock between her two hands. Lighting: three wooden Tiki torches on sticks, set up in a triangle around the pit. Sound effects: wind blowing leaves and twigs about, the howl of some animal. Scratch-and-sniff smell effects: manure, urine, the feral scent of forest.

"How can I help?"

"We thought you weren't coming," said Miya, staggering into the circle of light.

"We *knew* she was coming," said Gillian. She straightened up, dug the tip of the shovel into the ground. "I would have licked her down if she didn't."

"Sorry, had to sneak out." Aliya held out her hand. "You done? My great-aunt told me the jinn are afraid of metal—we don't want it anywhere near this place."

Gillian passed the shovel over. "You're going to need it to unpack the shit first."

"I thought you were going to do the shit? I'm blood, remember—"

"Come on." Miya's voice cut through the rustling wind, the hooting owl, the squabble. "It's almost midnight."

Seven seconds, six seconds, five, four, three, two, one. Dressed in black, arms and legs carefully covered, Miya drizzled the bucket of urine into the shallow pit. They watched while the urine foamed, puddled, seeped into the hard forest floor.

Aliya looked across at Gillian's face, staring down. She rubbed her lips together, lips Trevor had once traced with his forefinger. Then she took firm hold of the shovel and began transferring shit to pit, scoop by scoop. The black clumps sunk and spread with each scoop. Aliya threw the shovel as far as she could—not very far, because it was heavy and hit a tree anyway. Time to find a jinn, get him to pass the message to Trevor. Great-aunt Reem again: *Don't forget to thank the jinn for their gifts.*

"*Ya jinni, tusaidani ma hatha al hedaiya.*" God willing, the jinn would make out her poor Arabic.

Gillian crossed the flat land between herself and the bucket of blood, balanced between the roots of a tree. When she brought it back, she was dragging it, not paying attention to the drops that spilled over the top, the red streams dripping down the side, soaking into the white paper pasted there: Al-Ansari Halal Meat.

"*Only obeah can reveal the truth I seek,*" sang Gillian as she tilted the bucket toward the pit and a stream of blood flowed away. She waited until the stained-red metal bottom was nearly empty. "*Only obeah provides the hope I need.*" She threw the bucket over by the shovel and held out her hand. Miya passed her an envelope. Gillian tried to lift the flap but it stuck, so she tore it. She used her thumb and forefinger, carefully, delicately, tweezing out the hairs Miya had found in Trevor's room. Leaning over, she dropped them, one by one, on top of the body fluids.

Gillian looked up, looked out into the forest. "Now the wood," she said. She moved to a small pile of logs over by a bump in the forest floor; Aliya helped her carry them back, place them inside the pit they'd made. Miya came right behind them, her arms full of brush. It too went into the dark hole below.

Gillian upended a Tiki torch and brought it close, closer, closest—the wood caught fire, crackled, a tiny spark in an enormous forest.

Aliya held still in the almost dark. If she closed her eyes, she'd have believed she was alone. Then she smelled it, so strong she almost tasted it, Baldessarini for Men. She caught her breath, realized: Baldessarini was cedar-tinged; must be the wind rolling through the cedar trees, carrying their scent.

But Trevor had worn Baldessarini.

Aliwhooo, said his voice. She looked at Gillian, glanced at Miya. One of them must have noticed, must have heard Trevor call her name. But their heads were bent, intent, as they watched the wood in the pit alight.

Aliwhooo.

Something touched her neck, stroked it, caressed it. Not the wind. She reached up to grab his hand and—

CRACK.

She was interrupted by the sky. Harsh, angry lightning shot through the dark clouds above, lighting up their small circle.

She, Gillian, and Miya were alone.

SEVENTEEN

MIYA STARTED to move. From famous dancing cultures, both of them—Gillian, with her Carnival and her soca music and her wining; Aliya, with her Arabic orchestras and her scarf around the waist and her belly dance—but it was Miya, the girl who'd been kicked out of ballet class, who led the dance. Gillian had her obeah, Aliya had her jinn, but it was Miya, the atheist, the Unbeliever, who broke the lightning spell and decided what to do next.

Her first movements were sharp, jerky, as she raised her arms over her head. Was this how spirits moved? Of course not. Think: the sweep of the wind, the dance of the air. But she wasn't trying to be a spirit, was she? She was trying to summon one. Or was it . . . Fine, she didn't know what she was trying to do. *Feel the music*, Mom would have said. Miya threw back her head and felt, but the music was still. Wind lifted her hair, cold air brushed her nose, and nothing more.

She let her arms drop in a kind of half circle, out in front of her, still stylized but a little more graceful than before. What would she do if she believed all of this? Bow. Bend over, pay homage. Touch her knees, elbows, forehead to the dirt.

She did. Waited for some sign that she'd done it right; when none came, she got up, moved a little faster. Spun around, and caught a surprising sight: two girls following her, copying her movements. Miya almost stopped. She was used to going where no girl dared to follow. Lightning flashed and framed the two girls beneath swaying trees: dark eyes burned into their faces, tangled hair standing on end. Was that a shadow behind them, towering over Gillian, holding out a protective arm to Aliya? Lightning faded, and the night swallowed them up—the two girls and whatever tree Miya had mistaken for a man.

Miya bowed her head and shuffled through the dirt. Veering right, she headed up an embankment, hands reaching up to the nearest trees, clutching at a handful of pine needles, pulling herself up.

The girls behind her passed in and out of view as she spun around. Gillian, moving with rhythm, Aliya, climbing with grace. Gillian muttered something—was it, "Is this how they do it in Japan?"

How would Miya know? She'd been to Japan just three times, and only the last trip, Ojii-san's funeral, had made an impression on her. Flying into Tokyo exactly seven days after his death, being escorted everywhere by relatives; catching her own cheekbones in someone else's face, her habit of chewing pencils in her young cousin's mouth. Then the funeral itself. The smell of *senkou*, sharp like sandalwood, the creak of respect as old bones bowed before his photo, the rustle of envelopes as incense money passed to Obaa-san; that was the first time she realized it wasn't just her mom who was Japanese, it was she, Miya, too. Even if she was just "that Asian girl" to everyone else—"that smart Asian girl" to her teachers, "that slutty Asian girl" when she started wearing the tight shirts with the scoop necks.

The embankment was a bad idea. Miya struggled on until her feet plunged into a shallow indent, a kind of puddle. Cold, wet mud spilled inside the tops of her boots. One small gasp, and then she took hold of herself. Stopped, spread her arms wide, looked over her shoulders. Behind her, the confined fire had grown much stronger. It flickered red and orange in its circle of stones, lit up the forest between here and there. She'd half lost both her followers: Aliya had her arms around a nearby cedar tree, face pressed against its trunk, branches of needles spilling over her neck and shoulders; Gillian was spinning down the embankment, black hair matted against her head, clothes spotted with mud. Something dark stained her hands.

Miya lowered her arms, returned to the dance. Back down the embankment by herself, squishing with grace, stumbling with rhythm. The trees, smacked and whipped by the howling wind, began to sound like music, moving branches thumping out the bass, crackling leaves playing the melody. Miya gave herself up to it, swayed, stumbled, spun, thought no more. Eyes half-closed, she twisted through the leaves, turned back, saw, too late, the thick trunk of a pine tree. *Slam.* Her head thudded, her knees buckled, and she sank into the mud.

And then Miya wasn't in the mud at all. She was rising through the air, buoyed by a faraway voice saying, *I never meant to screw up your life, I just wanted the mom I loved back, the one who wasn't entranced by a fat old man.* Her voice. Growing louder, growing angry. *Fine, Trevor, whatever, go drown yourself in the lake if you're going to feel so sorry for yourself. Do you think I'd care? Do you think anyone would?*

She held there, high above the trees, peering down as though through a high-powered lens. In the clearing below, one girl danced and spun around the fire, arms waving, mouth moving, hair and hands flying. Closer by, a second girl splashed through the leaves to save a third and final girl. A close-up on the last one. Her black hair had tangled into ropes, her head bent at an awkward angle, a spot on her forehead was already turning red. That girl, there was something about her . . . She'd been melting into forest floor, but now, without warning, she stood out: bathed in light, encircled by color, a pale yellow that grew dark, strengthened into a gleaming gold. She moved her head, moaned, and the light shimmered with her.

Then Miya felt the hard ground beneath her, and her face started to throb. The moment was over. There was Aliya, cold hand clutching hers. "What happened, Miya? Are you all right?"

EIGHTEEN

THERE WAS NO MUSIC, but Gillian heard it anyway. George Aiwa pounded away inside her head—*Wave your flag, wave your flag*—Alison Hines ordered her to *Roll it on, gyul, roll it*, David Rudder insisted she was the girl from Bahia, The Mighty Sparrow crooned about saltfish. The fire drew her like a band at Carnival, and there she was beside it, in front of it, around it. Jumping up. Mums, all those years ago, in Auntie Ruby's kitchen: *What kind of Trini yuh are, yuh don't know how to wine? Wit the hips, gyul, wit the hips—wine yuh waist.*

She got it, and she never forgot it. She was wining now. Her hips swung in perfect rhythm, here she was circling the fire, once, twice, there she went round again. *Like Soca Baptists*, she was shouting, sweat streaming down her face, arms in the air. Superblue was right: religion and music were the same damn thing. Shaker Baptists jumped up for their love of the Lord in church, soca-loving Trinis jumped up for song on the Carnival trail. Gillian jumped up for—she was jumping up for Trevor, wasn't she? Jumping up for a chance to find her money, a chance to remake her life. If there was healing in dancing, salvation in singing, obeah in any of this, she was here to find it.

Round and round the fire she went, cheeks burning, face wet. She stumbled, almost fell headlong. *Yuh moving too fast, gyul.* That was Mums too, at Gillian's first Kiddie Carnival. She'd been wearing green satin pants and a long tunic with wide sleeves—dancing dragons, they'd been. *Hurry,* she'd called to Mums over her shoulder. *Ah don't want them to start without meh.* And there was Mums, trailing behind, canoodling with that Stephen. Or was it Dwight? Or, no—that memory couldn't be right. She would have been seven, her first Kiddie Carnival, and Mums and Dad were still together then.

She spun around. No dancing dragons tonight, but who needed costumes when you had the real thing? Something smashed, crashed, crumpled: the jumbies stumbling through the forest? Fire behind her, she could see nothing in front but dark shadows, enormous, shaking. Good Lord, what was she doing? She stopped, ears, nose, eyelids tingling, skin shimmering, fear shaking down till it came out her fingertips. Crash, boom, *agggghhhh. Oh my G*—

Aliya's voice: "Miya, are you all right?" Right. Of course. Miya and Aliya, how could she have forgotten them?

Gillian turned back to the fire. The obeah man had taken Aliya's e-mail with slow, careful hands; his face twisted in concentration as he held it over the fire. She moved again, slower now, more deliberate, eyes screwed closed, mouth twisted, breathing in the urine-fecal-bloody-but-alive scent of the undead. The song in her head: Calypso Rose's "Fire Fire in You Wire." Fire. It crackled and popped to the soca rhythms as Gillian's body circled, as she willed herself to think of Trevor.

Somehow, he eluded her. *Yuh burn yuhself, gyul, yuh not careful.* That was the time Mums had lived up to her promise and they'd roasted goat over an open flame in Dwight's backyard. They'd spent half the afternoon chopping herbs and grinding spices to season the meat. Of course—Gillian's nose wrinkled—they hadn't watched it carefully enough, and the meat had charred. Mums ate it, sitting in the grass, leaning back on Dwight's knee. *Anything tastes good, yuh got enough rum to go wit it.* But Gillian hadn't had rum. She'd had the burned rice from the bottom of the pot.

She twisted, spun, picked up speed. Alison Hines again: *Nothing, yuh getting nothinnnnnng.* And this wasn't the time to think about rum. There was never a time to think about that last night, Mums coming through the door, hair askew, clothes rumpled, looking like she'd swallowed the rum bottle whole. Saying: *We got a thing to drink in this house?*

Yuh, yuh cut off, Gillian had told her. Nicely, really nicely. But Mums couldn't take nicely, could she?

Swish. Wind whistled through the leaves, lifting them, swirling them, letting them groan. Gillian wined through the darkness and into the warmth of the fire. *Oh yo yo, ah ya yi.* Crackle, hiss. *Hiss.* That's exactly how Mums responded. *Yuh cutting meh off, gyul? Yuh think Ah won't put yuh black ass out? Fifteen years old and yuh trying to tell meh how to run meh life?* Across the kitchen floor, over by the oven, fencing with insults and cusses and blows. Gillian, nasty eyes, smoldering face, had slashed with, *Look at yuh, yuh cyar even go one day without the rum?* Mums, ugly with her fat lip out, parried back: *Yuh just like yuh dem father, so above it all.*

Gillian waved her arms higher, harder, in the smoky night. It was Dad to blame, it was. Had to be. Leaving Mums, like he the big man, too good for she. Leaving Gillian to dote on Mums, to adore her—to love her, yes, she'd loved her. Hidden the bottles from the boyfriends, called in sick to the zoo for her, and okay, maybe she'd overstepped her bounds with her *Yuh cut off*, but *Yuh think Ah won't put yuh black ass out?* That went too far.

Gillian danced even faster, wilder, her feet kicked up mud that landed in her hair, splattered down her back. Her chest tightened, shuddered. Almost like it was still that day in Trinidad, Mums backing her up against the stove, waving a finger in her face. She'd bitten back the anger then, but no need to bite it back now. Kitchener pounded in her head: "Ten To One It's Murder." Now was the time, here was the place, for anger. She sank into it, as she had sunk back against the stove, felt the heat coming off the top burner. Hell, she could feel it now. It burned her feet, rose up, began to transform her. It was—

What the devil are you doing? No, wait, Mums didn't say that. That was Aliya's voice, coming from far away. Gillian opened her eyes—blinked once, twice. Something was way wrong. Aliya again: "Gillian, are you out of your mind? Get out of there!"

Spin. The fire had leaped out of the pit, ignored the rocks surrounding it, started snaking toward her, burning the ground just beyond her Nikes. What the hell—? She stared around wildly: had to be something to put out the fire. The pee. Miya had only drizzled it into the pit, there was plenty left.

She lunged, scrabbled for the bucket's handle, caught it— *Agh!* Hot like hell. The metal seared her fingers and she winced in pain, dumped the pee on the fire, almost gave up the whole cursed effort, but at the last minute clutched the plastic rim with her fried fingers. She held her breath.

The fire dampened slightly, yes, but it soon raged back. She skirted it while she still could, stuck her feet off the path into moss and thorns, bucket bouncing against her legs. Head for the lake, it was the forest's only hope.

Miya and Aliya were both shouting now—warnings, maybe, or voices raised in supplication to God or devil—but she ignored them as she filled the bucket with water and then started running back. If the wind blew the wrong way, yes, she could be trapped. But if she turned, took her last step home, who knew the damage the fire could cause?

It sputtered and spit. A flickering spark landed on her cheek—she flinched, but, funny, it didn't hurt. Was this just the beginning? Had they opened themselves up to some other realm, one where fire wasn't the foe of life but its fuel? More flame, more ash on her neck, her hair, her fingers. It fell gently, with the soft touch of rain.

Maybe because it *was* rain.

Gillian tilted her head back and, sure enough, drops of water sprinkled her face. In the next moment, the rain grew serious, and it began to pour. Gillian stared into the fire, twisting and spinning and fighting, just as she herself had done a few minutes before. She took just a minute to sing it to sleep—*like soca Baptists, like soca Baptists, ah ah ah ah ah.*

Then she turned in the mud, her Nikes so ruined they almost slipped off her feet, and trudged back the way she'd come. What had happened down there? She couldn't get her head around it. They'd cordoned off the pit with rocks, she'd lugged some of them herself. And what the hell were they thinking in the first place, building a fire in the woods?

She'd expected to see Aliya and Miya watching the spectacle from the safety of their cars, or at least half way up the hill, but here they were, two dark shapes beside her. "So sorry," said Aliya, when Gillian could finally make out the words. "Blasted tree fell in our path." Looked more like Aliya'd been the fallen one. Black squishy stuff dotted her elbows and her arms, and covered every inch of her from the waist down. Aliya went on. "I can't believe you tried to put out the fire like that, all by yourself. Are you all right?"

Miya said nothing, just rubbed her lips together and looked over her shoulder. Gillian copied her: the pit was dark, the fire dead. Not every rainfall could trounce a forest fire, but this one had.

"Let's get out of here," said Aliya.

They challenged the steep hill again, struggled through the sheets of rain, finally found themselves back at the lookout point, where they climbed into their cars without saying good-bye.

Gillian should have been thinking: stupid rain. Beating against her back, freezing the skin on her neck. Stupid weather, always changing. Stupid New England, couldn't it get with the global warming thing and heat up? But instead she was shoving the key in the ignition, turning on the car, putting her hands on the steering wheel.

Her hands. She held them up and peered at them in the dark. Dirty hands, sticky hands, but whole, uninjured, unscarred hands. She'd grabbed that metal, hadn't she? Winced and screamed as it bit into her skin?

She flicked on the overhead light. Sure enough, her hands were absolutely fine.

PART II

NINETEEN

7B. UNDERNEATH IT, smudged black letters on a white label: *Yoko Kano.*

Miya raised her hand to knock, held it. In that moment of hesitation, the door opened. "Welcome." Miya looked up. The woman was tall and willowy, with long, disheveled black hair spilling over her white kimono. "I've been expecting you."

Why was she here, in this paint-peeling hallway, instead of at home with a remote and a mug of hot something? The séance, wind whistling around her ears, the crackle of fire behind her. That out-of-body moment, when she saw herself surrounded by light and glowing. Miya shivered. She was involved, like it or not.

"Uh, hi," she said. "Interesting, that, since I just now decided to come here."

"I've been waiting for you for a long time," said Yoko. She held the door open politely while Miya slipped out of her shoes. Then Yoko stepped back and Miya entered the sanctuary. A tiny room, this front one, but serene. Yellowed Japanese tatami mats covered the wooden floor, dry and a little worn. A scroll hung on the wall, painted with a single kanji character—that was one she knew, wasn't it? Stamped on the boxes of detergent Mom brought home from the Asian grocery: *yuki,* "snow." The faint smell of incense scented the room. In the corner, a pot of tea sat steaming on the floor, three ceramic bowls already filled.

Miya swallowed.

Yoko led her across the room. Did she walk with a kind of inhuman grace? *Stop being ridiculous.* Science, that was Miya's god. What about Sociology last year? All that about collective consciousness: how when people gather together for religious ceremonies, their collected energy can make it seem like an outside force is present. That's what happened Friday night. Aliya's frenzied grief, Gillian's desperate homesickness, and her own powerful guilt all linked arms and lit up their wild imaginations. Made perfect sense. Except all the logical explanations in the Soc curriculum couldn't shake those vivid moments in the forest out of her head.

Miya sat down on the mat.

Yoko lifted one of the bowls and passed it across to Miya, then took the second bowl in her own two hands. Miya found herself raising eyebrows at the lone bowl on the tray. "Yes, yes," said Yoko. "My third guest will be here. Sooner or later. Fortunately, he doesn't mind his tea cold."

He. She couldn't possibly mean Trevor, could she? Miya wrapped her hands around the bowl and stared down into the dark liquid.

"You're only half-Japanese, right?" Yoko asked. Miya looked up. "I've been waiting for you many years." She closed her dark eyes and a stillness settled on the flat planes of her face. "Yes, I'm sure you're the one in my dreams, the one who will carry on my tradition."

What could she possibly mean by *tradition*? Nothing so mundane as a tea ceremony. Was it possible—Miya tried to read her hostess's face, but the shuttered eyes, the tight, expressionless mouth gave her nothing to work with. Was it possible that Yoko had had that same experience, floating and being at the same time? Was there really something in this?

Or was it just a concussion, brought on by banging her head into a tree?

"It will be a long, difficult challenge," Yoko told her, "but you, you will see it through. You have great gifts, although you perhaps don't recognize them. One day, *ao wa ai yori ideshi*. You know what that means?" Miya stared back into her bowl. Yoko must have read her mind: no. "You have a pool of navy blue paint, and you take out a speck of it. That speck shines brighter, more powerful, than the original pool of almost black. Sometimes it is the student who outshines the teacher."

Great gifts. That wild sense of something other in the forest—had Gillian felt it, had Aliya? Close her eyes, and she heard Aliya's plaintive call as she stormed down the hill; saw Gillian dancing in circles, arms outstretched—illustrated in that one wild instant when the fire behind her ignited, shot up. They should have placed the stones closer together, should have been more careful to brush all the leaves away.

Both Gillian and Aliya had been silent over the weekend, each of them retreating to her own little world. But she'd walked into school beside Gillian this morning; the girl's brow thundered when Miya mentioned obeah. And she'd bumped into Aliya after gym and heard some vague mutterings about Trevor's presence. *Trevor.* Miya swallowed, tugged the ends of her hair. "I came here to ask you about a friend of mine," she said. She licked her lips, rubbed them together. "A boy, he died recently. It may—well, it may be he took some things I said too harshly, in ways I didn't mean." *Face reality, Miya.* "Maybe his death was my fault. My mom, she's the Japanese one, she told me that sometimes there are special prayers you can say to put dead people at ease. Since you're a kitoshi, I thought maybe . . ."

Yoko waved away the idea with swift, angry arms. "Later, later," she said. "For now, you must begin your training. You need to gain control over the spirits as soon as possible—if they tap into your untrained power, it could be disastrous. You must fast, twenty-four hours." Yoko dropped her arms but kept on talking. "Then you will go at dawn to the waterfall by Oak's Ridge, take off your clothes, all your clothes, and stand underneath it. As long as you can. The water will wash away your past, prepare you for your future. You won't be ready for this transformation, oh no. Perhaps the first day, you'll be able to stand one minute only. Then three, then five, as your body becomes stronger, as you think less of pain, and more of possibility. And then . . ."

A waterfall, in the winter. She'd catch pneumonia. No, not pneumonia, but maybe hypothermia. Shivering, goosebumps, muscle mis-coordination. Pale skin, blue toes.

"Later, there will be more challenges."

"It's twenty-eight degrees today," said Miya.

"Yes," said Yoko.

Miya brought the teacup to her mouth, but she didn't drink. *You must fast, twenty-four hours.*

Yoko leaned forward, spoke with a new intensity. "You are hesitating. I see. But it will be worth it. Think of the power. The great mystics of the past—Ozuna, who flew around on a cloud, who controlled the weather, you've heard of him, of course. There were no limits to what he could have done. In Japan, many kitoshi are held back, able only to speak with the spirits, help ease their suffering and the bad luck they put on the living. But here in America, the spirits are more powerful, able to change everyday things, conditions, and that makes us more powerful, too. I believe it's their contact with other spirits from all different parts of the world."

Miya heard a sharp, indrawn breath. Her own.

"All kinds of possibilities," Yoko told her. She looked over Miya's head, threw her arms wide, as though talking to a large audience of spirits. "Maybe make a boy who hasn't spoken tell you he loves you." Love? She wasn't interested in love. She was a sex-is-life kind of girl. But she found herself thinking of Luke's pale face, his sad, green eyes.

The kitoshi waited. Not until Miya looked up did she say, "Or find a way to punish the one who broke your heart, who made you hate yourself. Or even find some new, special way to make the dead rest in peace. Everything is possible. But first, first you must begin your training."

Miya stared. She reached for the sociological argument— *the collective consciousness . . . ancestors . . . the sacred*—but her vaunted memory failed her. Nothing but words on a page anyway, in a book published a hundred years ago. She'd been there, in the forest, floating above the trees. She'd seen her powerless self, seen—maybe—her potential. Was that a nod she just gave?

The kitoshi, at least, took it that way. "Of course, I will need many things to start your training. Incense, and prayers, and special fabrics. But we can begin for, let me see, maybe one thousand dollars. Very cheap, compared to what it would cost you back home."

A thousand dollars. Miya's first, gullible thought: *Where am I going to get a thousand dollars? If I ask Mom, she'll want to know*—and then, *Fraud!* She shook herself and pushed back on the mat, hard enough that she crashed into the wall. She plunked the bowl back down on the ceramic tray and scrambled to her feet. "Well, thanks for the offer, *Kitoshi-san*, but I think I'll have to pass."

"But you're the one . . ." Yoko kept repeating variations of the sentence as she followed Miya to the door. "Maybe I could buy everything I need for eight hundred. You think this is all about money? Of course not. If I had the money, I would gladly pay for everything myself . . ."

Miya slipped through the door and into her shoes, and Yoko called after her. Taken in by a charlatan! Unbelievable. She, the girl who'd always been so skeptical.

She ran down the stairs and through the magic shop below. The cashier at the register called out something, but Miya ignored her. Safe in the street now, she looked up overhead, half expecting Yoko to poke her head out the window and call down, *Really, you're my one and only.* With perfect timing, Glimmer's friend Savannah was passing by across the street, offering Miya yet another chance to be great fodder for the gossip-column crowd.

But Yoko must have accepted defeat. All Miya heard was some car honking at the light, the tinkle of a bicycle bell, classical music drifting out of the bookstore next door.

Miya buttoned up her leather jacket and headed down Main Street. Time to be satisfied. She'd gotten what she came for, right? Grasping, greedy kitoshi just proved that anything can happen when you let a tree bang you on the head.

Except there were those three teacups already set out on the mat. And the kitoshi's comment about making a boy fall in love with you. Not that she was interested in love, of course not. But . . .

Not evidence, these things. Just coincidences.

Miya reached her car and went to open the door. Someone had stuck a flyer on her windshield. She ripped it off. *Special offer*, it read across the top. *Ditch the Winter Blues and head to the waters of the Caribbean on a special tour of spectacular waterfalls.*

Miya crumpled it up without reading any further. Another coincidence.

Right?

TWENTY

ALIYA STOOD in the woods beside Trevor's driveway, staring at Mrs. Sanders' car. Not the first time, this. The week of the funeral, she'd practically camped out here, watching mourners come and go, trying to figure out who was related to Trevor, tracing his features in their eyes and noses and foreheads.

Remembering the fall day they'd cut school in the afternoon and Mrs. Sanders came home for lunch. They beat it out the back door, rushed around the corner, and covered themselves in leaves in this exact spot. *No giggling*, he whispered sternly, and then he added, *I'd do you right here, you know, but then, I'd do you anywhere.* How could she keep from giggling after that?

Down the street, a car roared around the corner. Aliya melted a little deeper into the woods.

She should be done with all this.

If only she didn't have the feeling that the house had something to tell her. If only she wasn't so sure that Trevor had been at that séance, hovering over her, about to take her hand. She'd heard him in those moments leading up to midnight, felt him, sensed him. But what had happened next? Did the jinn cause the fire to explode? Were they mocking her when she'd called on them for help? What did they know that she didn't? The secret of Trevor's last night, she was sure of it—a secret tied to the redheaded girl.

She had to see that torn-apart room for herself. Maybe it held a clue—a secret diary, a scrapbook, a video journal. Miya said no, but what did she know? There had to be something in it, Trevor's room in ruins, like Aliya herself . . .

The car purred down the road, slowed as it neared the house. No need to panic. Unless someone was looking for her, she blended in with the trees.

"Hey."

She looked over, had to. A black sedan with the windows rolled down came to a complete stop. A new black sedan, the one Nabile had just bought for Mariam.

"Aliya?"

Two choices: She could run till her feet fell off, but knowing Mariam, she'd probably gun the car and chase her through the trees. Or she could find out what her cousin was doing here. Aliya made her way past the trees and brush, sloshed through a puddle, and leaned in the passenger window. No *salaam*s today. "Are you spying on me?"

"I used to see you come this way after school sometimes." Mariam met her eyes without the hint of a smile. "*Salaam aleikum, ya Aliya*. We're not all fools, you know." Fear hit Aliya, so sharp, so abrupt, it felt like pain. Who else knew? Her parents? "You're too young for this, too innocent. Someone needs to look out for you."

"I can look out for myself," she said.

"Can you? Can you, Aliya?"

The weather seemed harsh all of a sudden, the cold bit her nose, froze the ends of her hair. "I don't like spies," Aliya said. "Or gossips." The fear spread until even her fingernails shook. Had Mariam followed her around like this when she was with Trevor?

"He wasn't worth it, Aliya. He still isn't."

Of course she had.

"You don't know anything about him."

"I know enough," said Mariam. "Sometimes I'd run into him at the butcher shop; he'd come in and buy fresh meat for his dog. Demented American. People are starving all over the world—people are starving right down the street—and he's giving choice lamb to a dog." Aliya stared at her. She remembered thinking the exact same thing, those precise words. Until she saw Trevor curled up on the couch, his arms clutching that dog like a climbing rope. She couldn't help but like Rambling a little after that. The week before Trevor died, she'd even bought Rambling a leather collar and leash, to replace the ones he'd chewed through. She'd never had a chance to give them to Trevor. Her last present to him, still hidden in her top drawer.

"How did you know about . . ." She couldn't say the words. *Trevor and me.* She didn't like this, her carefully delineated worlds crashing into each other.

"He was a donkey, Aliya. I saw him in the library once with this redhead—"

Aliya's head swung up. "What? Who? What was her name?"

Mariam put both hands on her leather padded steering wheel. "No idea. I pretended to look up a word in the dictionary and hovered around their table for a few minutes because . . . Well, I thought if I told you he was with someone else, you'd drop him."

Aliya's heart broke. Literally. One piece headed up to her brain to chop it into little pieces, the other down to her stomach to set off a riot. "They were together? You're sure?"

"No, I'm not sure. That's why I didn't say anything to you. They didn't hold hands or kiss, but they sat close together, laughing too loud, even though it was the library. The looks she gave me . . . she didn't say 'ninja,' but she might as well have." Mariam blinked her eyes, gave two tight shakes of the head. "So rude. He didn't say anything to her, ask her to stop, even though he was, the two of you were, well, whatever."

Wow. Aliya was still alive, breathing even. "I need to find out who she is."

Mariam clicked her tongue against the roof of her mouth. "No, you don't. You need to get in the car and let me drive you home."

Aliya turned her head and stared at the front yard. What she needed was . . . well, whatever it was, she wasn't getting it from Trevor's house. At least not while his mother was there. Still, climbing in the car with Mariam seemed too much like giving up, too much like letting her cousin win. Mariam was trying to talk her out of Trevor.

Then again, wasn't she trying to talk herself out of Trevor?

She eased herself back a little and opened the door. Her chest felt heavy, like it had doubled, tripled its weight. The air stretched between them, put a million extra miles smack dab in the space between the front seats. She finally managed to say, "I don't know why you care so much."

"I'm your cousin," said Mariam, "and your sister in Islam. Of course I care." Her mouth screwed up, but maybe she was just moistening her lips. "This whole boyfriend thing, it never works out. You love him so much, just looking at him makes you smile, and you do whatever it takes to make him happy. He loves you back, of course he does, when love means stroking your hair, or buying you illegal martinis, but when you need him . . . suddenly he doesn't recognize your number on the Caller ID." She smoothed her hijab into place then started the car. "I've seen it happen to a million girls."

"Trevor wasn't like that," said Aliya. She couldn't, wouldn't—didn't—think of his e-mail: *I can't come tonight either. But soon . . .*

But never.

Mariam snorted as she pulled into a three-point turn. "They're all like that, Aliya." She pressed the gas, and they roared down the road. Aliya wanted, oh, how she wanted, to look back at the house one last time, to see the Secret Truth about Trevor Sanders escape from the windows, to jump up and catch it as it tried to float away like a balloon. But she didn't.

"The safe thing to do is get married, love your husband," said Mariam. Her pompousness spilled into unbearable.

"The fact that you let them railroad you into marrying some FOB with a mustache just because he has a residential surgery doesn't mean I'm going to."

"You have no idea," said Mariam. Was that a tremor in her voice? Her lips—yes, trembling; her eyes wet? Aliya blinked, and the whole world changed.

"You're not talking about me," she said. "You're talking about you."

"Don't be ridiculous," said Mariam. "I'm an *adamiya*."

Too late. Aliya had pressed the rewind button on her memory, and scenes from last year scrolled across the screen, garbled. Mariam had been erratic, hadn't she? Exuberant at times, like the day she brought Mama that vase full of roses, despondent at others. The plate of stuffed grape leaves she threw across the room, the screaming match she got into with Mama over—well, what *was* it over? The stress of exams, must be, Aliya had thought. Then she'd tuned out the noise, buried her face in her phone, sent more texts, sent them faster.

Mariam had had a boyfriend, of course she had. An Unbeliever, somebody at school. Maybe he'd been on the literary magazine, stayed late to read manuscripts, bumped elbows with her as they went to draw the same red line on a novella.

Had Mama known? Had Baba? The screaming match had been followed by a locked-door session in the living room, Mama emerging sorrowful, telling them Mariam might be too sick to take exams. She wasn't though, was she? She starred on every one, though she'd been so pale and distant and snappish through the spring. *By God, could you leave me alone?* she'd said, more than once, when Aliya'd brought her hot milk with sugar on Mama's orders. Brought it upstairs to her own bedroom, where Mariam lay with the curtains pulled down and a cold compress pressed to her forehead.

After the fight, she lay about for a few more days, then she cheered up. Everyone said it was because she'd gotten engaged.

"Oh my God," Aliya said. The words came out Arabic. Mama had broken up Mariam's relationship, broken her heart, then bought her off with a man from abroad. Or the boyfriend had broken her heart, Mama had descended on him, shrieking—Aliya was sure of that—threatening to cut off his testicles and then got Baba to cheer her up with a new husband. Did it even matter? Because Mariam was crying now, tears spilling out of her dark eyes, making lines on her sharp nose. "I never loved him," she said. "Not the way I love Nabile, never."

"Who else knows about this?"

Mariam didn't answer. She pulled up at a stop sign, took a sharp, angry left turn. "I wanted their 'freedom,'" she said at last. "And all I found was a straightjacket. There's a reason Allah forbids boyfriends, Aliya, and I know what it is. Do you really want to end up like that? Chewed up and spit out? I came so close." Mariam swiped at the tears on her cheeks. "You're the lucky one, Aliya. God spared you what I went through."

Aliya stiffened. What was she saying? That God let Trevor die in order to keep Aliya away from an Unbeliever? Hardly likely. And anyway, all boys, all Americans, weren't alike. Trevor wouldn't have chewed her or spit her or crumpled her. Remember the night rain had pounded the basement windows so hard they shook? And Trevor had bundled her tightly in a blanket, secured her with his arms. Brushed her cheek, teased her nose with his cologne. She breathed deeply. Was that Baldessarini she was smelling now?

Mariam drove right past the end of Aliya's street. "No, I'm not taking you home yet," she said. "Not before I talk some sense into you. Your parents, I don't think you have any idea how much you're upsetting them."

Her parents. That's who she should be thinking about. The parents who grounded her after the séance when the car didn't clean up quite as nicely as it should have. Baba, grabbing his jacket without a word, storming off to the pizza shop. Mama, shrieking, wringing her hands—anyone would have thought the car was alive and her daughter dead.

"I know you don't believe it," said Mariam, "but they're just worried about you."

Of course she believed it. Wasn't that worry, those expectations, part of the problem?

"I'm worried, too," her cousin continued. "Everyone is. Sherine wants to know why you're avoiding her in the halls, whispering in corners with that Caribbean girl."

What had Aliya been thinking, getting into this car? An enclosed space on wheels—she was at Mariam's mercy. No surprise, Mariam took her trapped silence for an invitation to go on. "Trevor was more of a *kelb* than his dog was," she said. "You deserve someone who respects you, who respects women. You deserve a good Muslim who obeys God's law." Aliya crossed her arms, looked out the window as Mariam kept going. "A million girls in school who would be happy to swing it with him, but no, he has to go and pick a decent Muslim girl."

Decent Muslim girl. Where had she heard—

"You wrote to him, didn't you?" Aliya said. "You told him to stay away from me or you'd chop off his head."

"Of course not," said Mariam, but it was her shaky voice she used, the same one that had denied ever having had a boyfriend.

"It was you who broke into Trevor's room and smashed it up, wasn't it?" She hadn't been thinking about Trevor's room the right way. All concerned with what might be hiding there, she never asked: Who hated Trevor so much that they'd beat up his pillows after he died? "Pull over," she said.

"Of course I didn't! I would never go in the room of a non-*maharam*, a man who's not a relative. If my husband ever found out . . ." Mariam drew a hand across her throat. Her voice was steadier this time, more earnest, but didn't liars improve with practice?

Aliya opened the door.

"Aliya!" The car came to a stop just in time; Aliya's legs were already on their way to the ground. She didn't bother slamming the door closed, just took off down the road. Mariam had taken Davis Drive; if Aliya jumped the fence by the corner house, she'd find herself in the maze of alleys behind the downtown shops.

"Aliya!" Behind her, Mariam was swearing. And putting the car in park and getting out to close the door because, really, she had no choice.

Ba-da-di-da-da. A text message. She glanced over her shoulder, saw Mariam climbing back into the car. No time to check it now. The red house was in sight. Time to pump her legs and run a little faster.

TWENTY-ONE

GILLIAN SET her chai tea down on the corner table. Almost a week since the séance, and she'd finally marshaled the courage to tell those girls what she was thinking. Of course, she'd been texting them all evening, and had she heard back even once? Here it was going on nine thirty, and not a skinny Arab girl, not a trendy Japanese one, in the place.

She pulled a pack of cigarettes out of her bag and placed them next to her cup. What was wrong with this *chupidee* table? There, that leg was higher than the others. Maybe if she pressed down here . . . oh, shit. The paper cup bobbled and there you were, tea all over the table, all over the cigarettes. Stupid table. Stupid tea. Stupid guy behind the counter, filling the cup to the very top.

"Let me get that for you."

A firm hand wiped away the mess with a paper napkin. An expensive silver watch clinked against the table. Gillian looked up. "What the hell are you doing here?"

"I saw you through the window," said Nick. Shrimps, man. Just when she'd most wanted to avoid him, too. "You didn't return any of my calls—did you even get my e-mail?— so I figured I better grab you while I can." He crumpled the napkin and tossed it in the nearby trash bin. "Like I told you, I've got your evidence."

"I'm meeting friends," said Gillian. "Two friends. So, sorry, no room for you and your evidence."

"There's room," said Nick. "Better be. I think you have something for me, don't you?" He looked up at the menu board. "Three forty-nine for a latte? Then I'll take . . . two thousand, eight hundred and sixty-five of them. Keep the change." Smug, stupid boy. She hated it when he rang things up in his head, like a cash register with legs and a little piggy between them. Did he actually think he impressed people?

He did. He sat there and preened, stroking his chin. Jackass.

She took a deep breath and a sip out of her half-empty cup at the same time. Not like she'd forgotten Nick's threats, just that she had other things to worry about.

He leaned over and pulled up a briefcase. *Briefcase*? And the guy couldn't figure out why girls blew him off and he ended up romancing the screen? He edged his chair around so that his back was to the room. "I've heard interesting things about you lately, Gillian," he said. "Going places, doing things that aren't quite the norm for you."

Gillian caught her breath. Caught her cup, too, which was about to bobble itself off the table. Had Nick been spying on her? Had he climbed into his car and followed her as she drove out of the bright lights, big city, through the winding roads of the countryside, up, up, up into the state forest? Had he watched from the top of the hill as three girls lit a fire and danced?

She shook herself. Ridiculous. He'd be blackmailing her now, if he'd been there, something about vandalizing state property. Instead he was lining up the numbers on the lock, flipping the briefcase open, pulling out a sheaf of papers. "First things first," he said, passing her an orange folder.

"Photo evidence." He cast a quick glance around the room. "My guess is, you don't want anyone seeing those, so you should be careful—"

Gillian yanked the photos out of the pocket. The first was a blond, shot from behind, hair swept up in some kind of chignon. Emmie, clad in pale lingerie that didn't quite cover her bottom. *Gorm, man.*

"Told you so," said that smarmy ass. He punched some buttons, held the shiny black iPhone to his ear. Jeezan ages, she needed to find a way to pin all this on him. Visiting a prostitute was a crime, too, wasn't it? She'd love to see his face when they took all his possessions and handed him an orange jumpsuit in exchange.

Back to the photos. She grimaced. She wasn't a prude—even if she'd left T and T when she was too young to wear the really sexy Carnival clothes—she just thought most people looked more attractive with clothes on. Especially people she had to see at school every day.

Photo 2: Full-length Emmie doing some kind of strip tease. Photo 3: Emmie and fat Ronald from Am Civ class, his surprisingly long legs stretched out on the bed. Photo 4, photo 5, photos 6, 7, 8, 9: More of the same, Emmie with some naked guy. Nevil Carter, uglier than ever with that hairy chest. The pale ass of Haroun Suresh. Geoff Seaver from behind—no, not Geoff, the shoulders were too broad. And what did it matter anyway? A sigh of relief as she turned over the last one. No Trevor. Not that she expected to find him there, but you never knew—and then she'd have to tell Aliya about it, and Aliya had such mistaken ideas about the kind of guy Trevor was.

"So? What's this got to do with me? Go blackmail Emmie."

iPhone still at his ear, he took out a red folder with the other hand. "Financial records," he said.

Gillian took up the thick folder and pulled out another sheaf of papers. Copies of credit card bills on top—bills for rooms at the Holiday Inn.

Underneath, receipts printed out on paper with a formal *The Matchmaker* letterhead. Signed in thick black ink, *Trevor Sanders*. Copies of checks—made out to Trevor, yep, $1000 each.

None of them had known the bastard they were dealing with.

Underneath the checks, bank statements. The one she was looking for, though, the last one, wasn't there. Where the fuck had Trevor hidden the money?

"Again, so what? None of this has anything to do with me."

Yellow folder. Thickest of all. Pages and pages of her e-mails to Trevor. *i got cat wilks to sign*, she'd written a couple of months ago. *hotter than lava, that gyul. we can ask the cash for dis one—we gonna be rich.* And another: *don't go for flat boobs meh-self, but haroun suresh lapped up pix of melinda tanner (saint sebastien day school, no?) i think he'll pay double.* Haroun Suresh. The very same Haroun Suresh who was lapping up Emmie in the photo . . .

Gillian felt a little sick. She turned over all the pages in turn, went back to the bank statements—sure enough, Nick had removed all evidence of his own involvement. So much for the john charge.

"So," said Nick. He'd finally let go of the stupid iPhone and was leaning across the table to take his folders. Maybe she should have tried to steal them, snatched them up and run out the back door? But what good would a bunch of copies do her? How had he gotten those e-mails, anyway? Damn that Trevor, she'd told him and told him about Internet security, but did he ever listen? "I'll take my money in crisp one-hundred-dollar bills."

"I don't have your money, mook," said Gillian. Then regretted it. Sweet Jesus, he could probably have her arrested, the evidence in those files. Procurement, they called it, so they didn't have to use "pimp" in public. Even if she got off, that word would haunt her. Down in Trinidad, they read the *New York Post*, the *National Enquirer*, too.

And imagine if she didn't get off? If twelve people in a jury box couldn't make out her accent and believed Nick's white-skinned lies? She'd be the one claiming the jumpsuit. "I mean, Trevor hid all the money. My money, too. I'm looking for it." She swallowed. Swallowed her anger, swallowed her disgust. "When I find it, of course I'll give you yours back."

"And I'm supposed to believe you because . . ." When she didn't answer, Nick leaned forward, face balanced on the palms of his hands. Who did he think he was, Lord Drake of the gothic novel? "Of course, there are always other ways to pay."

Anger bubbled back. "I don't think so, jackass. I am not some kind of—some kind of Emmie." Damn, she'd have to call that girl, see if she could get some evidence of her own. "I don't take money for sex, and I sure as hell don't use sex to pay my debts. I'll get you the stupid money, Nick, I have more than a few maps in my treasure-hunting kit." Like obeah. Her stomach clenched. That unexpected rain running down her neck, seeping into her clothes, putting out a fire that might have enveloped the forest tree by tree. Her hands, burning on the metal handle. She found herself opening the right one, then the left. Still uninjured, still unmarked.

Nick had the gall to reach across the table, to touch her fingers, still wrapped around the paper cup. "Well, it wouldn't be all about sex." He was touching her—damn him, making her skin crawl—but not looking at her. "I mean, I'm in it for the whole thing. I'm looking for a girlfriend. You wouldn't have to think about it as paying a debt, Gillian. You could just think: he's my boyfriend, he's trying to help me out." Nick gave a corny little laugh. "And my parents are very liberal, so you wouldn't have to worry about the race thing."

Gillian shuddered. From over her shoulder, someone said, "Hey, what are we missing?" and someone else said, "Hey Gillian, hey Nick."

Miya and Aliya to the rescue.

"I didn't know you guys were friends," said Aliya as she pulled up a chair and swung her legs over the side. She wore black jeans and cowboy boots.

"We're not," said Gillian.

Nick gave another little laugh. "Not exactly friends," he said, so coy he sounded like a girl. "I was just asking Gillian out to dinner on Saturday night, an intimate twosome at P.F. Chang's." Aliya's look: straight out of a horror movie. Miya bent her head and tried to fix the uneven table leg. "I'm thrilled to say she told me yes." He scraped back his chair and stood up. "Six o'clock okay?" he asked Gillian.

Say no. Say, *Never in a zillion years.* Say, *Here's the ten thousand I owe you?* "I'll call you," she got out, between her teeth.

He swept up his briefcase, dodged two tables full of people typing on their laptops, and made it to the door.

"So," said Miya. "You and Nick, huh? Young love, how inspiring."

"Oh, shut up," said Gillian. "Where have you *chupidees* been all night? It's almost ten."

"Hiding from my parents," said Aliya. She reached over and grabbed the tea, flicked the little plastic piece open, drank. "Want some?" Miya shook her head. "I told you like five times that I was grounded."

"So how'd you get here?"

"My window."

Gillian swiped her tea back before Aliya drank the whole thing. "What'll you do if you're caught?"

Aliya pulled her hair off her face. "I'm not sure I'm going back."

Gillian drained the tea. She'd been thinking the same thing. Time to find her own way to get out of here. Maybe she could get Nick drunk and put the plane ticket on his credit card.

"Hey," said Aliya. "You sent us about five hundred texts. 'Urgent,' you said. 'Must meet.' Speak up—what's going on?"

She'd meant to tell them she was getting out. Leaving the obeah to them if they wanted it, and to the man in the white turban if they didn't. How had her hands survived unscathed? Someone—some*thing*—had to have intervened. *Step back, jumbies,* she'd planned to say. Gillian Smith got the message.

The tea in her belly should have warmed her, but she went cold instead. It wasn't really possible to say good-bye to obeah once you'd welcomed it in, was that it? *Kill that thought.* But the stupid thought lived on, echoed, reproduced. What had given her the crazy idea that she could hedge her bets with magic, with obeah of all things? Obeah, whose very purpose was to upend the future.

"Gillian?" said Aliya. "We're not mind readers over here." Something flashed on the other side of the table: Miya's ringed fingers, her oval eyes.

"Sorry," said Gillian. She rearranged her thoughts, stuffed the dark one way down in the back. Aliya and Miya were in this too, weren't they? "Did you guys notice anything strange the other night?"

Stupid question. The whole idea, them in the forest, was strange. But Miya's eyes widened as she said, "You felt it too?" and Aliya, sure, sad, said, "Trevor."

Gillian locked eyes with Miya. "When I picked up the bucket of pee, the metal handle was branding-iron hot. Scars-on-your-palms-for-the-rest-of-your-life hot." She lifted her hands slowly, held them up to the other girls. "By the time I got back to the car, they were absolutely fine. It was obeah that made them whole, had to be."

Miya ran one finger across her bottom lip. "Maybe it wasn't as hot as you thought," she said. "Heat can be tricky, like when you cross a beach on a hot day—feels like your toes are going to burn right off, but once you stick them in the water, you're fine."

A comforting idea. Gillian stared into her smooth palms again. She heard her own screams echo in her ears, felt the sharp bite of searing metal. And found herself shaking her head. "So you think nothing happened that night? Just us playing dress up and pretend?"

Miya looked away. "I didn't say that."

And anyway, that didn't explain the fire, did it? Carefully cordoned off by rocks, and then—swoosh. Out of the pit and raging toward the trees.

"It wasn't something strange that happened," said Aliya. "Trevor was there."

A little shiver ran down Gillian's back. Did the crazy girl think he was really going to *come back*, hold her hand and be her boyfriend and give her some necromancer lovin'? Even obeah had its limits. At least she hoped so.

"I don't know," Miya said. "It wasn't what I expected, that séance, not exactly. I keep thinking: Isn't there a simpler explanation? The red-haired girl, the one Trevor was fighting with. If we knew who she was—"

"I'd like to know who she was," said Aliya. Her shuttered eyes stared down at the table where her fingers rapped a short, angry beat.

"Ask Luke," said Gillian. "He's the one who brought her up in the first place."

A long, silent minute passed before Miya said, "Maybe I will."

"And Aliya—"

But Aliya had crouched down beside the table, and the next thing, was heading toward the back door. Down on hands and knees skittering like a crab. "Al—," Miya started to shout, but Gillian slapped a hand over her mouth. The girl might be brilliant, but she needed to pay attention. *The door.*

Two tall, bearded men in long dark coats stood there, speaking gibberish.

"Oh," said Miya.

Gillian's hand came off, painted purple.

"I'll tackle Luke," Miya said. "And if Trevor's going to contact anybody, it'll be Aliya."

"You really think Trevor's going to contact her?" A jumbie coming to call wouldn't be so bad if Gillian wasn't the one who had to feel his cold fingers. Of course, if he did get in touch with Aliya, the girl would be so *basodee* she'd never get any straight answers.

"No," Miya said. "At least, I don't think so."

Then she was gone, too—the normal way, on two legs. Gillian watched her collide with a stranger at the door, hang back, let the redhead in the black cap pass through first.

Redhead? Couldn't be. Gillian grabbed her bag and rushed past the foreigners, broke through the long line of high-school kids waiting for lattes. There must be dozens of redheads in town—then again, wasn't it the least common hair color?

No matter. By the time she pushed her way into the street, both girls were gone.

TWENTY-TWO

MIYA SETTLED into position on the bench outside Gold's Gym. Three times a week, seven to eight a.m., said her source. (Aliya.) Miya checked her watch. Give Luke ten minutes for a shower, another minute to stuff everything into a bag, and—

Here he was, coming down the steps two at a time.

Miya pushed her hair out of her eyes and started across the street, sprinting when she realized that she just might miss him. Man, he was fast. He'd reached the bottom step and turned toward the corner before she jumped the curb. "Hey," she said.

He kept walking. A little more speed, and she grabbed the back of his jacket. "Hey," she said again.

He stopped, even turned around. "Miya." Was he pleased to see her? Angry? Remembering their conversation down at the lake when he stormed away? She stared down at her hands and watched herself twist the strap of her pocketbook around her wrist.

"Hey," she said, for the third time. She swallowed, looked back up. "How's it going?"

"You taking up kickboxing?" he asked. "I think you can still make the eight fifteen class."

She pulled the strap tighter, felt her fingers go a little numb. "No," she said. "Not kickboxing."

"You seem like a kickboxing kind of girl." His brown hair hadn't been cut in a while, and it curled up on his neck. Shone in the early-morning sun. "Fiery, ready to take on the world."

What was she supposed to ask him? Right, the redhead. "I'm so glad I ran into you," she said. *Inject some warmth, Miya. Sound real.* But all she could see in his face was Trevor. Behind his glasses, Luke's green eyes went gray; his brows arched a little higher, his cheeks filled out. She blinked once, twice, three times. "There's something I've been meaning to ask you about . . ."

He'd been staring over her head. She took it in only now, that distance in his eyes, as he brought her into focus.

"You know, Miya," said Luke, "you might be just the person I need." *Need.* Not a word you used lightly. "Can you do something for me? I need you to talk to this guy who won't give me a straight answer. Pretend you're a reporter or something? You're good at that, right—projecting one thing but staying yourself inside?"

Staying yourself inside. It was like he saw the Miya she wanted to be, not the Miya that she was. The Trevor-like parts of his face faded, full-on Luke emerged.

"Miya?" Luke waved a hand toward the parking lot. She recognized that green Mercedes parked in the end space, the one that used to belong to his father. "What do you say? The clerk at the Handi Mart swears he never saw Trevor that last night, but I got a ride with Trevor to Mal's party—the tank was practically empty then. He had to fill up somewhere."

THEY WALKED into the Handi Mart together, her shoulder inches from the elbow of his jacket. A tinny *bing-bing-bing* heralded their arrival. The store was not the clean-

est: it smelled a little like sour milk, and the floors were
streaked with dried mud, although the rain had cleared up
two days ago.

"Gas?" asked the clerk behind the counter, not lifting his
shaggy head from his crossword puzzle.

Luke took a sharp turn and headed straight to the drink
machines at the back of the store. One coffee for her, no
cream, no sugar; one enormous slushie for him. "We're from
the high school paper," said Miya. "Fillmore High. We're
doing a story on Trevor Sanders, the boy who died in the
state forest a couple of weeks ago." Her lines came out all hesitant, like an actress on her first big break.

The guy didn't seem to care, as he filled in half a dozen
boxes. He looked up. Midthirties, dark eyes, pockmarked face.
"You knew him?"

"No," said Miya. "That's why they assigned us the story."

"Sad," he said. "Kids today, they have everything. That
boy tossed it all away. Should have been careful—the night
was too foggy, and he'd been drinking."

In the back of the store, the slushie machine wheezed.
"You saw him that night? You were working?"

"Never saw him." Shaggy's head shook. "The police came
by after the crash and showed me his photo, though. Nice-
looking boy."

Luke came up behind her, touching her elbow as he placed
two cups on the counter, one Styrofoam, one plastic. Was that
touch on purpose? Miya bit her lip and went on with her job.
"Who else came in? Was there a girl with red hair?"

"How would I remember that?"

Inspiration struck. She reached into her purse and
thumbed through her wallet until she found the picture she'd

stolen from Trevor's bulletin board. "What about her? Was she here?"

Luke took a breath so fast he whistled. *Catastrophe.* Trevor's bulletin board, Luke's house—of course he knew the girl. Miya refused to look up at him. "Was it her?"

The clerk shrugged. "Two hundred people in here a night—I can't be expected to remember every one, can I?"

Nothing left to do but leave.

The door opened and closed behind them, automatic of course, but it felt like magic. How to distract him? Miya reached for the sexy look, the arched back, the three open buttons on her blouse.

None of it worked. Less than three steps and he was saying, "What the hell were you doing in my house, Miya? You completely freaked out my mom—she's convinced that it was Trevor's ghost."

Miya stepped up on the platform with the gas tanks and leaned back against the nearest one. *Say something.* Except that she couldn't.

"She thinks he's all pissed at her for letting his room get trashed. The woman can barely hold her life together as is. She's late to work three days a week, spends every night crying on the phone, can't even pay the bills on time. Why would you want to make her more miserable? Why do something like that?"

Like what? Break in? Repair the model ships? Steal the photo?

"Can I have my cousin's picture back, please? What did you want with it anyway? Jeez, Miya. Don't you think the police would have asked Katelin first thing? She wasn't there, she was taking her boyfriend to the bus station."

His cousin. At least Aliya would cheer up.

Miya mustered an apology. "Look, I'm sorry, I have this friend who was in love with Trevor—they were together and she's so afraid he was cheating on her. . . ."

"Uh-huh." Even with the six inch advantage she got from the platform, he looked down at her. "Your friend."

"Are you saying I'm lying? You think I'm making her up?" And Miya, the liar, poised herself on the brink of truth.

Luke punched the gas tank with his right fist, hard, direct, like the steel tank would go down for the count. Not the smartest move, but who was interested in smart these days?

Miya tugged the ends of her hair. *Make a boy who hasn't spoken to you tell you he loves you.* Maybe the charlatan kitoshi knew Miya better than she knew herself. If that kitoshi had real power, what would Miya be asking her now? Raise Trevor from his watery grave, but then give Miya the will to demand what she might want the most: *Ignore my warts. Love me—yes, love me—even if I break into your house and steal family photos.*

"I'm not calling you a liar," said Luke. He turned his back on the tank. "I mean, the whole thing, it's so unfair. It should be Trevor alive, cheating on girls, if that's what he was doing, taking their shit himself, and having all the pleasure of convincing her she's wrong. I mean—"

He was crying. His face was a mess, tears spilling out beneath the glasses, mouth crumpled up with something painful. In a rage maybe, or shock. Miya had never been much good at reading faces. Books, that's what she knew and loved; texts from horny boys, she could read those.

"It was me who trashed the room, you know," he said, voice shaking. "The morning of his memorial service—God, I was so angry, so unbearably angry. I don't know why I went into Trevor's room in the first place, but I was standing there, my whole life laid into a freaking waste. I threw every damn thing I touched, which was almost every damn thing in the room." He turned his head away. "I ended up standing in a pile of trash."

It was the easiest thing to round the gas tank, close the distance between them. To reach up and wrap her arms around Luke, squeeze. "Sorry, sorry, sorry," she said. The stiffness of his shirt crushed her cheek; she inhaled the fresh, clean scent of soap. "I shouldn't have taken the photo, shouldn't be playing Lulu Dark, so, so stupid. And it's not what you think, I swear, not just curiosity or even a girl with hurt feelings, it's more than that, it's . . ."

She shut her mouth just in time, so he wouldn't look for the men in white coats over her shoulder. Where she went very wrong was to let her fingers trace a sexy curve up Luke's back, to twist her head around, let her mouth taste the salty tears on his face, to kiss him.

He shrugged her away. "No, Miya, I can't, I've got to think."

"You mean, not me."

He had his back to her now, but she saw his hand move, wipe his face. Then he hurled the slushie against the gas pump. "We're so different, Miya. You're all about fun, about the next guy on the list, and me, I'm finding it hard to think about fun these days." He stared at the green liquid and ice trickling down the side of the pump, pooling on the ground. "I'm finding it hard to think about anything except Trevor."

She too. She'd dreamed about Trevor's flailing arms, his sinking head; replayed *go drown yourself, do you think I'd care?* like a song stuck on infinite loop. She'd even abandoned reason for Trevor. But all she said was, "So you think I'm that shallow?"

He reached into his pocket and pulled out the car keys. "I'm not calling you shallow, Miya, just because you thrive on the chase. And think of it that way; it's not me you want, it's the satisfaction of a race well run." One raised hand cut off her protest. "You used to chase prizes and grades, now you chase guys. All it says is you're a person with goals and ambitions. You're a winner."

"Isn't everyone all about the chase?" Her voice wobbled, but not so much that she couldn't get away with it. "Whether you're chasing love, or identity, or an end to global warming? Whether you want a million dollars or a date for the prom?" *Or the truth about why a seventeen-year-old ran his car off a cliff one night?*

"You could put it that way." Luke was striding across the parking lot, heading for the car. Miya had to scramble to catch up. It wasn't until he pulled his seat belt across his chest and started the engine that he spoke again. "But I don't want to be a goal."

He pulled out of the parking lot, took the first right and hit the highway full speed. They ripped past the break in the road that marked the secret entrance to the state forest. Was it really less than a week ago that she'd peeled out of there, wet clothes sticking her fast to the seat, hands barely touching the steering wheel as she raced to the bottom of the hill? Unable to get the memory of floating out of her head as she ran a red light, went the wrong way down a one-way street. There *had* been something to that night, hadn't there? Maybe there was even something to the kitoshi, something more than greed.

She snuck a glance at Luke, his face grim, his head bent over the steering wheel. So close she could feel the warmth coming off his skin, so close that if she moved half an inch, she'd brush his elbow. But she didn't dare. Tension seeped off of him, filled the air of the car with weight. If she touched him, they'd both sizzle.

Her mouth set in a straight line. Time to do away with the feminine wiles, once and for all. Bury them, the way she'd dumped her college bowl trophies in the back of the closet and piled clothes on top. There were other paths to the Miya she wanted.

Her voice under full control, she said, "I see your point." She did. And very soon, he'd see hers.

TWENTY-THREE

STUPID EXPEDIA.COM. Did it have to take all day to call up a new page? Finally: Boston to Columbia, Columbia to Caracas, Caracas to Curacao, Curacao to Port of Spain . . . $619, one way.

Vol-ca-no. Gillian's ringtone, courtesy of soca king Red Plastic Bag. She swept up her cell, looked at the Caller ID— **out of area**—and snapped it open. "Good night," she said.

"Hey, hey, hey," said Mums. "Good night. How yuh doing in the land of the free and the brave?"

"Mums! How goes my sweet TnT?" Something sharp and uncomfortable shot through Gillian's side. A pang of guilt? What had she been thinking, giving free reign to all those negative thoughts at the séance? She'd swept all her textbooks off the bed and made herself comfy with a couple of pillows up against the headboard before she realized Mums wasn't talking. "Mums?" she said. "Everything okay?"

A scary sniffle came from the other end of the line, then two. "I all right, gyul."

"Mums? What's wrong?" She'd been after Mums to go to the doctor for a long time—those headaches, that loss of appetite. Had she finally gone?

"I ready to cuss," said Mums. "Worst day of meh life today. Yesterday too. Bad things piling on, gyul. This place, things ain't like they used to be."

"What are you talking about?" Gillian pinned the phone to her ear.

"People. Used to be, yuh could trust people. Trinidad was full of good people, honest people."

Gillian was on the edge of the bed now, bare legs dangling. "What happened?"

"I telling yuh," said Mums. She sighed so deep, Gillian's cell phone almost shook. "I told yuh about meh new job?"

"At the roti shop?"

"Two days ago, lunchtime, three of us working, crowds pushing through the door. Money went missing from the till. For some reason, Sebastian—he the boss—decided I the culprit. Outrageous. Sent meh home then, and didn't pay meh for meh time, the whole week."

"But Mums." Gillian crossed her legs, then dragged the comforter back to cover them. "Didn't he search you? Couldn't you prove you didn't have the money?"

"Sebastian, he doesn't think like that."

There was some silence. "Well," said Gillian, to cheer her up, "you still have your job in the zoo gift shop. This part-time thing was just to help Dunstan, right? He'll have to—"

"Dunstan." Mums laughed, or maybe she was crying. "That cheating rat's ass?"

Gillian didn't like Dunstan, but she'd thought he knew a good thing when he hooked up with Mums. "Cheating?"

"He been bullin' meh for weeks, telling meh Nancy stories, then he cut a night here, cut a night there. I know there's another girl he talking to at work. I don't go for drama, but I went to see she, let her know she boy a blasted rat. Well, she didn't like that—"

"Is Dunstan gone?"

"He gone," said Mums. "And meh TV gone wit him, and the iPod yuh sent meh last summer, and all meh U.S. dollars. I having bad luck like Christmas. Someone out there put *maljo* on meh, and when I find out—"

Maljo. The evil eye. Underneath her warm covers, Gillian froze. A phrase, that's all, one Trinis used all the time.

Nothing to do with her ham-fisted attempts at obeah, with three girls in the forest calling up spirits they couldn't control. With her thinking harsh thoughts about Mums as she danced around the fire. Wasn't enough that she'd abandoned the woman, she had to bad talk her to the jumbies too?

Mums was still going on, talking about a bake and shark stand that might take her on, run by the friend of a cousin, but the pay, not enough to live on, so maybe she should take up private cooking?

"But what about your job at the zoo? You're still working there, right?"

"Didn't I tell yuh about meh bad luck?" said Mums. "We on strike at the zoo. Big boys think it's okay to cut we salaries, so that they can keep their fancy cars. We said no, we want we money, and we out. That was, let's see, the thirtieth."

The thirtieth. Gillian scrambled over to the desk, clawed through some papers and found the calendar. Please let her be wrong—

Just as she thought. The thirtieth. Saturday, the day after the séance.

". . . so yuh know I hate to ask. But the rent money, I don't have, and the landlord, he telling meh, yuh got a daughter up in the Stars and Stripes, why not go on up? With this crazy weather coming—"

"You want to come here? That's *loca*, you've got no idea what it's like . . ."

"That's why I said, I hate to ask, but this is no time to be out on the street." She was proud, Mums, she'd eat stale porridge for breakfast and nothing for lunch rather than ask for a bite of sandwich. "If yuh got a bit of spare change, well, more than a bit, I'd need at least two hundred dollars. Three, I mean. US."

Good Lord. How could Gillian be such a *chupidee*? She hadn't been paying enough attention to the malevolent force, or at least not the right kind of attention. Out to get her, she'd assumed. But the obeah man had seemed to think *she* was the malevolent force, or was aligned with it, or some such—wasn't that why he kicked her out? And then she'd piled on with all those negative thoughts in the forest. She winced. Anything was possible. Maybe she'd sent the malevolent force after Mums, all inadvertent.

What had the obeah man said to her that first day? Don't interfere with what you know nothing about.

There was still a chance she could snitch a credit card, buy that ticket on Expedia, make it to the gate before someone called, *Stop thief.* "Maybe I could come down, help out—"

Look ting! Finally, meh daughter coming home. But instead, she heard: "Gwan wit yuh. Come down here to what, call out for change in the street?"

"I want to come home, Mums, I really hate it here—so cold, the weather, the food, the people. I want to swim in Maracas Bay, jump up at Carnival—"

"Life isn't Carnival every night, Daughter." Another sigh, a tired voice. "What's that man been telling yuh? I let yuh go away so I could party? I let yuh fly up there so yuh could learn something, and live in a house with heat and AC." A sudden noise crashed in the background, like someone was carrying a roomful of steel drums past the phone, then it vanished. "I know yuh ended up only half a Trini, wit that Yankee accent, and that hardass cheapness, and that American sense of superiority. But that's the price we had to pay. Both of us, meh and yuh. Yuh think I'm gonna lose out on every-thing, and get nothing back for it but missing yuh? Yuh keep that black ass freezing in the cold, where it belongs."

The coverlet above Gillian was torn, the cotton insides straining to jump out. Funny, she hadn't noticed that before.

"Besides," Mums was speaking up again, "now is not the time to come to Trinidad. Don't yuh get the news up there? There's a major hurricane heading straight this way."

TWENTY-FOUR

MIYA STARED into the rushing water. Hard, pounding, and . . . cold. Very, very cold.

Was she really going to do this? Of course not. But she sat down on the nearest boulder and started unlacing her black boots anyway. She'd been up all night, her thoughts tossing between Trevor and Luke. How could she get Luke to forget his brother if she couldn't forget him herself?

Wash away your past, the kitoshi had said. A greedy woman, that kitoshi, poised to psychic out all the cash she could, but that didn't mean she was a liar. It didn't mean she was wrong. These last few days, Miya had been researching Japanese mysticism every chance she got; she'd found plenty of web sites about pain and asceticism and purification.

Miya pulled off the right boot. A sharp blast of cold curled her toes. She grit her teeth and tugged at her sock. Her bare foot shivered in the open air. A con artist would say anything to make a sale, true enough. But whom could it hurt? What if, a little cold water and Miya forgave herself? Became a purified body, a transparent human vessel, and Trevor came and did the forgiving for her? She'd be at peace, and for nothing more onerous than an early morning in the rain.

She ripped off her other boot, other sock, let both feet dangle above the sand. People in Boston did this all the time, to toast the New Year. What were they called? Walruses or polar bears. They didn't get frostbite or hypothermia. They

wrapped themselves in towels, drank a little hot chocolate,
and toasted each other on the morning news shows.

Not a foot away from the boulder lay Miya's backpack. She leaned over and pulled out a towel and a thermos. Then she pushed her butt off its stony seat, buried her feet in the cold, cold sand, and reached for the zipper of her jeans.

Shiver, shiver. She was no Gillian Smith, but it was freezing. Bare bottom, bare thighs, bare calves. She shrugged out of her leather coat, lifted her pink-and-white V-neck sweater over her head—with all the ghostcraft research, there'd been no time to buy a white kimono—and sharp air gushed across the sensitive skin on her stomach. *Click* went the catch of her bra, and she was naked.

Naked, shivering, and scared.

Enough. Hadn't the now-believed kitoshi said it was all about degrees, moving forward one tiny step at a time? Wasn't exposing her backside enough for one day?

Only if she could live with herself until tomorrow. Twenty-four hours of thoughts going round and round her head, that infamous sentence replaying itself like the message on a customer service phone. She kicked her clothes aside, walked through the sand till it gave way to gravel. Sharp, jagged pieces of rock poked her, prodded her a little faster than she meant to go. Two more boulders and there she was, at the stream.

Dip your toes in . . .

She eased both feet into the water and gasped as it closed over her toes, the tops of her feet, her ankles. Tiny drops of water from the waterfall sprinkled her arms and back, and she bent over to protect her chest and stomach.

Take the plunge, Miya, or stop playacting and go home.

She stepped through the stream and hesitated for one final second. *Now or never, Miya.* It was now. The freezing water pelted her shoulders, her lower back, her ass. Her hair, drenched, whipped around her neck like a wet towel. She was screaming, or was that her teeth, clenched and grinding down?

Ten seconds, Miya, and holding. The pain shifted, her body shivered, her feet froze. Just when she was sure the waterfall would push her block-of-ice body down the stream and out to sea, something happened. The water was still cold, but no longer painful. She couldn't see herself, she wasn't flying, but she'd left her body behind. Again. She became more, not less, herself. She raised her icy hands in homage to the sun. *Shine.* Without limits, she shone.

She'd assumed, she'd been sure, that this was all about Trevor, placating the dead, letting go. Only now did she realize: it was about holding fast. Her frozen body, her tortured mind—what importance did they have? Asceticism was the route to power. She'd read that somewhere, and it came crashing back to her, resounded with the rhythm of the pounding waterfall. In the glittering water, she caught the faintest glimpse of what it meant.

She stepped out of the icicle shower and made her way back to the beach. The stones, ineffective now, made no imprint on her impervious feet. She hadn't expected to feel, to be, this different.

She was a whole new Miya, ready to take on the world.

BY THE TIME she got to school, her hair was almost dry. She clutched a fat book under her chest: *Asceticism, Pain and Power.*

"Hey, Miya, wait up." Aliya popped up out of nowhere like Tinkerbell, but in a wool jacket and jeans. "Did you talk to Luke? What'd he say?"

Miya dragged Aliya to the relative peace of the bushes at the side of the school steps. Would Aliya notice anything different about her? Sure, the fishnets were gone, the tottering heels, the bare-my-belly-in-the-cold tops, but Aliya'd never raised eyebrows at those before. It was the under-the-skin radiance Miya hoped shined through.

"Well?" said one-track Aliya.

Miya broke her silence. "I tried IMing you last night."

"My *judba* parents." Aliya crossed her arms over her chest. "They took my cell phone, and now they've unplugged the computer, too. They think I'm going to the bad."

"Well, aren't we?"

Aliya gave a little laugh, like she wanted to take it as a joke but couldn't, quite. "So what did he say?"

He didn't want me. Had he said anything else, really? She shifted her feet. Their scratched bottoms ached a little, brought back the rocky streambed, the screaming water. Reminded her that she—all of them—needed to deal with Trevor, help him find peace, before they did anything else. "He dragged me to the Handi Mart and I showed the clerk the photo."

"Did he recognize her?"

"Luke certainly did. It's his cousin Katelin."

"Oh my God." Aliya clapped a hand to her mouth. "His *cousin*. But Trevor never mentioned . . ."

"Luke said it wasn't her at the Crescent, she was out with her boyfriend that night. I'm not sure I believe that; what are the chances Trevor was involved with two different red-heads?" Only two percent of the US population had red hair, right? If you assumed Trevor knew two hundred people, and—

Aliya tugged on her arm. "The clerk?"

"He didn't say much, just implied that the accident was Trevor's own fault; he was wasting his miserable life on drinking and drugs."

Someone climbing the steps behind them called Aliya's name, but she didn't look up. "Trevor wasn't miserable," she said, her voice low. "He was with me."

"Right." How could Miya have been so tactless? "What does the clerk know?"

"Aliya!" The voice calling her turned sharp. Aliya arched her neck, Miya, too. A girl's face, shaded by a scarf, hung over the side of the banister. "Aren't you coming in?"

"Uh, yeah," said Aliya. "Just a minute, Sherine."

The girl said something in Arabic, but Aliya didn't answer back; after a minute, footsteps clicked upward, faded away.

"You're screwed now," said Miya. "Talking to the school piece of trash. Wait'll your parents hear. They'll ship you back to Syria."

"Don't be ridiculous," said Aliya. Right away, not like she had to think about it. "Who cares if you had affairs with this one and that one—I don't know why you'd want to, but that's your business, not mine. My parents think every American girl's like that anyway, no matter how many times I tell them different."

Nothing wrong with sleeping around, as long as you did it for the right reasons. Of course, to do that, you had to know what the right reasons were. "Falling into someone's arms because you couldn't bear to be yourself one second longer" probably didn't make the list.

What the—Big, thick hands landed on her shoulders, jolting her out of contemplation. They managed to skim her breasts as they moved from her shoulders down to her waist.

"Hey, kitten." A voice she knew: Rodney. And here she thought he'd finally taken the hint when he stopped texting her. "Wow, you're looking your fabulous self today. Like the perfect before-school snack." He jerked his head in the direction of the parking lot, where his SUV, with those tinted windows, gleamed in the morning sun. "What do you think? Little pick-me-up to start the day?"

Once, Miya would have made a joke of the whole thing, and wondered later whether the attention made up for the cackles in the hall.

Now, she pushed his hands off with her elbows. "I'm not in the mood."

She blinked, and there she was again, emerging from the waterfall, blood frozen, skin razor sharp, self something altogether new. Blink, blink, and she was soaring over the dark and shifty forest, eyeing that shining girl below. How many years had Miya let her desperate need for approval boss her around? Trying to please her teachers, her mom, Rodney and every other horny boy in school, Trevor . . . *She could be that shining girl*. She wasn't all the way convinced, but she wasn't willing to let the possibility go.

"Since when? Come on, I thought you were supposed to be the adventurous type." He knocked back his head and laughed. "Remember the fountain in Town Center Park?"

Miya had read Chapter 7, "Pain Leads to Power" twice. Now she rooted in her pocketbook—yes, here it was, the safety pin she'd dropped in her coin purse last week. "Haha," she said to Rod. She unlatched it, took a deep breath. Drew blood. Ahhh . . .

Was that Aliya, asking if she was all right? No matter. *Gather your power*, the book said. What did that mean? Miya closed her eyes, concentrated every ounce of thought on the pin. *Stitch his mouth closed*, she told herself. Her lips even moved. She saw the pin piercing, clipping, silencing. *His bad luck; don't let him speak again.* Eyes opened, raised to the sky, she concentrated on her ancestors, the lingering dead of Japan. Used to spreading misfortune in their random way . . . Let them fall into line, spread bad luck and trouble at the feet—in the mouths—of her enemies.

Seal the deal with the power of words, Miya. "Shut the fuck up, Rodney," she said. Then she slapped him.

His mouth dropped open and nothing came out. Nothing moved, not arm, not leg. He stood, stuck to the spot like the frozen twig he was, his mouth the only fluttering thing.

"Let's get out of here," she said to Aliya.

They climbed over the banister as the final bell rang. "Wow," said Aliya. "I can't believe you slapped him. He's a hockey player—they beat people up for a living, you know. He couldn't believe it either. He looked stunned." She turned around, leaned back. "*Ya Allah*, he's still there."

Miya swallowed, felt the hole in her sore thumb. Not playacting after all. She didn't turn her head, though; she wasn't about looking back, not anymore. "Of course he is," said Miya. Her voice gave her confidence. "Didn't you feel the spirits when I invoked their power?" Her breath came rasping, jagged; she tried to catch it but fell short. Unbelievable morning. Or maybe this was the toll that invoking spirits took: their starved souls lapped up her energy. She let herself think one last *Am I crazy?* Images flashed again: the waterfall, the rocks, a frozen body impervious to wind; a rush of power, the sense of New Miya. All these hours later, she still tingled. Not imagination, not insanity.

She banished doubt forever.

Aliya's eyes widened. Miya could see her thinking *What the . . .* as they walked through the front doors. Inside, Ms. Martitius was hurrying people to class with snapping fingers. Gillian, pacing in front of the office, ignored her. "Sistren, yuh finally reached," she said. "I've been waiting half an hour gone. Did you tell her about yesterday? Katelin? Luke? The hurricane?" To Aliya: "Why the hell don't you ever return your messages?"

Aliya was still staring at Miya. "No phone," she said. "My parents took it."

"Well, thief it back."

Aliya shook her head. "What hurricane?" she asked.

Miya had forgotten all about the hurricane and Gillian's three phone calls, each louder and more frantic, last night. "There's a late-season hurricane heading toward Trinidad," she told Aliya. "And Gillian thinks it's all our fault." Last night, she'd soothed Gillian with talk about centurial shifts in weather patterns. But now, who knew?

She sensed something behind her, a movement, a swish of air—a something so sad and forlorn, she whirled around. *Do you really think I care if you drown?* Her heart clutched, her breath came quicker. Here she was, thinking of Trevor again. "If we really want to contact Trevor, we need to do it at a place that meant something to him." Chapter 10 in *Asceticism*. "The book I'm reading says spirits don't draw their powers from the place where they died, but from the place where they lived. We need to hold the séance in Trevor's house."

"Jeezan ages," said Gillian. "Keep your tail quiet."

Miya looked over her shoulder and down the hall. Kids were rushing by. One girl read a textbook as she walked, two had headphones in their ears, a couple of guys argued about who was hotter, Belinda or Stephanie. No one even glanced their way. "What difference does it make? Who cares what they think?" Her confidence stepped up another notch. *Nobody can stop us now.*

"You seem awfully sure," said Aliya, who never seemed sure about anything. Miya tugged on her hair. Was she crazy after all? What did she know about magic, about mysticism? Their mothers had fed them belief with their breakfast milk, wrapped up with the chickpeas and hot sauce for Gillian's doubles, fried with the fava beans for Aliya's falafel. All Miya got was a faith in information and the little black dress. Religion, especially Christianity, was a waste of time said Mom. But Mom wasn't always right, was she? With all her sighing and *Oh Miya, if you'd just junk the glasses and wear contacts . . .* and look where that got her.

"I am sure," said Miya. No more doubt, remember? She kicked its conniving little butt right out of her brain. "We can reach Trevor, I just need to think a little more about—"

Quick steps came up behind them: somebody suddenly paying attention. "Okay, girls, move along now," said Ms. Martitius. "It's time for class." When the girls didn't stir, she flapped her book of detentions against her thigh. "Let's get going. Move those legs like the athletes I know you are. Ms. Chonan," she added, recognizing Miya with surprise, like she was a movie star in sunglasses. "I've been looking for you. Come into my office."

That didn't sound good. "Text me," Gillian mouthed, as she and Aliya moved off down the hall. "As soon as you can."

Ms. Martitius held her door open. As Miya lifted her hands out of her pockets, her thumb clung a little where it had bled against the lining.

If Ms. Martitius said anything she didn't like, well, Miya would put a stop to it.

TWENTY-FIVE

ALIYA WAS GROUNDED. No cell phone, no computer, no car. Except they couldn't take her voice, which she used to ask Gillian for two dollars, and they couldn't take her feet, which ran down the long hallway leading to the cafeteria, jumped the chairs piled up in front of the janitor's closet, and snuck out the back door. A whole building away from where Mariam was waiting for her, probably fixing her lipstick or gabbing with Sherine while she scanned the crowd of high schoolers.

They couldn't take her hands either, which gave the bus driver the bills and received her seventy-five cents change. She stuffed the quarters into the pocket of her jeans and didn't bother to find a seat. Good thing Miya the Google goddess had tracked down Katelin's address and paper air-planed it to Aliya on her way to the library.

Then again, Miya owed her. The only reason they'd lost the stupid picture was because she had it all up for that Luke. "But you could have any guy in the school," said Gillian over lunch, which the three girls brown-bagged in the darkest corner of the caf. "Why him?"

"You could have any island in the world," said Miya. "Why Trinidad?"

Gillian would have actually answered the silly question if Aliya hadn't jumped in. "What happened with Ms. Martitius,

Miya?" Miya launched into a wild story, one she seemed to believe, saying that Martitius admitted Miya had the highest grades and the best essay, but she couldn't compete for graduation speaker because she didn't have a "moral reputation." So Miya pricked her finger and channeled the power of the spirits—yes, she actually said that—and Martitius shut herself up and didn't say another word.

"Pricking your finger?" asked Gillian, sounding even more irritable than usual. "There's no pricking your finger in obeah."

"You are totally messing with us on this, right?" Aliya shouldn't have had to ask that, but Miya looked so serious, she did. Miya didn't answer either of them, just went on about how Ms. Martitius looked a little dizzy, then came to. "Ah, Miya Chonan," she'd said. "What can I do for you?" Then she'd looked up with a quizzical tilt to her head and reached for a pencil.

"Not perfect," conceded Miya. "I need more practice. But if I work hard, discipline myself, anything can happen. Wait till Friday night."

"You talking nonsense, girl," said Gillian.

"Ask Aliya, she saw me shut Rodney up this morning."

True, Aliya had seen. Quite remarkable. After Miya stuck her hands in her pocket, Rodney had stood there, tongue waving, either mute or an idiot. Of course, Miya had also slapped him, a very surprising, unMiya thing to do. Maybe Rodney was in shock?

"If you can really do this thing, this obeah," said Gillian, who still hadn't ditched her all-magic-is-obeah idea, "then addlepate me right now, Aliya as witness. Let me see for myself." But Miya said no. Got angry, too, which wasn't like Miya. But then, basic black, magic-using, manipulating teachers—none of this was the Miya all the boys loved. "It's not a game, Gillian," said Miya.

"Cumberland Street," said the bus driver. Aliya leaned over two seats and dinged the bell, brought the bus to a stop, and jumped off. According to MapQuest, 114B Mansfield should be the second left. Not the best part of town, this: three-story duplexes crammed into tiny lots, geezer cars—black, blue, white—breathing their rusty last at the side of the road. The still-wet ground didn't help either: nasty puddles, filled with floating debris. A cigarette carton stranded here, a Fritos bag washed up there.

Skip, skip, splash. She looked around, sniffed the air. Ripe garbage, wet dog. It was lonely without her iPod or cell phone, without her ghost. "Trevor?" she whispered into the wind. "Trevor?"

Her feet stopped short at 114, till she realized B was around the back. Had Trevor come here, skirted the nasty mud pie of a front lawn by holding onto the fence like this, found the basement stairs in the back, right here?

My cousin, Luke said. *Not there*, Cousin told the police. Assertions with no more substance than Trevor's ghost. She found *114B* scrawled on a piece of cardboard next to the door. She knocked.

And knocked. What had she been thinking? Cousin Katelin—if cousin she was—would be in class, at work, ordering a latte at Starbucks.

The door opened. A girl in an extra large T-shirt and bunny slippers said, "Do I look like I have the money to buy your stupid magazines?"

"I'm not selling," said Aliya to the girl, a girl with crushed red hair and almost perfect skin and big black circles around sad eyes. Talk fast. "I'm a friend of Trevor's—"

"Trevor? My cousin Trevor?" The sad eyes narrowed. "He's dead."

"I know that." Would she be here if he wasn't? "I heard you saw him the night he died and—"

"Nope." Katelin wasn't blowing bubbles, but she sounded like she was. "You heard wrong."

"The thing is," said Aliya, "I'm a friend of his. A good friend. A . . . uh, his girlfriend." First time she said it out loud, and he was three weeks dead. *May God have mercy on my unchaste soul.* "I need to know, his last night—"

"Wasn't me," said the girl.

Katelin moved to the side and gestured Aliya in anyway. It smelled like spaghetti sauce, burned, and more garbage, spilling out of the corner bin. "I told the police: I was driving my asshole boyfriend to the bus station. Ex-boyfriend. Anyway, I don't do that shit anymore, smoke up at the Crescent. Trevor and I used to . . . but that's over now, for both of us."

Aliya looked around the apartment: crumpled blankets on the floor, stained paper plates in the sink, an enormous collage on the wall over the sofa bed. Someone scrapbooked: the collage was edged with gold, matted with olive green. Fancy calligraphy ran down the side and, with true professional restraint, the collage used only five photos. Aliya found the one she was looking for right away, smack in the center: Trevor and Katelin, arms around each other, faces smeared with the same maroon and white paint.

The girl snapped on an overhead light, and in the dim, dirty room, Trevor's smile glowed. "He was a bit of a shit these days," she said. "Drugs, stealing from his mom—not that Aunt Patty didn't deserve it, talk about cheap! She wants me to take Trevor's damned dog off her hands. Do I look like I have room for a dog?"

She didn't.

"Right. Drugs, theft, sleeping around . . ."

Aliya's back stiffened. "I was his girlfriend."

"Mmmm. Sorry. Could've been before you. When we were younger, we were close. That picture was from my last semester at BU; he took the train in so he could come to the game. We had—we had a good time. He would have straightened out eventually." She smoothed back her frizzy hair. "Sucks rotten eggs that he didn't have the chance."

"Yeah," said Aliya. She swallowed. "You think he was high when it happened?" What she really wanted to ask: *Do you think he misses me?*

"No idea. Don't think about it, it'll mess with your head." Katelin tucked the hair behind her ears. Then she crossed the room, took a cell phone off the dirty counter, checked the Caller ID display. "Nothing. Bastard called me from Mexico this morning, said he loved me but he needed time to think, to find himself. *Find himself.* Ha, I could hardly hear him over the tequila party in the background. If he loved me he wouldn't go backpacking for a freaking year. Shithead. That bastard Jack, I'll never forgive him." Aliya didn't know what to say; luckily, Trevor's cousin didn't much care. "God, it's three thirty already. I've got yoga at the Y."

Aliya showed herself to the door, stood in the wet backyard.

"What'd you say your name was?"

"Aliya."

"Katelin. See you around."

Aliya sludged back through the mud.

Would they have ended up like this, she and Trevor? Wasn't that Islam's argument? Boyfriend Boulevard, also known as the detour to misery. Without God's rules, without the protection of the marriage contract, was this what you got: cheap apartment, swearing over the phone, cheating in Mexican tourist traps? An incompleteness that hours of long-distance pleading couldn't assuage. That same incompleteness Aliya felt right now, the one that caused her to remind herself: yes, ten fingers, two kneecaps, one solid chin. Her physical body still held together.

Had God taken Trevor to save her? Couldn't be. Even Mariam knew that God didn't work like that: He was neither so protective of Muslims nor so callous with uninformed Unbelievers. But Aliya felt very far from Trevor as she wandered past the front fence, let her feet sink into the sludge. She came all the way to the edge of the street, checked out the traffic. It seemed deserted. No cars, no trucks, no buses.

And no ghosts.

TWENTY-SIX

MIYA OPENED the shed door. Bikes, skates, that big box of Halloween decorations, and, yes, here it was. She pushed the box aside with one knee, reached behind it, yanked hard. The grill rolled out onto the grass.

She lifted up the cover. The smell of burned hickory drifted out from under the metal grates. Miya took off one and then the other; both were a little rusty. Their last barbecue, Mom had just set out the burgers when the rain poured down, drove the whole party into the house. Miya had ended up in the doorway, watching the angry rain storm the backyard, hearing the crack of thunder—What was that?

Nothing like thunder this time. A soft stirring brought her back to the here and now. Not much more than a puff of air, it tripped up her back, tickled the blades between her shoulders.

Don't get ahead of yourself, Miya. But she found herself smiling as she carried handfuls of coal from inside the grill across a short space of brown grass and lined them up in even rows. Now the lighter fluid—*drizzle, drizzle, gunk*—and . . . wait, had she forgotten the matches? Yep. Back inside the house, where she retrieved them from the vase on top of the refrigerator and brought them out. She set fire to the coals. As they flared up, she was thinking of rain again, of clouds opening, drops pelting, girls running. That magic night, float-

ing above the trees, seeing her true self, a self that glowed
with power, with possibilities.

There had to be a way to do that again.

She kicked off her shoes, stripped off her socks. Touched the red coals with her fingertips: still cold. She stepped across on tiptoe, for practice—the coals scraped her not-tough-enough skin, but she made it all the way to the end. She closed her eyes, hunched her shoulders, concentrated as she went over the coals again. Nothing. Not yet. Of course, she wasn't exactly sure what she was hoping for. So far the spirits had been shy, wary, untamed—sliding up to her at brief, unexpected moments, their closeness like the tenderest caress. She whispered *Welcome*, waited for the *pss-pss-pss* back, for words that would curl up inside her ears, encouraging her, empowering her.

Time to try again. She readied herself. The coals had darkened with the heat—and yes, they burned her skin—thank the spirits for the chance. A second step; sharp, searing embers, roasting feet. She pulled her mind into a single point of concentration, reached for the words to charm the spirits, to corral them and—

Crash.

Miya found herself spread out on the ground, hands pressed against her ears like a metal vise. Stars danced above her, in front of her, on the grass beside her—she blinked once, twice, and they resumed their place in the heavens. Slowly, the banging inside her died down.

What happened? She'd been reaching for the spirits—how long had she been balanced there?—when something had launched itself in the way. The single note of a discordant symphony erupted, a dozen incompatible instruments blaring all at once, rampaging inside her head. It had lasted a single second, it had gone on a million years. Some force she'd never sensed before, dark and shady and—what was the right word? *Malevolent.* She found herself shivering. A little at first, and then her hands were trembling and she had to tuck them under her arms, her teeth were chattering and she had to clench them together.

Miya rolled onto her side, nose so close to the coals if it'd been a little longer she would have singed it. They must be blazing hot by now, she should test herself again. But somehow she couldn't. There was something else she needed to do first.

THE SUN WAS SETTING behind the white church. Thick pine trees on three sides cast long shadows before blending into forest. The church wore that shuttered look, doors and windows closed tight, a small placard in front announcing *No prayer group this Thursday.* Out in the deserted parking lot, the wind tossed needles, small stones, pieces of yellow paper.

Aliya and Gillian were already sitting on the front steps when Miya arrived. She circled the church, wondering if she would get a hint of Trevor—that unhappy, dead feeling that pressed against her body now and again. By the time she rounded the last corner, she was sure: no Trevor. The heavy atmosphere of Christian God must have driven him out. There was blood here, and pain, but it was the pain of holes in the hands, thorns in the head. For the first time, Miya felt affection for the body on that cross. Not creepy, just another ascetic trying to gain power.

Gillian, punching buttons on her cell phone, didn't look up when Miya joined them, just pressed the phone so tight to her ear it looked as though she were trying to weld it in place. "Straight to voicemail," she muttered. "Again. The woman's got no job, no man, where the hell can she be?"

Aliya met Miya's eyes. "He's not here," she said. "I can't feel him at all."

"No," Miya agreed. She sat down next to Aliya, almost reached out and took her hand. "This place is hostile to spirits, I sensed it as soon as I arrived." That was a slight stretch. There was no "as soon as" in power, at least not for her. Everything was about patience, about focusing her mind, reaching out, finding, feeling. "But anyway, that's not why I called you guys."

"You can still smell the flowers," said Aliya. She brought a hand to her nose as though it held a bouquet. "Gardenias, lilies, roses. Trevor liked roses, yellow ones. His mom would have had yellow roses."

Gillian put down the phone and looked across at Aliya. Concern creased her face. "Memorial service was weeks ago, girl. The sweet stuff you're smelling could be from half a dozen funerals since."

"The yellow roses, those were Trevor's," Aliya said stubbornly. She sniffed. "And the cedar—no, it's not there, I can't smell it. It's gone. He's gone." Her lips trembled a little. "He's gone," she said again.

"It's not that," said Miya. Wind picked up, fluttered one of those yellow pieces of paper across their feet. The sun's pink light dipped behind the church, the grass and trees and gravel around them went gray. "I told you guys about the techniques I'm working on, the books I'm reading. I've been trying to figure out how to help Trevor, to ease his distress." Sometimes that hint of Trevor came with a sense of pain, with faint moans, with futile fits and starts, as though, in trying to slip away, he was always jerked back.

Go drown yourself. No, she needed to stop thinking that. It drained her power every time she did. Still, she couldn't help picturing this church as it must have been a few weeks ago, the parking lot crammed with cars, solemn girls in dark dresses filing up the church steps, Trevor's mother leaning on someone's arm as she made her way down the aisle.

Not someone's arm, Luke's arm. Dressed in a dark suit, sunglasses hiding those bloodshot eyes. An hour or two before, he'd been storming around Trevor's room, tearing pillowcases, smashing picture frames, throwing computer parts against the wall. Passionate, tormented Luke. If only she could have spared him that.

She should have come to the service. Shouldn't have been afraid of what Mrs. Sanders would think, what other people would say—

Enough with the regret, Miya.

No one spoke. Gillian flicked her fingers over her cell phone as though she could obeah up the message she was waiting for. Of course, maybe she could. Aliya had picked up one of those yellow papers and was twisting it back and forth between her fingers. She straightened it out on her knees. *In memory of Trevor Sanders,* Miya read over her shoulder. *Beloved brother, son, friend.*

Miya cleared her throat. "I've been trying to increase my power, and it's kind of worked," she said. Her voice sounded banal, harsh in front of the empty church. She lowered it. "The thing is, though, I'm not sure if I'll be ready this weekend; that's what I wanted to ask you guys about. There's something that's blocking me, I don't know how to describe it. It's like some kind of malevolent force."

Gillian looked up, her round eyes as infinite as two black holes. "Malevolent force?" she echoed.

Miya grimaced. "I knew I couldn't describe it properly," she said. She tried again. "It's not something powerful, not something chasing me, not a spirit, not really. It's more like it's just in the way."

"Trevor," said Gillian.

"I told you, Trevor's not malevolent," said Aliya, but her lips trembled.

Miya searched for another way to define the force, failed to find it. Still, she knew it didn't have the dense, mournful presence that Trevor did. "Not Trevor," she said. "Something blocking me from reaching the spirits, from advancing to the next level." She frowned, tried one more time, but it eluded her. "I don't think it's a spirit at all."

A *wheet-wheet-wheet* echoed in the churchyard. They all started. "Oh," said Aliya. "My watch." She peered down at it, trying to make out the numbers in the almost-dark. "Seven o'clock. Must be."

Gillian stared at her, muttering to herself. "'Lined with silver, smelling of soy sauce'—oh. 'Something black crowing in his ear'—*oh*. Stupid mook, stupid obeah man, stupid, stupid Gillian."

Had Gillian's obeah taken over? Miya couldn't see auras yet, couldn't command spirits, couldn't even overcome this new blockade. She spoke more sharply than she meant to. "What are you talking about?"

"Sorry," said Gillian. "No, it's nothing, really. I mean, I just figured something out. Something that I totally misunderstood the first time. I think I know what your malevolent force is."

"It's not Trevor," said Aliya. Hadn't they already agreed on that? She twisted the yellow paper in her hands again, and it tore in half.

"No," said Gillian. Her face took on a grim tinge. "It's not."

"So this weekend is out?" Aliya asked. The paper was in half a dozen pieces now, a few of them scattered at her feet. "I just feel—I can't help but feel—he's fading away. If we wait till next weekend, he may be entirely beyond us."

"We can do it this weekend," said Gillian. Her voice was as grim as her face. Cold too. "I'll take care of the malevolent force."

"If you want to meet tomorrow morning before school," Miya said, "we could—"

"No." Gillian was shaking her head, cutting her off. "This is something I need to deal with by myself."

Miya shut up. For the first time in days, she felt uncertain. Control snaked its way across the stone steps toward Gillian, stepped daintily over the yellow pieces of paper between them. Should she struggle for it? But the *kitoshi* had said something about this—what was it? The words floated back to her, haunted her, comforted her: *Here, in America, the spirits are more powerful . . . I believe it's their contact with other spirits from all different parts of the world.* Still, she asked, "Are you sure?"

"Oh, I'm sure," said Gillian. Fair enough. Miya gave a little ground to obeah.

"I'll bring something that Trevor loved more than himself, we'll need it," said Aliya, as though she'd been reading *Asceticism, Power and Pain* over Miya's shoulder. She'd bring it? For one scary second, Miya thought Aliya meant she would bring herself, but then she added, "Well, it's already at the house. But I'll take charge of it."

Miya started to ask for details, *What do you*—but no. Not tonight. Aliya was already standing up anyway, already brushing off the seat of her jeans. "I better get out of here," she said. "My parents are going to have a fit if they realize I'm not in my room."

"Will you be able to get out this weekend?" asked Miya, but Aliya was already tumbling down toward the road, already running after the bus screeching to a stop around the corner. Gillian fumbled in her purse, came out with her keys. "You need a ride home?" she asked Miya.

"No thanks." Miya stared up at the dark blue sky. Somewhere in those trees behind the church there must be spirits. Why not climb the highest tree, up, up, up, until she was swaying with the wind? *Conquer your fear*, another vital step in her quest.

"No thanks," she told Gillian again. "I'm not quite done yet."

TWENTY-SEVEN

FRIDAY AFTERNOON. Nine hours to midnight.

Gillian leaned on the bell again, and the chimes echoed inside the house. *Ding-dong, ding-dong, ding-dong.* He had to be home, right? *Ding-dong.* And if he wasn't? She'd force the door, go right inside and wait.

She tripped down the obeah man's steps and followed the neatly laid stone path toward the side of his house. There was a fence, but it was the work of a minute to scale it. Reversing the *maljo* spell, that was most important, of course. Save Mums, save Trinidad. Let him curse her out, as long as he told her how to fix things. She took a deep breath, stepped over a bed of dried dirt. Obeah man probably grew chives here, in the summer, spring onions, Cuban oregano, maybe even *chado beni*.

Trust a New England winter to make it look like nothing had been grown here in a long time.

The stone path wound between a couple of oak trees. Obeah man had a vast expanse of lawn back here, brown this time of year but still behaving itself. Gillian reached the back door, rapped on the glass window. Her last visit flashed before her—smell of garlic, sound of drums, the obeah man telling her, *What's this malevolent force that brought you to see me?* Stupid Gillian, thinking it was Trevor interfering with her. Stupid, *stupid* Gillian, not having the presence of mind to ask how to negate it.

Still no obeah man. Gillian raised herself on her toes, peered inside. Big white box. She squinted—the refrigerator, this was the kitchen. Clean stove, clean sink, clean counter. Too clean.

It was almost as though no one lived here at all.

She pushed herself through the thick shrubbery—scratch, scratch against her hips—to look in the next window. Rubbed a fist against it, but no matter: the room was bare. Not a stick of furniture, not a wisp of clothing, not a chicken. The obeah man had packed up shop.

Who'd have thought him a damn coward? Obeah runs a little wild, and the man takes off. Gillian felt a certain grim satisfaction that she'd disrupted things all the way to Trinidad. Unless something more serious had hit the obeah man. Gillian intertwined her fingers so tightly, her nails left marks in the skin. No time to think about that. Tonight's séance was only nine—no, eight and a half—hours away, and who knew how it would ricochet if Gillian didn't neutralize the malevolent force? Mums, wading into Maracas Bay for an innocent swim, being tossed up on the rocks battered and bruised.

Gillian thrust her hands up into her hair. At least she'd discovered whose nasty personality was throwing interference into all her plans. Should have figured it out from the start. Nick. *Lined with silver*: his wristwatch, glinting in the dimly lit coffee shop. *Smelling of soy sauce*: ". . . something intimate at P.F. Chang's." *Something black, crowing in his ear*: that ever-present iPhone.

She took a deep breath. Sure enough, things were out of control. Trinidad slipped more and more miles past the equator every second that went by. She should never have gotten involved in the first place, should have left Trevor to rest peacefully in his watery grave, let her money lie buried too. *Give up the regret, Gillian.* Now wasn't the time to stand around ruminating—now was the time to act. She peered into the empty house one last time. She was on her own.

How to get rid of Nick? Her eyes swept over the back-yard. Pine cones, rolling in the wind. Bare stone path, empty flowerbeds. Leaning up against the house, the tools obeah man must have used to rake up the last of his herbs: rusty hoe; rake with missing prongs; and beside them, a pair of shiny hedge clippers.

Hedge clippers. Now that was an idea.

TWENTY-EIGHT

GILLIAN HAD sexy clothes. She'd had to ransack the bottom of her closet to find them, but they were there. A leather miniskirt in hot pink. A black bustier. Fishnet stockings. It was too cold to go out like that, so she added here and there. A fisherman's sweater over the bustier, the heavy wool coat she'd stolen from her dad.

She stood in the corner of the motel lobby, eyes pinned to the wall. If she couldn't see the motel clerk, he couldn't see her either, right? She shifted the backpack over her shoulder, and the bottles inside clinked together. Goddamn Nick, where the hell was he? Only four hours till midnight. Make that three hours, fifty three minutes.

"Hey, Gillian," said Nick. He had a smug grin on his face. *I win.* They'd see about that, wouldn't they?

Gillian crossed her arms over her chest. She could handle Nick, the panty man, the mook. She twisted her head a little, taking in the chipped wall beside her, remembering that open bag in the supermarket, the thin stream of brown rice spilling out.

"We didn't have to come here," Nick was saying. One hand touched the wall, just above a bit of peeling paint. "I really think you'd like P.F. Chang's, it's my favorite Asian place. The fried duck dinner is out of this world."

Of course this was the new, tamed Nick.

"Here is fine," said Gillian. Not much chance to get Nick drunk at P.F. Chang's, thanks to American laws against under-age drinking. Alone in a motel room with Nick and a bottle of rum—what if she *couldn't* handle him? *Stop*. Nick was nothing more than a teenage boy with an attitude. "Pay for the room, and let's go."

"Okay," said Nick. He leaned in toward her, hesitated, leaned in a little more, finally kissed her. The faint taste of Chinese fried rice lingered on her lips. Yuck. "You smell nice."

"I had asparagus soup for lunch."

"Right," said Nick. "Love asparagus." He collected the key and quicker than she would have thought, they were inside the room, the door shut tight, the walls closing in . . . no, it was just the musty-bathroom smell going to her head. Gillian slid the backpack off her shoulder and set it down. *Clink, clink*. On the other side of the double bed, Nick had snapped open his briefcase and retrieved a small radio. He held it in his hand, scanning channels. "I've got a subscription to XM," he said. "Believe it or not, they have a—yes, here it is." The low sultry sounds of the Baron calypso "Sweetness Is My Weakness" filled the room. "It's a Caribbean station." He pulled a candle out of the briefcase. "Island breeze. I thought it would remind you of home."

"How . . . sweet," she said. At home the music would be loud and throbbing, the boy brown and charming, the salt air inviting. She looked away. Was that what was up with Mums? A brown boy on a beach somewhere? If only Gillian could believe that.

If only the damn phone didn't ring and ring every time she called her.

"You said you'd be bringing drinks," said Nick. "Or if you want, if you forgot, I could—"

"No, I brought them." Gillian unzipped her backpack, took out two bottles of Angusturo old oak rum and placed them on the cheap bedside table. She rummaged in the bag, past a pair of plastic cups, a few crumpled napkins, the folded white robe she'd borrowed from Kevin—there they were, a pack of cards. The cards thunked against a piece of heavy metal in the side pocket as she pulled them out.

"Any ice?" she asked. Without answering, Nick swept up the ice bucket and disappeared through the door. Gillian took the opportunity to fill the cups: his, from the bottle filled with pure rum, hers, from the bottle filled with colored water. Then she cracked open the cards.

She was shuffling when he came back in. Great way to hide nervous hands. What if this didn't work, was one more thing that didn't go according to plan? What if—

"Strip poker, is that it?"

"Not exactly," said Gillian. "You know how to play All Fours?" He looked blank, of course, so she explained the rules.

"Three points if I take your jack," he echoed when she was done. "And cheating is okay?"

"Blind men don't play All Fours," said Gillian. She moved on to scoring. "You win a hand, I take off a piece of clothing. I win, you drop my debt by a thousand dollars. I get you all the way to zero, we go home. You get me down to nothing, we don't." She held back the shudder. "Either way, we each take a sip after we play a card." Either way, she won. Three rounds of All Fours, he'd be passed out on the floor.

And then . . . "If you forget to drink after you play, other person wins the hand."

"Sounds like a great way to score to me," he said, leering. Or maybe he was trying to look romantic. He took a sip of rum, managed to not make a face. "But do you mind if I inspect the cards?" Ten minutes poring over the cards—man, the mook was anal—and then they started to play.

"What happened to the old Nick, by the way?" Gillian asked as he shuffled like an expert. "Do-as-I-say-or-go-directly-to-jail Nick?"

He dealt six cards each, one at a time, American-style. "Sure you're not afraid to play me?" He winked. "Or maybe you're secretly hoping to lose?"

She looked down at her cards. Stupid mook—clubs was trump, and all he'd given her was a useless seven. She'd have to knock. "Asshole Nick?" she said. "Whatever happened to him?"

"Did it ever occur to you that maybe, underneath all my bluster, I just wanted to get to know you?"

Something wobbly in his voice made her look up. Was he kidding? Not kidding, his pockmarked face was serious. "All your money, couldn't you find a dermatologist?"

His back straightened, his face went still. "I see a dermatologist regularly. Thanks for the advice. Did *you* ever think of going to a speech therapist?" What the hell had she been thinking? Antagonizing the crazy man with the red hot temper was brilliant strategy? Damn nerves, made her come out with exactly what was in her head. Even if he was a jackass . . . nothing wrong with frank, but there she'd verged on cruel. She should apologize. Except that old Nick rolled away, and the new, creepy Nick said, "There are some things that money can't buy." He turned up the ten of hearts. "Suit you this time?" He played the queen, took a sip of rum.

"Really?" She cleared her throat, sorted her cards. Slapped down the ace, took a sip of cold water, pretended to wince. "I think money can pretty much buy anything." Except protection from obeah.

Final round, he won with the jack. "Pay up, Caribbean Queen," he said.

"You pay up—I got low and game." He took a long sip of rum, playing pirate. Another. He drank the plastic cup in one long gulp, refilled again. Maybe this would go even faster than she'd thought. "Down to nine thousand bucks."

He shuffled, dealt again. "I'm going to win this game, Gillian—go on, raise your eyebrows, see if I care. I get what I want." She picked up her cards. Two aces, one ten—that was better.

Nick hadn't even looked at his cards yet. He tapped his fingers on the table, said, "Whenever I want something, Gillian, I start by acting like it's true. That's the only way I know to make it real. Whatever it takes: money, imagination, hard work. You do that, you *believe* it enough, it'll happen."

You're crazy, she wanted to say. She wanted to storm out of the room, out of the motel, out of this crazy scheme. Only the thought of Miya, opening her arms to obeah—a twisted, mind-of-its-own obeah that might, even now, be smashing Mums against the sharpest rocks—kept her still. "Drink," she told him.

He drank. Over the next hour, she lost her wool coat, her shoes, her fisherman's sweater, even her fishnets. He lost five thousand dollars. Finally his speech began to slur, he dropped six cards on the floor, his head dipped, and he held it in his two hands. "Think I'll just take a wee nap," he told her. "Lie down beside me?"

"Sure," she said. She pushed the covers over, helped him to the pillow. Then she made it to the backpack before he started to snore.

Side pocket. She unzipped it, reached inside, felt the cold steel against the palm of her hand. Was she really going to do this? Miya's voice echoed in her ear: *There's something that's blocking me.* Mums: *Someone's put maljo on me.* Something, someone. Obeah man: *What's this malevolent force that brought you to see me?* Lined with silver, smelling of soy sauce, something black crowing in his ear. Nick. It had to be.

She pulled out the electric razor and plugged it in. Remembered Father Michael thundering in the pulpit about Samson and Delilah: *But even that wasn't enough for she! She had to take the very root of the man's power, she take he hair! Left him helpless as a babe.* Remembered being six years old, listening to Nana give Auntie Ruby licks for cutting the baby's hair too soon.

Gillian turned on the razor and began to shave Nick's head.

TWENTY-NINE

ALIYA WALKED UP the driveway slowly, Mariam's car to her right. She'd been sneaking off after school every day, all week, and Mariam had never once thought to check the football field or the back roads or the bus. She hadn't come crying to Mama, either, until today.

Looked like Aliya's free ride was over.

What would they take away this time? Her five minutes' peace before dinner? Her shoes? They did that in Cairo long ago, made it illegal to cobble women's shoes because barefoot women would have to stay home.

She paused on the doorstep, the metal handle cold between her fingers. Suppose they put her under armed guard instead of lock and key. Asked Mariam to sleep in her room. How would she sneak out to join Gillian and Miya? Maybe she should turn around, head to Trevor's now? But something seemed to draw her inside, some sort of organic magnet pulling her to the scene of parental meltdown.

Through the door, down the hall, into the living room. She was met by brilliant smiles, laughter. "Here she is now," said Mama in Arabic. "Aliya? How was your day at school? We sent Mariam to meet you, but she must have just missed you."

"Uh . . ." said Aliya. Mama crossed the room and instead of two tight slaps, kissed her on both cheeks. "Miss Levitt kept me. The lab, those centrifuges, what a mess." *Taqiyya*, the cursed wrong-headed Shia called it. When you lied to save your life.

"No matter," said Mama, still with that miracle smile. She looked younger than usual, maybe because her mouth wasn't set in a grim frown, her voice mumbling about ungrateful daughters. Or maybe it was her reddened cheeks, her blue dress, the bright paisley scarf on her head. Back up. What was Mama doing with a scarf in the house?

Then she moved back, and the others in the room, standing up, came into focus. Baba, still smelling of halal pepperoni as he climbed out of the chair in front of her. Mariam and her husband, Nabile. And a tall man Aliya didn't know, with dark hair and dark eyes, wearing a pressed suit. Pale blue, like he'd fast-forwarded out of the seventies.

"Aliya," said Mariam, beaming. "This is Rashid, my husband's very best friend from university. Rashid, meet the very beautiful, very talented, very charming, Aliya al-Najjar."

THEY RUSHED THROUGH their *salaam aleikum*s and into a complicated discussion of Damascus neighborhoods. Rashid came from someplace called Jobar, which, judging by the frown on Baba's face, wasn't exactly the Syrian Upper West Side. Nabile kept jumping in with comments like, "Amazing, all the way from Jobar-boy to doctor of medicine in the United States. What resolve he must have, what tenacity, what intelligence."

Rashid ignored all that. "I know other people look down on Jobar, and it is a poor neighborhood, *hajji*. And I won't hide it that my father worked in a machine shop." That's what Aliya thought he said, anyway; she had no idea what a machine shop was. "But our neighborhood was full of good people, pious, kind, religious people. I hope I can be a credit to them."

Aliya couldn't help admiring his loyalty. One of the things she had liked most about Trevor, after all, was that way he said hi to everybody, how he never shortchanged one person to please someone else. Like the time he was late meeting her because he'd been helping Mal jump her car. *Don't be mad*, he said. *So sorry you had to stand out in the rain.* She wasn't mad. She didn't even mind being wet, especially when he let down her hair, dried it with a towel, and the electricity crackled between them . . .

"Aliya?" It was Mama. "What do *you* think?"

"Oh, sorry," she said. She cleared her throat, turned to Rashid, sitting next to her. *Smile.* "My Arabic, very bad."

Mariam swept in before Mama could swat. "Oh, she's being modest, so you won't be embarrassed when you speak English. Don't worry, her Arabic is excellent, her accent just, you know, a little too formal, from all those years of Qur'an school."

Aliya met Mariam's eyes. They were a long way from Qur'an school, weren't they? The days when Mariam used to scribble stories in a notebook while the teacher droned on. Aliya would kick her under the table, *pay attention*, even as she giggled.

"That's okay," said Rashid, switching to English. "I was speaking of religion, and admiring how you've managed to keep your religion in America, where people are angry at the Muslims." His eyes swept over Aliya, and she expected him to say something about her jeans, her tight pink shirt. Her mother would be sure to, after all this was over. "Of course, I know it can't be easy, in secondary school, but Mariam was telling me about college, about MSA."

"The Muslim Students Association," said Mariam, as though Aliya didn't know. "Lots of girls feel comfortable enough to start wearing a scarf when they see other girls doing it, when they get to college."

"Uh-huh," said Aliya. "Sure."

"They want to before that, but they don't have the, well, it's so difficult, the way kids make fun of you."

Aliya thought: *Maybe I should hand her a frying pan inscribed with ALIYA WILL WEAR A SCARF IF YOU MARRY HER, and then she can hit him over the head with it.* Or how about this one: *ALIYA WILL TURN OUT LIKE ME?* Out loud she said, "That's not true, not really. My friend Sherine's been wearing a scarf since ninth grade, and she gets funny looks in the street sometimes, but the kids from school are protective. We were at McDonald's once, after school, when some middle-school kids started calling her a ninja. Three football players ran them off. Afterward, one of the cheerleaders said, 'How would they feel if someone wrapped them up in a burka? It's the same thing as trying to take yours off.'" That was Glimmer Collins, two years ago.

Funny thing, Aliya didn't hate her then.

She looked up. Mariam and Mama were both glaring, and she was pretty sure Mama was looking for a vase to throw at Aliya's head. Baba launched into some argument about the mosque, and how the uncovered woman they threw out today might be tomorrow's convert, or something like that.

Nicer than she'd expected, this Rashid. Cuter, too; black hair with a hint of wave in it, and somebody'd clued him in to shave the facial hair before he landed in the airport. He went on about praying now. "I wasn't religious for a long time, well, I wasn't *not* religious, but I was so focused on my studies, sometimes I would miss prayers. One Ramadan, I kept sneaking coffee, because there was no way I could stay up and finish my lessons unless I had some powerful *caff-a-yine* in me. Then one day, I was standing out on the balcony and I realized nothing, *nothing*, not twenty-four-hour-a-day study sessions, not all the *wastaa*, connections"—he looked at Aliya, her own fault, since she'd claimed her Arabic was poor—"in the world, would make me a doctor unless Allah decreed it so. From that day, I put my religion first."

He was still looking at Aliya, his dark eyes nervous, as though afraid she wouldn't agree with him. Well, she didn't. She was younger, and didn't have a medical degree, but she'd already figured out something he clearly didn't know: you can't count on God.

She still believed. God's hand was evident everywhere: the trees that brushed the sky, her own convoluted body that pumped blood and digested food and grew skin without her even thinking about it. She liked the religious rituals that made sense out of her life. Okay, she didn't pray much any-more, and she'd cheated a little last Ramadan, and her chances of going on *hajj* were just about nil, but she liked the way they kept life in order. Or could keep it in order, if she let them.

But that didn't mean she wanted to marry the guy.

"What a coincidence," Mariam twittered. Aliya looked over, and even Mama raised her eyebrows. "Well, Aliya's recently made a new plan to be more devoted to religion . . . sorry, Aliya, I know that's private." So private Aliya herself didn't know. *Come join me in this nice, safe box*, Mariam seemed to be saying. *The one where you know everyone and everyone knows you. Sure it's a little crowded in here, the air gets stuffy, but you'll never be lost, never be alone.*

Mama's giggle rose above the talk. Conversation continued, and they left Aliya out of it. Proper enough for the blushing bride. A few minutes later, after Rashid said for the seventh time that he had to leave, they all got up and walked him to the door, Mariam and Nabile too, since Rashid was so new in the States, he didn't have a car. Aliya came, trailing. Mama pushed her forward, made sure she shook hands all around, pinched her elbow until she smiled. "I'm going to show Aliya the new dress I bought," said Mariam, pulling Aliya outside, toward her car. "It'll just take a minute." Aliya thought she was talking to Mama until Nabile said, "Be home in ten minutes," over his shoulder. Mariam waited until he and Rashid had disappeared into Nabile's small green car at the bottom of the driveway before she asked, "So? What do you think? Much nicer than you expected, right?"

Easy to say yes, more accurate, too. But it wouldn't answer the question Mariam was really asking.

"I know what you're thinking. It's what I was thinking, too." Mariam watched Nabile drive off down the road then turned back. Aliya tried very hard not to think of Mariam's secret past. "Trust me, once you've fallen in love, really fallen in love, you'll forget all about it. You won't even remember his face."

Trevor's sharp cheekbones, his green eyes, his black hair flopping over his forehead—were they fading already?

Never. She'd never forget.

Aliya looked up at the porch, where Mama was standing at the screen door, her mouth pressed into a grim straight line. "I've got to go," she said.

"We'll be back tomorrow. If your parents agree, maybe we can—" Something about a movie, something about ice cream afterward. Then Aliya was waving good-bye, trudging up the steps. *If you don't look at her, maybe she'll let you walk right by.* But Mama reached out, grabbed her by the arm.

"What are you, *majnuna*?" Mama asked. She didn't smack Aliya upside the head, but Aliya raised her hand to ward off the imaginary blow. "You come home late and alone, too, when I *sent* Mariam to get you. And what are you wearing? Jeans, jeans, jeans again, and a T-shirt I can see your under-wear through. When I *bought* you one million pretty dresses especially for wearing to school! All of them hanging in your closet, might as well be in plastic, the way they're worn. And there you are smirking and *takalluf* "—Takalluf? What was that? "Simpering?"—"and can't even be polite and ask ques-tions to a man we *found* for you, a doctor and all. He'll help you go to school and be happy, but no, all you can do is think about whatever *boy* you were out with that night, in the mid-dle of the night, in the dirt and the mud."

"I told you, Mama"—and told you and told you—"I wasn't out with any boy. It was a school project, we had to go get certain plants from the state forest. I didn't tell you about it because I knew you wouldn't let me go, and I didn't want you to know that I'd completely forgotten about it and if I didn't have them on the teacher's desk by the next morning, I would have gotten an F." Aliya twirled her fingers around and around the ends of her hair.

"You think I'm stupid, to believe all this pack of lies? You think I won't go to your school and ask your teacher what nonsense she's talking, assigning young girls to go to the forest alone?"

So much for *taqiyya*. Aliya yanked at her fingers, only to find them stuck in her hair. Tug-tug they came out, pulling a few strands with them.

"Now I find you a man, a proper man, a *doctor*, and you do everything you can to deny him, to deny me." Mama grabbed Aliya's ear and pulled. "You too," she said to Baba, pointing a sharp finger in his direction. "You're the man. Put your foot down."

"No," said Aliya.

"What? What?"

Baba raised his hands in the air. "This is a mother's responsibility," he said. "You bring her up right, she knows what she can do, what she can't, that's your job."

"My job? My job? My job to raise the family while you work all night, making big dough circles? What about your job, putting your foot down hard, locking doors at night? Eh? What about that?"

They couldn't even talk to each other—how could they ever talk to her?

"Blah, blah, blah." Mama was fuming along, furious at both of them now. She ignored Aliya's defiance, Baba's discomfort. "What has gotten *into* you, Aliya? You used to be such a good girl, an *adamiya*, only two weeks ago. You think a bad reputation will take you out of the marriage trade? Rashid will hear about your game with the car, the day you stay out all night; he'll think, 'This bad girl is not the one for me'?"

"If that's what I wanted, I'd come straight out and tell him I'm not a virgin."

Slap.

Okay, that was a stupid thing to say.

Aliya raised her hand to her stinging cheek. Mama's voice grew shriller. "The Muslim girl does not go with boys!" That was too much for Baba, who turned his back and stumbled out of the kitchen. *Mama, I didn't mean it that way.* But she couldn't make herself say the words. Because she did mean it that way. She was a girl of faith, but she was also a girl who loved a boy.

"Stupid girl," said Mama. "You think I'm going to go through all this again? Once was not enough?" For a minute, Aliya didn't know what she was talking about, and then she did: Mariam. "Another sick girl, throwing up her breakfast all over the bathroom floor? Another ruined girl I have to stitch back together? If I knew America would carve girls up with a snaggletooth saw, never, never would I come here." Wait. Mariam's secret wasn't just that she'd had a boyfriend. She'd had an abortion, too. Aliya clapped a hand to her face, trying to keep her shock from showing. Mama didn't notice—or maybe she did—as she ranted on about family honor. When she took a breath, *I Love Lucy* sputtered on in the next room: Baba, ignoring the family crisis as usual.

Aliya didn't care. Mariam's voice, harsh, breathless, echoed in her ears. *There's a reason Allah forbids boyfriends, Aliya, and I know what it is.* No wonder they saw Rashid as a safe harbor for the SS Aliya. For the first time in a long time, Aliya got Mama. She understood that impulse: roll her daughter up safe and whole and fresh smelling, like a cigar in that box of

Mariam's, and never worry that she'd end up burned up or shredded on the floor.

But was the only alternative to be lonely and in pieces?

Mama stormed on. "And what do you have to say for yourself? Nothing. You stand here and you say nothing. You don't know what's good for you, you don't, you don't know what you want."

How could Aliya know what she wanted from life when every inch of her skin, every ounce of her blood, yearned to talk to Trevor?

"Not in my house." Mama was shouting. Rant, rant, rage, rage. "Not in my car, not if I have anything to say about it."

Only one way Aliya could move on with her life: she needed to tell Trevor good-bye.

"Where do you think you're going? Aliya? Aliya, you come back here right now! Aliya, I'm not finished talking to you."

Aliya passed through the living room, where Baba looked right through her, bounded up the stairs, crashed into her bedroom. Yanked open her top drawer, rooted around. This is where she put them, had to be here—aha. She swept up the thick pieces of leather, weighed them in her hands. Rambling's collar. Rambling's leash.

From downstairs: "Aliya! I'm not finished!" punctuated by Ricky and Lucy laughing on TV.

What was that Miya had said about wearing white? Aliya flung open the closet, pulled out the *abaya* she wore to the mosque last Ramadan. She came back downstairs, slow but resolute. "Foolish, disrespectful girl." Mama followed her through the house, trying to grab at her arms, but Aliya shook

her off. She walked down the steps, down the driveway,
closed her ears to the yelling behind her.

She took one chance, looked back. Mama, futile against
the door, head bent, mouth crumpled. No rage, no anger, no
fear. It was failure that etched every line of her body.

It took all of Aliya's remaining anger to keep her march-
ing down the driveway. All the rules, the pointless admoni-
tions, all the no-visits-tonight and the fiddling with Aliya's
clothes to cover a bit more chest, a little more leg—she loved
her mother anyway. Loved her, but couldn't bear her. Bore
her, but couldn't bear herself.

At the end of the driveway, she turned left. Good thing.
She had no idea how long Gillian had been parked there,
waiting for her. So much time was wasted when they took
away your cell phone.

"Yuh finally reached," said Gillian. "Get in. Miya's sending us on a mission."

THIRTY

THE HOUSE was dark, just as she'd planned it.

Miya came around the corner, shuffled through the wet leaves in her embroidered slippers and stretched out her arms. Concentrated. Had Luke and his mother left the house? Last night, she'd spread out the coals to try again, fired them up, sat still in the damp grass.

I will not be afraid.

The old, weak Miya, the one caught up in lies and deceit, in pleasing people, that one, she was gone. "Miya, honey, what are you *doing* out here?" Mom had come out on their little deck, peered into the darkness. "Aren't you cold? Is that our old barbecue? What are you doing with it?" *Almost* gone. Miya dredged up some excuse about a party and a football player, but Mom's face set in a frown. She came down the couple of steps. "Really?" she said. "Why is all the coal on the grass? Hot, too, someone could get hurt out here. And why have a barbecue in the middle of the winter, anyway?"

Speak the truth. Her mother believed in kitoshi and in spirits: Would it be such a stretch for her to see her daughter seeking enlightenment? "Miya-chan," said Mom. Her voice was gentle, hopeful. "Come on inside. Why don't we try out that home spa kit you bought for my birthday?"

Miya came, but she made her excuses. This morning, up at five, down to the waterfall. She took off her clothes, ducked under, held her breath one minute, two—how long could she take it? One last instant of concentration: *Sanders, head out of town.* Had the spirits heard her? Then she was out, spinning on the gravel until her body grew warm and dry, her head dizzy and drunk.

She crossed the lawn now, heading for the side door, the wind whipping her white kimono around her legs. A flickering touch, so light she wasn't sure—yes, there it was, stroking her forearms, darting across her shoulders, settling in at her neck. Sometimes the spirits comforted her, but now . . . What comfort was there in powers that crossed her body so easily? She tensed. What if she misstepped, misspoke, misunderstood? Was it wise—

She made her way to the side bushes, swinging her drawstring bag, the one with "Lipstick" scrawled in multiple colors. She stopped just outside the door to double-check her mystical items one last time: the sage she'd bought at the market, the cedar bark she'd chipped off the trees the other night at the church. At the very bottom, the belladonna she'd found on Craigslist. Belladonna, a hallucinogen used for centuries by men and women seeking power.

Drawing on multiple traditions could only amplify their power.

The most vital items, she'd left to Gillian. Hours ago, must have been, when Gillian called, breathing hard. "Hey—"

"Can you do something for me?" Miya asked from her bedroom, where she was pressing the kimono. "I meant to ask you before—we need drums, nothing expensive."

"Drums?" said Gillian. "Will steel pan do?" Then she added, "Look, I've taken care of the malevolent force. Steam on, girl."

Miya pulled the drawstrings tight, took a deep breath. Fished a key out from under her kimono. It didn't come from Luke, though she'd thought about trying. Tempting, to stand side by side with him, smell his soapy skin, focus her mind: *The key, the key, give me the key.* Tempting, but not tempting enough. And anyway: not yet. She felt that fleeting, sad presence join her now, pressing up against her body. Trevor. He moved in close, backed away, impatient, unruly. She pressed her lips together. She'd played a part in this sadness, and it fell on her to cure it. Tonight.

She pushed the key, the one Rodney had filed with a series of careful cuts, into the keyhole. Pulled out the screwdriver recommended on how-to-lockbump.org. The flutters at the back of her neck beat harder, faster. She steeled herself. Would something go bang, knock her to the grass, leave her bewildered with a cacophony burning out her eardrums? *Press on, Miya.* One hard tap with the screwdriver and the dead bolt unlocked, the door gave. *Thank you, Gillian.*

She came through the doorway. The house smelled slightly dirty, with a hint of rotten fruit, of wet dog. She raised her arms out straight. *Oh spirits*, she prayed, bowed her head, tried to be powerful, couldn't help being human. *Flutter, flutter, flutter* upgraded to a constant pressure. That was a good thing, right?

Miya closed the door behind her and made her way into the dark living room. She banged her knees—*ouch*—into the coffee table. Paper plates went flying, something sticky smeared her elbow: *sniff-sniff*, ketchup. Not on the kimono, thank the spirits. She dodged through the obstacle course—laundry basket, high-backed armchair, pile of empty bottles—and reached the stairs. Impossible not to think about the last time she'd snuck through this house. How puzzled and naive she'd been, how powerless. She'd never stood naked beneath a waterfall then, never crossed hot coals on bare feet. She'd add another "never" to the list tonight.

Up the stairs, one by one. Down the corridor, the one she'd been trolling nightly in her imagination. Trevor's unlocked door. That sound—where was it coming from? He'd been here. She didn't sense his sadness, but there was something else, some other clue, it was . . .

It was gone. Then: *Tick, tick, tick* came from behind the door. Was it—could it be—a heartbeat? *Don't get carried away.* Her hands shook, her heart pounded, but she stepped inside. A cold wetness seeped through the soles of her slippers, up their sides. Wetness? The ticking grew louder. Wetness, ticking—this made no sense. She reached out a hand to flip the light switch. Nothing.

"Lights don't work," said a voice behind her. Gillian, clattering up the stairs, a dark shape—make that Aliya—at her heels. "Should have brought a torch," said Gillian. She came close enough for Miya to smell the perfume clinging to her clothes. She bent over the backpack she'd brought, fiddled in one of the pockets. A candle flame flared to life. When she stood up, Miya saw they'd followed instructions: Both wore white—Aliya had some kind of Middle Eastern robe left open over her jeans and T-shirt; Gillian, a white sheath that she'd belted around the waist. Their hair had been pulled back, and they wore no jewelry. Gillian's backpack bulged a little, and when she lifted it, it sagged. Heavy.

"You got the drums?" Gillian nodded. Then she raised her hand, and the thin streak of candlelight gave them a view of the room. At least an inch of water had flooded it.

"Someone must have been using Trevor's bathroom," said Aliya. "Maybe Luke."

"Not Luke," said Miya. She smelled damp clothes, dirty rug, mold. The cramped, wet room was no place to spin. She held still, hoped to feel the flutter at her neck—had it gone? A very faint thump sounded overhead. Miya raised her eyes to the ceiling. Branch crashing into the roof, must be, unless it was a hint.

That fire escape had gone up as well as down, hadn't it? "Come with me," she told them.

Gillian came, so quick they almost tripped each other, but Aliya turned to the top of the stairs, snapped her fingers three times. "Let's go, Rambling," she called. A short bark, followed by the clip of toenails on stairs and a whiff of that wet dog smell. *Pant, pant,* shudder, and tiny droplets of something that felt like rain landed on Miya's cheeks, her forehead, dampened her hair. "Why on earth did you bring him inside?" she asked.

Gillian swung the candle around, and Miya saw Aliya's face up close. Red around the eyes, swollen nose. She'd been crying. "Trevor loved this dog more than anything," she said. "I told you I was going to bring him."

A dog on the roof? But Miya didn't stop to argue. She was down the hall almost before she noticed, inside the bathroom. She'd swear no one had been here since her last visit—over there, under the window, there was even a dark clump of something that might have been dirt from her shoes. "Come on."

Miya opened the window, pulling herself up onto the fire escape. The lightest caresses patted her head, tiptoed across her face—or was that just the wind? She climbed up, balanced her knees on the metal grating, took the fire escape steps two at a time. Behind her, Gillian swore, "Stupid, stupid fingers." And: "Jeezan ages, Aliya, can't you keep that dog from chewing up my shoes while they're still on my feet?"

And then Miya was on the roof. The night was clear and cold, lit by a bright, angry moon. The side of the roof facing the road sloped up sharply, gray shingles layered one over the other. It hid the flat back half of the roof, the perfect place for a midnight séance. In one corner, a handful of bricks had been tossed into a small pile.

A breathless Gillian, a shaky Aliya, and an overexcited Rambling joined her. "What about the neighbors?" asked Gillian. "Aren't you worried they might hear something?"

"Don't worry about the neighbors," said Miya. She laughed, her own ordinary laughter at first, and then a high-pitched giggle that seemed to go on and on. Nerves, must be, unless one of the spirits was using her for its own purposes.

Get control of yourself, Miya. She turned to Aliya. "How are we doing for time?" Aliya raised her wrist to check her watch, and the moon disappeared behind a cloud.

They were surrounded by darkness.

"I've got matches, hang on a second," said Gillian. "Let me get the stupid candle out of my pocket." The roof flamed to eerie life; the other girls' faces were shadowed and gaunt, the flat area behind them faded into nothing.

"It's eleven forty-two," said Aliya. She pushed at her already tied-back hair. "Eighteen minutes to midnight."

"It has to be midnight?" Miya asked. "Are you sure?" *A sacred place*, she'd read. *A quiet night, no distractions.* Nothing about midnight.

Aliya rubbed her lips together. "Old Aunt said midnight," she told them. "And the first time, the time that worked, it was midnight." Rambling pressed up against her legs, whimpered. Aliya reached into his fur with her fingers and rubbed him hard.

"The last time, the time that twisted, that was midnight too," said Gillian.

The dog barked. He stood between Miya and Aliya, his wet nose buried in Miya's kimono now. "Can't we use something else?" she asked. "Put the dog back and get something else, something from his room? I don't know, his favorite sweatshirt or something."

"Rambling was more important to Trevor than some stupid sweatshirt," said stubborn Aliya. "Trevor cared about him deeply; that has a special power, Old Aunt said." She looked down at the dog, pulled him close. "Anyway, I have him on a leash." She raised her hand to show them the leather cord wrapped tightly around her wrist. "He'll be fine—I'd never let anything happen to Rambling."

Miya had ceded power to obeah in front of the church; now it was time to listen to the jinn.

Gillian set down the candle, crouched down and opened her backpack. She took out half a dozen additional candles with one hand, passed them to Aliya. "Here are your candles." Two small metal vases went the same way. "Your incense burners. You want everything here in the corner?"

Aliya took the candles. "We need to set them out in the shape of a pentagram," she said. "Here and here, like this. And then we each sit outside, looking in. And wait, let's use these bricks—this one over here, like this, so the wind doesn't blow them out."

Gillian passed a candle to Miya. *Pss-pss*, said the spirits. For the first time, Miya could make out the words: *Your time has come.* When she looked up, Gillian was holding a flat, steel pan in one hand and a leather drum, with a round top and a curved base, in the other. A *tabla.* "Aliya didn't want steel," she said. "So we drove across town to someone she knew, and got this Arab thing."

Aliya tilted her head back, said something into the wind.

Gillian moved closer to Miya. "Are you sure about this?" she asked. "Sure, sure, sure?"

"I'm sure."

She was. She'd never been surer of anything in her life, not that William the Conqueror stormed Hastings in 1066, not that $e=mc^2$. Not that all it took to get Rod Crew to do her bidding was a kiss right there. This, *this* was what Miya Chonan was meant to do.

The candles glowed on the rooftop, giving their corner a ghostly feel. Behind them, the roof stretched into darkness. With a suddenness that surprised her, Miya felt Trevor, pressing as close to her back as he ever had.

"This is it," she said. He wasn't trying to escape, not this time—she felt something on her waist, almost like fingers, clutching her. "This is our chance to finally reach Trevor. To apologize for the way we treated him. To make amends."

"This is our chance," said Gillian, "to untwist the obeah. To protect ourselves against the unexpected. To let Trevor go his own way." She tossed the tabla to Aliya, who caught it with one hand.

Aliya's quiet voice echoed in the night. "Our chance," she said, "to say good-bye."

Miya felt on the roof beside her, found her drawstring bag. "The offerings." She handed the sage to Aliya, the cedar bark to Gillian; she kept the belladonna for herself. She fed it to the candle in front of her: each leaf lit up, glowed with purpose, crumpled into ashes. The sharp, pungent flavor of burning bark, burning leaf, enveloped her.

From behind: *thump, thump, ching*—the steel pan. Aliya said, "He's here, I can smell him," and then the tabla started up with quick, hard beats, eager, intense. Miya's leg kicked out; she began to spin.

She'd practiced spinning in her room, in the backyard, down by the waterfall. But nothing had prepared her for this atmosphere: for the dark, the wind, the whimpering dog; the presence of the other girls, the presence of the spirits. Her pulse raced its way out of her bloodstream, her heart pounded hard enough to break her chest. She was reaching for the arms of the spirits, for the chance to set Trevor free.

She heard the beat of the drums, the *swoosh* of the air, the *click-click* of the dog at the side of the roof. Far below them, something cracked. She smelled the candles, the incense, the sage, the cedar, the belladonna. She felt her body twist to the rhythm of the drums and the wind, rise up off the roof. Then it no longer mattered. She heard, smelled, felt nothing. She was approaching the moment of peace. She felt the tug of Trevor as she spun harder, faster; he clutched at her shoulders, her back. *Set me free, Trevor. Set yourself free.*

Spin, spin, twist.

"Miya!" The spirits were calling her name.

The drumming stopped abruptly, and Trevor was gone. Miya jerked back into her body with such suddenness she almost toppled. She felt again: the wind whipping around her head, sweaty hair on the back of her neck, sore, tired legs. She heard: Rambling howling, a crack from the other side of the house. She opened her eyes and saw: candles flickering, incense steaming, a wet and winded dog pacing. The moon had come back out, and it lit up the two girls, wild-eyed, stumbling toward her.

"Miya! What the hell are you doing?" She looked down. She stood at the very edge of the roof, balanced on one foot, one spin away from launching herself into air and sky. She could hardly make out the ground below, but there were no dark shapes, no long shadows. Her best guess: no bushes to break a fall, nothing but hard ground.

"*Arooooooooooo*," howled Rambling. He bent his head back, howled into the wind, pain and longing—and something else—in his call.

They'd stopped her just in time, saved her from a broken leg, a broken neck, a broken self. Or they'd prevented her from saving them all.

"Miya, get away from there, would you?" Then, to the dog: "What's wrong, boy, are you afraid?"

"*Arooooooooooo*," howled Rambling, again. He pulled on the leash. More noises filtered up from below, loud enough to outspeak the wind: *Crack. Sizzle. Clunk.*

"What the hell—?" said Gillian. They'd all three turned now to look at the far side of the roof, the side with the fire escape. *Scrabble, scrabble.*

With one final burst of spirit, Rambling pulled his head free of his collar and bounded across the rooftop. "Rambling, no!" shouted Aliya, but sure enough, his scrambling feet kicked the bricks in that corner and knocked over the candles. He paid no heed, and neither did Miya. She couldn't. Like Rambling, her eyes were fixed on the large, dark form pulling itself up onto the roof.

THIRTY-ONE

THE JUMBIE'S HANDS appeared first, thin and white, then his face, his shoulders, his chest, as he crawled over the edge. He glowed with the light of the moon. After one stopped moment, Gillian's heart crashed back to life, her blood rushed through veins and arteries. A jumbie. It had worked: the spinning, the chanting, the drumming. The shaving. Obeah come back again.

She opened her mouth to name him *Jumbie*—it's important to name the dead—but Aliya got in the way, tearing across the roof like Rambling. "Trevor, Trevor, Trevor!" She grabbed onto him, tossed her arms around his neck, buried her face in his chest. Gillian let herself look at him full-on. Death had left him skinnier than she remembered. Dark shadows circled his eyes, stubble dotted his chin. Substantial, not transparent; feet planted firmly on the roof's edge, not hovering in the air.

His hands shook as he pulled Aliya close, closer—then she almost disappeared into his arms. They were kissing, Aliya bent backward, like that girl in the painting. Rambling, not one to be left out, thrust his nose into the jumbie's fingers, belly, crotch, sniffing for boy. Only Miya kept calm. Her dark, tangled hair gleamed in the moonlight. "Ozuna triumphant," she said. Whatever the hell that meant.

The jumbie looked around the roof. It was a long moment before he seemed to take in their faces, longer still

214

before he said her name. "Gillian?" His brow wrinkled. "And Miya? What the hell is going on here? Is this some kind of . . ." His voice sounded low, frazzled, like he hadn't used it for a long time. "It's almost a reception, with all those candles. Or a wake." He dropped Aliya, pushed past Rambling. "Have you guys been in my room? I took a chance earlier, took a shower—the place is a huge mess, looks like someone died in there."

"Trevor," said Miya. Shrimps, man, her voice sounded so loud, bouncing across the roof like that. "I'm sorry, I know this is hard to hear, but someone did die. You."

He pinched himself on the back of the neck. Pinched Rambling through his fur. Pinched Aliya's cheek softly with his other hand. "No," he said. "Not me. Not dead."

Famous for playing tricks, jumbies. "Pinching is for pick-neys, to wake them up from nightmares." Gillian's voice still worked, please God. "Nothing to do with living or dead."

"You want me to prove it? You want to see me bleed?"

Aliya cut in. "No need for that." She linked her hand through one ghostly arm, reclaiming her lover. "But you went over a cliff, Trevor. The car, Mitsu, there was almost nothing left of her. Almost nothing." The moon ducked for cover again. Gillian's gaze moved from Aliya to the pale and flick-ering face beside her, fading in and out of the light of the nearby candles. A chill crept up her spine.

The jumbie turned those odd eyes on her. Eyes the same shape as Trevor's, the same color, taking up the same space in his face, but not the same. Empty. "Poor Mitsu," he said. "All these years, she was good to me." He shook his head, and the silver dagger pinned in his ear flashed. "She deserved a better end than that.

Lined with silver . . .

"I don't blame you if you hate me," he said. The obeah man was gone, but Gillian couldn't forget him. *What's this malevolent force that brought you to see me?* A sudden, panicked conviction erupted in her bones, reverberated outward till she knew it in every pore of skin. She'd been right about Trevor, wrong about Nick. She'd shaved the wrong head. They'd meddled with obeah, raised a jumbie—a malevolent jumbie, look at the flashing white teeth, those hooded eyes. The malevolent force involved with the fire in the forest, with those unanswered phone calls. What would be easier than for him to destroy them all? Aliya, nestled in his arms. Miya, lost in thought. Sheself, shivering in the cold.

Sheself, the only one with all the clues, the only one who could stop him now.

Jumbie let Aliya go, dropped to his knees, embraced the exuberant Rambling, buried his face in the animal's fur. "You don't hate me old boy, do you? God, I've missed you. Who did I have to fetch me the remote in that smelly old hotel room? Nobody, that's who." Aliya's eyes were half closed, Miya's riveted on Trevor. No one noticed as Gillian reached for her backpack and unzipped its side pocket. She pulled out the battery powered razor and turned it on. *Hold his head, slash at the roots of his hair.* She lunged. If that didn't work, surely something in the steel—

"Gillian!"

"Agh! What the hell—"

She sliced through the air, met skin, felt something wet—drops of blood. Somebody screamed. A sharp blow to her arm, and the razor clattered to the roof. She tumbled over on top of the jumbie, heard his ragged, unused voice: "For God's sake, Gillian, what are you trying to do, kill me?"

An odd thing for a dead boy to say.

Her hands came up to the sides of his face, pinned it in place. Perhaps she could tear the hair out by the roots? Her fingers met soft, flaky skin, roughened with tiny bristles of hair. She smelled the onion, pepper, anchovy on his breath. More real, all of it, than she'd expected from a jumbie.

Then someone was dragging her off—Miya, with surprising strength. "Don't hurt him!" she shouted, and their arms locked in a wrestling match, the same one she'd fought in the kitchen with Mums. They moved two inches this way, three inches that; over Miya's head, she caught sight of Aliya awash in moonlight by the edge of the roof, cradling her arm. Patches of red showed through her fingers.

Gillian stopped, dropped her arms; Miya let them go. Girl stepped back a couple of paces, breathing hard. "Lord Almighty," said Gillian. "Aliya, I'm sorry, so sorry. I just wanted to shave his head. I didn't mean to—"

Aliya shook her head. "I'm okay, I'm fine." Trevor had tossed aside his jacket, stripped off his long-sleeved shirt and was using it to mop up the blood on her arm. He wrapped it tightly in place. "Ow." Aliya winced. "No, really, Gillian, it's nothing—it doesn't even hurt. You got carried away, I get it." She let Trevor tie the T-shirt in a knot, then sank back into his arms. "It's just a surface cut, really. And I know how much that money meant to you."

"What the fuck, Gillian," said Trevor. "What'd I ever do to you that you wanted to attack me with a razor?"

"It wasn't about the money, not really," she tried to tell them, but Aliya, at least, wasn't listening. She asked Trevor: "The money you were keeping for Gillian—where is it?" Jumbie said nothing. Aliya's hair had come unbound; she pushed it off her face. "Don't we get an explanation? What makes you think it's okay to pretend you're dead?"

"I'm not pretending I'm dead." Trevor took her hand and pressed it to his heart. "It was just a stupid misunderstanding that spiraled out of control."

Out of control. Gillian flinched—he might have been talking about her. One *malevolent* from the obeah man, one flash of silver, and she was jumping the boy. What hard evidence did she have that he was out to get them? His eyes, his teeth? The fire that could have been an accident, Mums who might have lost her cell phone?

When would she learn to keep her tail quiet and wait things out?

"Trevor?" said Aliya. Behind the two of them, Miya settled herself up against the sloped side of the roof, face shining with sweat.

"Uh, okay. I was flying up the road—"

"Start with the party," Aliya said. She didn't move her hand, but it looked dead there—funny, since it was a living thing against a dead boy's chest.

"The party? What party? Mal's? Nothing happened there. Well, except for that stupid fight with Miya." His eyes slid off Aliya; he half-turned toward Miya. "You remember that?"

Miya bowed her head, like she was looking for some kind of truth in the shingles on the roof. "Of course I remember."

"I felt terrible after that," said Trevor. "Man, I felt like a piece of shit."

"I'm the one who should be saying sorry." Miya's lips hardly moved, but her words were clear. "And I am. Sorry, I mean."

"Wasn't you," he told her. He ran his fingers over the bandage on Aliya's arm. "Wasn't just you, anyway. Aliya wouldn't even admit I was her boyfriend, my dad hadn't called in months, no way was I passing Calc. I started thinking, and I couldn't stop." His voice was stronger now; more confident, almost human.

Gillian put her hand to her heart—no longer banging away, but settled back in place. Her breath, too, came smooth, regular. She lowered herself with care to the rooftop, settled down. Listened.

"I couldn't stop drinking, either. A couple of Sam Adams, and then some shots—vodka, maybe a couple tequila. I didn't take off till my head had cleared, though, I swear it."

Miya leaned across the roof, scooped up Aliya's tabla. "Hard to have a clear head when you've been polluting it with alcohol."

"Not like you didn't have your share of shots, too," Trevor fired back. "And I told you, I was fine by the time I left. I wasn't *polluted*."

"You must have been tired," Aliya said quietly. "Why didn't you go home? Or call me? I could have slipped out the window."

"I felt like being by myself." There was a long silence. Trevor wasn't the alone type, not even when he was depressed. He was the one-more-for-the-road type. He was the—

"All right," he said. "Fine. I went to the Crescent. I heard Glimmer was going to be there, and I heard she had some high quality stuff."

Aliya shifted her body, breathed in sharply. "You couldn't see me that night because of *Glimmer?*"

"I couldn't come see you because of *your parents.*"

More silence.

Gillian couldn't take her eyes off Aliya, off the bloodied T-shirt stuck to her arm. Behind her, Miya began to tap on the drum—*padum, padum, padum*—and the sound carried across the roof. Gillian felt a sudden rush of affection. Funny how it had crept up on her, liking them. Brave Miya, ready to fight with those tiny fists. Tolerant Aliya, who never held grudges. The closest thing she had to friends up here.

The closest thing she had to friends anywhere.

Trevor was going on. "She wasn't even there," he said, "so it's nothing to get upset about. I pulled into the Crescent and just saw some guy shouting 'fuck you, fuck you' after a white car driving away. I didn't feel like being alone"—Ha!—"so I pulled up. Talkative guy."

Trevor dropped his head back, took in the stars like the story was done. Aliya and Miya, both stayed silent. Should Gillian say something? "How did you get from a conversation at the Crescent to the afterlife?"

"I told you, I'm not dead," said Trevor, but his voice was strained, once again hard to hear. "Jack's the one who's dead."

That got their attention. Even Rambling stopped his tail-rapping. On the road below, a car zoomed by, going at least fifty. They all leaned over to look at it, and Gillian caught herself thinking: *Did the jumbie conjure you up to illustrate his story?*

Aliya recovered first. "You must remember more than that. What happened next?"

Trevor sighed. "He got in the car, that was next. Then I drove into the state forest while he told me the whole story.

That was his girlfriend, dumping him because he was head-ing down to Mexico, not staying with her." Trevor linked his hand through Rambling's fur and let his face rest there for a second, half buried in dog. "The weirdest thing: turns out I actually knew the guy, and the girl dumping him, too. My cousin Katelin, and this was her boyfriend, Jack. We'd met at her sister's wedding, sneaking gin and tonics off the drink trays. Which made sense because the Crescent is hidden away; to find it, you have to know it's there. Katelin and I used to go there to smoke."

"I know," said Aliya.

Her words were soft, but they stopped Trevor in his tracks. Aliya ducked out from under his arm and the boy looked like she'd struck him across the face. Finally, he just said, "I offered to take him to the bus station. Least I could do." He sunk both hands deeper into Rambling's fur. "He said he had some time to kill before his bus, why not take a quick drive over the gorge, check out the moonlit visions of para-dise." Jumbie didn't sound malevolent, did he? He sounded sad, scared, like a reckless boy who'd made a terrible mistake.

"And how's the view from heaven?" Aliya, still Aliya, say-ing that. Her face gleamed paler now, almost ghostlike. Gillian could hardly make out her features. Did touching a jumbie make you fade away?

"We were racing, top down, I must have been doing a hundred. I mean, Mitsu wasn't a convertible, but she could convince you she was. Best ride of my life." Was that how the story ended? Trevor stared down at his knees—one heartbeat, two, ten. At last he said, "I barely remember what happened next. I spun around the corner, and, shit, there was nothing in front of me but air.

"The car headed down the cliff. I must have yanked open the door, must have shot out of the car just in time, but I swear I don't remember. The next thing, I was waking up covered in dust, spitting dirt, with a monster headache. Mitsu was gone. And Jack. Where the hell was Jack?"

Trevor rubbed his hands across his eyes. There was a moment of furious blinking before he said, "I found his backpack at the side of the road—must have flung itself out, same way I did. Then I remembered that he put his seatbelt on. *Jackass.*" That word, that tone, sounded like Gillian describing Trevor, every time she'd thought about him going over the cliff. Was he—he couldn't be—crying?

Aliya still wasn't looking at him, but she spoke up anyway. "How could you let us think it was you?"

Trevor raised his hands as if to embrace her, then let them fall. "I didn't. I didn't mean to. All I could think was that I'd been drinking, I'd been flying up the road, I was going to jail." And Trevor was off again. Now that he'd started telling his story, it seemed he couldn't stop. He went on, all about his flight to the bus station and using Jack's ticket and the three-day bus trip to the border. He crossed using Jack's passport without even passing over a bribe. Proof of what she'd been saying for years: all white boys look alike.

So he wasn't a jumbie after all? The whole thing was a mistake? Gillian frowned. Didn't Aliya say something about Katelin's boyfriend calling from Mexico? She couldn't quite remember. Either way, poor Trevor. She found her heart was big enough to feel sorry for him after all. He woke up one morning a rich white boy living in a big house, and by midnight he was either dead or on a bus to nowhere. Who knew that one spur-of-the-moment decision to pick up a stranded guy would spin out so deadly?

What was that Trevor was saying? ". . . found a place to live in Mexico, it took all the money I had." His eyes shifted around the roof: up at the stars, over to Miya, down to Rambling. They skirted right past Gillian. "Luckily, I got a kind of job. I'm settled now."

"But that can't be right," said Aliya. Said what Gillian was thinking. "Jack called Katelin . . ."

"How'd you know about that?" Trevor sounded almost angry. When Aliya didn't answer, he said, "I finally got the courage to google myself, and found out I was dead. And Jack . . . well, everyone thought—still thinks—he's in Mexico. I fobbed off his parents with an e-mail, but I knew I'd have to talk to Katelin or she'd have rushed off down to Mexico and found . . . me."

Rushed off to Mexico. Gillian found herself staring at Aliya's bloodied and bandaged arm. Bloodied and bandaged because Gillian had rushed to diffuse the jumbie's—Trevor's—power. Just the way she was always rushing somewhere, rushing into something. Always thinking life would be pulsing with joy if she could just get to the right place. Up to the land of the free, where she wouldn't have to worry about Mums. Back down to Trinidad where she'd sip rum punch, waves tickling her toes. Was it only last week nothing had mattered more? She found her voice, asked as decisively as she could: "What about me and Nick Loring? He says you owe him thousands of dollars or a bunch of girls." She almost pointed out that she'd shaved down that debt with her skill at cards, but no need to start a conversation that might lead to razors. She'd tell Aliya and Miya later. Instead, she said, "And he's not just talking money. He says if I don't serve up the saltfish, he's going to send his evidence straight to City Hall."

But weren't there other things she should be asking? About Mums and what the jumbie could do to protect her? Although if he wasn't a jumbie and he wasn't malevolent—he seemed to be neither, with his pizza breath and his verge of tears—then Mums should be just fine. Probably finer than fine, at an all night fete somewhere in Trinidad.

Ah, Trinidad. Gillian smelled the salt water, heard the Mighty Sparrow's latest calypso, tasted the sweetness of a just-opened coconut. *Trinidad is my land and of her I am proud and glad.*

"Gillian? Gillian, are you *listening?*" Trevor. She'd gotten so used to his voice droning on, it passed for elevator music now. "I *said*, what thousands of dollars?"

"Weren't you pimping Emmie? He showed me pictures, records . . ." Gorm, man. She'd been a bit of a *cunumunu* herself, hadn't she?

"Pimping Emmie? You didn't believe that crap, did you? He was stalking her for months—offered me five hundred bucks extra if I'd rearrange her schedule. Didn't I tell you? No, I guess I never got the chance."

Trevor wasn't waiting for her, he was pulling out his wallet, rifling through a thick sheaf of papers. "He didn't tell you about the restraining order Emmie copied for me . . . Figured it burned up with me, probably. Idiot. I was going to put it in Aliya's locker and have her give it to you. Seems stupid now, but I was worried about people seeing us together. I even sent

Aliya an e-mail from my cell phone, told her to look out for it." His head pivoted, and his eyes burned into Aliya's. "I told Nick I gave you the copy I had, but I didn't use your name, I said 'my girlfriend.' I used to like to say that, to pretend that we were for real, I wasn't just your walk on the wild side."

"You weren't . . ." said Aliya. She trailed off. Trevor found what he was looking for, a crumpled and torn sheet of paper that he tossed across to Gillian. She grabbed it—not one piece of paper, but two, folded up. She smoothed them out, then leaned over to read by candlelight. The top sheet, an e-mail from Emmie—Gillian scanned it quickly. Underneath, the restraining order itself. Taken together: Nick Loring had been sexually harassing Emmie, stalking her, and he'd been playing around with Photoshop—Photoshop! Gillian had been taken in by a scrapbooked collage—and posting fake pictures of her on random Web sites.

She found herself sitting back again.

"Wave those in his face, and he'll leave you alone. His filthy-rich parents settled with Emmie's family, enough for her to go to college on, so they dropped the charges."

No charges. That meant there was only one problem. "But what about my half of the Matchmaker—" But she figured it out before she got to the end of the sentence. *I found a place to live in Mexico, it took all the money I had.* Trevor had screwed her over after all. Damn selfish bastard, she would—

She unclenched her fingers, stretched them out one by one. Wasn't it the *she woulds* that had been getting her into trouble all this time? She'd been so busy dreaming about her island in the sun, she'd put her life on hold. She'd never had a proper boyfriend, had she? *Plenty of worthy guys in TnT*, she'd always thought. *Once I get there, I'll start looking.*

She'd never shouted herself hoarse over the Red Sox, never downed a stack of pancakes bathed in maple syrup, never learned to ski. Never stayed up all night baring her soul to her girlfriends. She looked at Miya, still leaning back against the edge of the slanting rooftop, at Aliya, cold-shouldering Trevor. That last one, at least, she planned to change.

She had a lot more to build a life out of up here than she'd thought.

Something rubbed against Gillian's back—what the hell?—her backpack, vibrating. Then she heard the *Vol-ca-no.* She fumbled in the pocket of her bag, came up with the phone. Sure enough—thank the Lord—it was Mums. "I gotta take this," she said, opening the phone. "Good night, Mums."

"Meh girl!"

"So," said Aliya. Gillian caught her words to Trevor just before she turned her back on the little tableau behind her. "You never said why you're back. You didn't come for us"— her voice broke on the *us*—"and you didn't come to give Gillian her money. So what did you come for?"

Trevor tightened his arms around the dog's furry body. "I came to get Rambling."

THIRTY-TWO

HE CAME BACK for Rambling.

It was the little things Aliya had always loved about Trevor: the way he draped his leather jacket over her shoulders without her even asking, the extra pizza he ordered so his mom would have something hot when she got home, the hours he spent calming Mal down after her date went disastrously wrong.

Risking his life—his freedom—for the dog he loved.

Aliya pressed her hand to her heart. It pounded wildly, as though she were still in that horrific moment when she saw Trevor rising over the side of the house, or that more horrific moment when Gillian lunged at him with a razor. Aliya found herself cradling her injured arm, still stuck in that most-unbelievable-of-all moment when she realized Allah had answered the prayers of a wayward *Muslimah*: Trevor was alive. After that, things had blurred, run together; she could only recall bits and pieces. Trevor's leather-clad arms coming around her shoulders, his lips pressing hers, fierce, urgent, like he wanted to brand her, being enveloped in the Baldessarini she'd missed so much.

Even while he told his story: she sighed at parts, she pouted, she slipped out of his embrace, withdrew her hand—but all she had *felt* was joy, relief. No seventeen-year-old body could have room for more emotions than one, when that one was this intense. Now, sheltered in the arms of the boy she loved, she looked around. A few feet away, Gillian was saying quietly into the phone, "Yeah, I get it, but even a new boyfriend, a party at Level Two, still you could have called me." Across the flat-topped roof, beside one of the remaining candles, sat Miya, eyes closed, face drained, leaning back against the slope. Here, a happy Rambling. There, a worried Trevor.

The tiniest pin pricked her happiness.

He was explaining: ". . . I couldn't just leave him. My mother, you know my mom, she doesn't like things that smell. I mean, she kicked my dad out, what would make her keep a dog? I kept thinking, I've screwed up so bad, but Rambling, he depends on me. A risk to come here, but Rambling deserves it, don't you boy?" Rambling licked Trevor's chin. "Friday night—I knew Luke would be out, seeing an indie band or something, and my mom would be in a bar with her friends, bitching about men."

If he could plan this rescue mission so meticulously, why couldn't he come back for real? Call his mom, hire a lawyer, figure a way out? She thought of Katelin: *That bastard Jack, I'll never forgive him, never.*

She let go of his jacket, moved a step or two away. What had she been thinking?

Aliya was in love with—had been in love with—a generous boy, a loving boy, but one who couldn't face his own mistakes.

"What are you going to do now, Trevor?" Her clipped tones, averted eyes, she could live with those, but she hated it that her voice bled hope. "Why not come and admit what happened? Maybe you wouldn't go to jail; it was an accident, after all. They can't prove you'd been drinking."

"And crossing the border on someone else's passport? They'll get me on obstruction of justice, try to make me out a terrorist." The words came quick and bitter, and she knew he'd been thinking about it. That said something, didn't it? He wanted to come home, he just—he couldn't bear it. Like her, and her two lives, and her inability to choose between security and independence.

No. Not like her. Not anymore.

"Here's the thing," said Trevor. "You could come with me. I, well, I dreamed it, but I never imagined . . . I was going to go by your house, stare at the place you live, let that be enough for me."

Hadn't been enough for her, though, when she thought he was dead.

"But now, seeing you, I can't, I don't want to give you up. Come back with me, Aliya, we'll pretend we're married. Hell, we'll *get* married."

"And what are you doing, *Jack*," asked Gillian, turning away from the phone for 2 seconds, "down in Mexico? And what would your new bride do?"

Aliya shifted a little, and the roof under her feet seemed to shift with her.

"I got a job on a boat," he said. "Crewing a catamaran. Doesn't pay that much, but we take tourists out, sometimes I get great tips. And you can't beat the weather . . ." He nodded, and Aliya noticed now how long his hair had grown, how dark the stubble made his chin. "Once I get a little capital, I'll get a boat of my own." Not the first time Trevor had talked about sailing. He had two shelves of model boats in his room, things he'd built himself. A pirate ship with a wooden plank, a British galley with a cloth flag.

He wasn't looking at her. Again. "You know what I used to think about, those first few days down in Mexico? A long time in the future, when I'm established, I'll come back and track you down, and make you love me under a different name."

Not that everyone had to be practical, but there were limits.

"Oh, Aliya," he said.

Oh, Trevor.

"That's ridiculous," she told him. "You've got to come home. You can't make a living as a boat bum. You can't make a life out of that."

"I agree," said Miya. Aliya twisted around. Miya's face looked wan and pale in the moonlight, exhausted, but it was the exhaustion that came with great achievement: crossing the finish line of a marathon, giving birth. She'd been so into the magic thing, used it like an enchanted rope to climb out of her pit of depression, Aliya'd expected its failure would crush her. Even wrapped in Trevor's comforting arms, she'd worried about it. But *I agree*, said Miya. Some people were more resilient than you thought.

"I can't make much of a life in prison either." His dark eyes swept her back to their first meeting in the bus lanes. "You won't come, will you?" he asked, but it sounded like *You don't love me.*

"You won't come back," she said.

There they were, on opposite sides of a divide that was steeper than the cliff he'd driven off. Not the cultural one she had feared; they could bridge that with prayer mats and prayer chains, dinners of microwaved falafel and movies with subtitles. But he was a boy of escape, and she—well, she'd come here tonight, hadn't she? She'd been lonely and confused and unable to go on, just the way he made it sound down in Mexico. But she'd realized she couldn't make a life out of loneliness, out of confusion.

She'd come to say good-bye.

She forced herself to look up, to look into his shadowed face. What about the time she stormed out of the gazebo and he chased after her, caught her just before she reached the white fence? He'd grabbed her with the fierceness of today. *I'll never let you say good-bye*, he told her between kisses. *Never, never.* What about the time—

But it was time she forgot about the times, wasn't it? Time she realized that Trevor was not the glue that would stick her life together. She pictured Mama's devastated face pressed up against the screen door, Baba's eyes gone blank as he flipped through TV channels. She'd made a mess there. Time to try to go home and fix it, try to make her point again.

Trevor bent his head and she was glad—*glad, I tell you*— that she couldn't see his face. He reached for Rambling's leash, picked it up and wrapped it around his wrist. Rambling pawed the floor a little, impatient for adventure. Miya sat up straighter, leaned forward. "You've been through an extraordinary experience," she said. "You'll carry it inside you forever." She folded her hands in her lap. "I'm so glad you shared it with us—it meant a lot to me, this chance."

Gillian snapped her phone closed and swung around. "You're going, then?" More words seemed to hover on her lips—another apology for the razor thing? Poor Gillian. It was so easy to get swept up, swept away by emotion. But in the end, she just said, "You're sure you won't—no. Everyone has to find his own way. Good-bye, Trevor." Aliya half expected her to tell him to look her up the next time he was in Trinidad, but she said no such thing. "Good luck, bredrin. You'll need it."

He stood up. He was still watching Aliya. Searching for some last chance in her face. "Well, I'll be going then," he said.

"Okay."

He reached out a hand and drew a line down Aliya's cheek. She shivered. "You never know—someday, maybe years from now, you'll check your e-mail and there'll be a message from me." That's exactly what she was afraid of. "So I won't say good-bye."

She bowed her head. Struggled, wavered. Could she really let him go? When she looked up, he was launching himself over the roof and onto the fire escape. For a few seconds she could see nothing but his hands. Then Rambling bounded after him, obstructing her view. Rambling jumped down, but Trevor was gone. She could only hear him: the clatter on the fire escape, the *click-click* of the dog behind him, the *clunk* as they leaped off the bottom step. "Shit," said Trevor when they hit the ground. *Yip, yip, yip.*

"Same old Trevor," said Gillian. "Everything the hard way."

"Maybe he didn't want to go back inside," said Aliya. She felt—well, she didn't know. There were still tears on her cheeks, but they were drying. That tight, can't-get-free band that had been binding her chest since the day Trevor died—no, she'd been wearing it since the day they met—that was beginning to loosen. Maybe someday soon she would breathe again.

She looked around the rooftop. It had an aura of party aftermath: a languid, did-we-do-the-right-thing atmosphere, three exhausted girls who'd rather go to bed than clean up the mess. Except, of course, there was no mess. Candles still flickered on three corners, but the smoke from the herbs had long since dissipated. There was one steel pan, one tabla, a backpack, a shoulder bag.

One exhausted girl moved. Miya. She pushed herself to her feet, smiling, then she came across the roof, handed the *tabla* to Gillian, who tucked it back into her backpack. "Trevor's mom deserves the truth, Jack's family, too," said Gillian. "But Trevor . . . they have extradition treaties with Mexico, right? They'd send bounty hunters or whatever down there to rough him up and drag his ass back to jail?" She ran her hand across the side pocket and frowned. "We all do things we regret," she added. "Not right, not brave, but . . ."

Aliya had already disappointed Trevor tonight, they couldn't ask her to betray him, too. "I suppose you're cheery because you don't feel guilty about Trevor now?" she asked Miya, who'd made her way back and was kneeling by the candles now. Funny how important that had seemed, setting those candles in the perfect pentagram.

Miya picked up the nearest one. In its flickering flame, her face looked like something out of a movie: Queen Galadriel, or the White Witch. Aliya added, "I thought you might be depressed or something. Not that Trevor's not dead, that's some kind of miracle. God is greatest and all that. But this magic nonsense . . . well, we wasted a lot of time and did a lot of stupid things."

"What are you talking about?" asked Miya. Not quiet-voiced, not serene, something else. She stared into the flame for one long moment and then blew it out.

"Weren't you the one who was all into this, 'We have to raise Trevor from the dead, free his spirit from its evil oppression'? Now we find out that he wasn't even dead, and all your Japanese spirit talking was just some modern myth."

"Who says he wasn't dead?" Miya's voice came out of the dark now. Exultant, that's what it was. Aliya gaped and even Gillian dropped her jaw. "Of course he was dead. Don't you get it? *We brought him back.*"

THIRTY-THREE

ALIYA STARED at her, open-mouthed. Gillian raised her eyebrows so high they almost disappeared into her hair. But their skin glistened, their breaths came hard and fast, their faces shone with power. Whether they knew it or not, they'd been part of something amazing tonight.

"Didn't you hear Trevor's story?" she asked Aliya. Miya spoke gently. Truth took some getting used to; look how long it had taken her. "He has no idea how long he was out, no idea what happened after the accident. He was dead, gone, nothing—you yourself said you could sense him, feel him, smell him. What about in the forest? Do you really think he wasn't there with us?"

"But then . . ." Aliya broke off. She pushed her heavy hair behind her ears, wiped the sweat off her forehead.

Had to give the girl some time—and some information, too. Miya picked up the nearest candle, blew it out. "Then we concentrated," she said. "Reached out to the spirits. We touched the fabric of time, erased it and rewove the past. We changed what happened." No small thing. "It's true, I didn't really understand what was going on. All this time, I thought Trevor wanted to be free, to make his own way to the land of the dead—or wherever the dead are, I'll have to learn more about that. I didn't realize that what he really wanted was to come back."

234

She stopped talking, dropped the candle into her draw-string bag. Reached over for the incense burners, popped them in on top of it. Trevor was gone. His physical presence had climbed down the fire escape, taking with it the sound of his feet, the smell of his cologne, but his spirit—that was gone too. She remembered his sudden disappearance on the rooftop, right over there, on that gutterless stretch which now had faded back to black. His sudden reappearance a few feet away, just above the fire escape.

She'd never forget the sight of him, coming up over the side of the house.

"I'll take that," said Gillian to Aliya, voice like a whisper, and the steel pan passed between them. They exchanged isn't-she-crazy looks, Gillian's hand went up to her ear—was she drawing a circle around it? But why should Miya care? They'd see it for themselves, in the end.

Miya closed her eyes, pictured Trevor-the-ghost one last time: coming up onto the roof like a pale phantom, hard to see at first, almost impossible to make out his words. He'd grown substance as he talked, as though feeding himself with words instead of food. What about those harsh sentences that had set him on his path to ruin, so many days ago? *Do you think I'd care if you were dead? Would anyone?* Nothing, no discomfort now, not even a sliver of pain. She had put it right. *They* had put it right.

She looked across at Aliya, head tilted back, staring up at the stars; at Gillian, stuffing the steel pan into her backpack. The three of them, such unlikely partners. Such successful ones. Taking up another candle, Miya said what she was thinking: "After this, making Luke fall in love with me will be first-round College Bowl." Puff, puff—she blew out the candle.

Aliya's eyes left the stars, came back to earth, back to Miya. "Are you joking?" she asked. "You can't be going on with this."

"So this was all about Luke?" asked Gillian. She zipped up her backpack. "Why not snare him in the old-fashioned way: the short skirt, the bottle of wine?" Her eyelids fluttered, like she had some secret memory. "Or better, be a bit Nancy Drew about it—tell him about Trevor, head down to Mexico together to look him up, something like that."

She didn't get it, did she? Miya wasn't looking for some superficial love thing.

"After all," said Gillian, "don't you think we've interfered enough? A hurricane in Trinidad, the obeah man packed off home, a boy loses his hair, a girl loses her boyfriend." Maybe she did get it, some of it, after all.

Aliya spun around, stared at Gillian. "Seriously? You believe all this stuff? Raising people from the dead? You think Trevor passed over and we brought him back?"

"I'm saying: Why interfere with it?" Something hovered on Gillian's lips—was that a smile? "I'm entering a new, mellow phase of life."

Miya leaned over and blew out two more candles. Sure, they were skeptics now, but that would change when they'd had a chance to really think about things. A little research and they'd get how extraordinary this night had been. She'd type them a reading list in the morning. She picked up the last candle, held it out in front of her like a fiery toast. "Here's to Trevor," she said. "May he live long."

Then she blew out the candle.